Bridgeport Public Library
1200 Johnson Ave.
Bridgeport, WV 26330
(304) 842-8248

"*The Big Kitty* is a charming, witty, exciting new entry in the genre, featuring the best realized and most personable fictional character on four legs. You'll love Shadow. And Sunny's fun, too."

—Parnell Hall, author of *The KenKen Killings*

"A paws-itively winning team! *The Big Kitty* deftly combines heartwarming humor and nail-biting suspense for a fun read that leaves you looking forward to Sunny and Shadow's next adventure."

—Ali Brandon, author of *Double Booked for Death*,
a Black Cat Bookshop Mystery

"Applause for paws—Sunny and Shadow take Best in Show!"

—Susan Wittig Albert, author of *Cat's Claw*,
a Pecan Springs Mystery

up and a tip of the tail."

t, author of *Dead by Midnight*

n this dangerous since Jes-
lead bodies in Cabot Cove!
, with the able assistance of
proves she has the skills to
leuth. Cozy mystery lovers
r many more adventures for

, national bestselling author of
the Cat in the Stacks Mysteries

W9-ARE-837

Bridgeport Public Library

The Big Kitty

Claire Donally

BERKLEY PRIME CRIME, NEW YORK

F
D7142b
M

THE BERKLEY PUBLISHING GROUP
Published by the Penguin Group
Penguin Group (USA) Inc.
375 Hudson Street, New York, New York 10014, USA
Penguin Group (Canada), 90 Eglinton Avenue East, Suite 700, Toronto, Ontario M4P 2Y3, Canada
(a division of Pearson Penguin Canada Inc.) • Penguin Books Ltd., 80 Strand, London WC2R 0RL,
England • Penguin Group Ireland, 25 St. Stephen's Green, Dublin 2, Ireland (a division of Penguin
Books Ltd.) • Penguin Group (Australia), 250 Camberwell Road, Camberwell, Victoria 3124, Australia
(a division of Pearson Australia Group Pty. Ltd.) • Penguin Books India Pvt. Ltd., 11 Community
Centre, Panchsheel Park, New Delhi—110 017, India • Penguin Group (NZ), 67 Apollo Drive,
Rosedale, Auckland 0632, New Zealand (a division of Pearson New Zealand Ltd.) • Penguin Books
(South Africa) (Pty.) Ltd., 24 Sturdee Avenue, Rosebank, Johannesburg 2196, South Africa

Penguin Books Ltd., Registered Offices: 80 Strand, London WC2R 0RL, England

This is a work of fiction. Names, characters, places, and incidents either are the product of the author's
imagination or are used fictitiously, and any resemblance to actual persons, living or dead, business
establishments, events, or locales is entirely coincidental. The publisher does not have any control over
and does not assume any responsibility for author or third-party websites or their content.

THE BIG KITTY

A Berkley Prime Crime Book / published by arrangement with Tekno Books.

PUBLISHING HISTORY
Berkley Prime Crime mass-market edition / May 2012

Copyright © 2012 by Tekno Books.
Cover illustration by Tony Mauro.
Cover design by George Long.
Interior text design by Laura K. Corless.

All rights reserved.
No part of this book may be reproduced, scanned, or distributed in any printed or
electronic form without permission. Please do not participate in or encourage piracy of
copyrighted materials in violation of the author's rights. Purchase only authorized editions.
For information, address: The Berkley Publishing Group,
a division of Penguin Group (USA) Inc.,
375 Hudson Street, New York, New York 10014.

ISBN: 978-0-425-24802-7

BERKLEY® PRIME CRIME
Berkley Prime Crime Books are published by The Berkley Publishing Group,
a division of Penguin Group (USA) Inc.,
375 Hudson Street, New York, New York 10014.
BERKLEY® PRIME CRIME and the PRIME CRIME logo are trademarks of
Penguin Group (USA) Inc.

PRINTED IN THE UNITED STATES OF AMERICA

10 9 8 7 6 5 4 3 2 1

If you purchased this book without a cover, you should be aware that this book is
stolen property. It was reported as "unsold and destroyed" to the publisher, and neither the
author nor the publisher has received any payment for this "stripped book."

ALWAYS LEARNING   **PEARSON**

Acknowledgments

Many thanks to Mom, who suffered through the first draft of this story, and to editors John Helfers of Tekno Books and Shannon Jamieson Vazquez of Berkley Prime Crime, who suffered through the succeeding ones.

Additional thanks to my niece Jackie, to Mike, Denise, Jack, Kathleen, and Bill and Karen for their cat stories.

And of course, to Lily, Mulie, Belle, Dinoot, and Theo—especially Theo—for practical cat demonstrations.

A Note from the Author

When I first discussed the idea of a cat mystery set in Maine, I thought, "What better location than the town of Kittery? It even sounds right!"

With all the outlet stores, the nearby city of Portsmouth, New Hampshire, and a naval shipyard bringing people from all over the country into the area, Kittery seemed ideal.

Except . . .

Kittery might be a little too real. It's a fairly small town, and it didn't seem quite fair, smearing a murder all over a real place. You can get away with killing lots of people (at least on paper) in large, impersonal metropolitan areas like New York, Los Angeles, or even New Orleans. But there's a reason why small-town murders tend to happen in fictitious places like St. Mary Mead, Pecan Springs, Texas . . . or Cabot Cove, Maine.

So I picked up Kittery and sort of smooshed it together with the neighboring township of York Harbor to create Kittery Harbor, a safely make-believe locale with its own politics, movers and shakers . . . and a cat lady. But as I worked on the plot, the specter of county politics arose, so I decided to secede the whole area from the real world.

Elmet is the name of an ancient Celtic kingdom that controlled part of what is now Yorkshire, England. So, Elmet County is a sort of parallel universe to Maine's York County. It's close to Portsmouth, there are lots of outlet stores nearby, and the town fronts on a harbor but there are still farms in the hinterland. Christopher Levett, an early settler in Maine, is commemorated with a fort in the real world. In Elmet County, he gives his name to the county seat.

I had a lot of fun creating a world that connects with reality in general, but definitely not in particulars.

No people were hurt in the creation of this literary crime (if you don't count the author's hair tearing), and all places and politics are definitely made up.

Any resemblance to real people, living or deceased, is purely coincidental.

However, some cat caregivers may recognize a few traits exhibited by certain feline friends . . .

1

The watcher crouched in the darkness between cars, staring through the plate glass of the storefront at the woman inside.

He liked the way her dark hair spread out in a mane behind her head, gleaming in the glow from the screen she was watching.

A splash of light from a passing car invaded his hiding space, and he crouched lower. Not that he needed to worry about passersby. All but two of the shops in this little strip were already dark, and the food store was down at the other end of the block. Besides, even if someone were to stroll by, it was unlikely that they would spot him in the shadows.

A puff of breeze brought the scent of the sea, never too far away. Then the wind shifted, pulling a bouquet of aromas out the storefront's open door. The watcher inhaled deeply, catching a mixture of dust and furniture polish, the sharp smell of electrical machinery at work, and then a whiff of the floral fragrance the woman was wearing, and under that the earthier tone of her own smell.

His head swam a little. The doorway was just a few yards away, beckoning him on this unseasonably warm evening. Maybe he should go in, make his move—

The breeze stopped being playful, turning into a gust that brought the chill of the ocean as well as its aroma. He hunkered down as it whistled around him. And as he did, the woman in the store moved to close the door, locking it and then rubbing her arms.

So much for that idea, he thought, turning to slink away.

Why do I keep coming back to her? he continued as he squeezed under a parked car and out the other side. *It's not as though I see her doing anything interesting—like eating.*

With a flick of his tail he crossed the road, ready to leave. But then he heard the rumble of a car engine and caught a whiff of exhaust . . . and other familiar smells. He knew this vehicle. Turning around, he settled down on all four paws.

This could be interesting.

*

Still rubbing her arms, Sunny Coolidge returned to her computer and the latest crisis. She should have been home an hour and a half ago, but that was before some jackass had started acting out on a flight from Paris to Atlanta, getting his plane diverted to the customs and TSA facilities at Pease Airport in Portsmouth, New Hampshire.

Frantic Web searches by stranded passengers in search

of nearby accommodations had led to a surge of e-mails at MAX—the Maine Adventure X-perience site—and Sunny's computer. Since the travel agency here in Kittery Harbor, Maine, was just across the state border and less than five miles from the airport in New Hampshire, she'd gone into overtime matchmaking passengers with local B&Bs, beating the bushes for whatever additional accommodations she could find, and arranging transportation.

Well, at least Ollie—Oliver Barnstable, a.k.a. "Ollie the Barnacle," the owner of MAX—should be happy tomorrow with all the extra revenue. And in spite of the late hour, Sunny was glad to help out the stuck travelers. It made her feel a little less like a mere Web lackey tending the site. When she'd come home to Maine eight months ago to take care of her ailing father, she'd only intended to take a brief leave of absence from her reporter job at the *New York Standard*. But unfortunately, the sickly state of the newspaper business had led her editor at the *Standard* to make her absence more permanent. And to pour salt into that particular wound, after he'd broken off their professional relationship, he broke off their personal one, too. Talk about a one-two punch.

When Sunny had tried for a job at the local rag, the *Harbor Crier*, Ken Howell, the editor there, had turned her down flat. Apparently after all his years of running the place, he didn't want some big-city "professional" sticking a nose in his business. But luckily Ollie, who was a major partner on the paper, had heard she was looking for work and had offered her the job at MAX. Compared to her old New York salary, the pay could only be called puny . . . but at least puny was better than nothing.

To tell the truth, it was a little odd to be back working just two doors down from the store where she'd had her first job. In high school, Sunny had spent Friday evenings and Saturdays behind the fountain at Barnstable's Sweet Shoppe, working for Ollie's father. Sometimes Ollie would come by, dressed in a suit and tie from his job down in Boston, and give his dad a break. He was a lot older than Sunny and plainly hated working in the place.

But even if he detested the work and could be a little skeevy—he used to creep Sunny out a little by telling her she was the sweetest thing in the Sweet Shoppe—Ollie was otherwise all business. Sunny remembered him always arguing with his father about how they should open on Sundays, something the elder Barnstable refused to do. In the end Barnstable Senior passed away while Sunny was in college. Ollie had sold the store, taken the insurance money, and gone off to New York City. Apparently he'd invested that money well, because a few years before Mike's illness, Ollie had come back to Kittery Harbor flush with cash and ready to do business around town. He'd invested in the faltering *Harbor Crier*, bought the row of stores where his dad's shop used to be, and put a lot of money into local real estate and other business opportunities, including MAX.

Sunny had been surprised that Ollie had even remembered her, much less offered her a job. Maybe he just wanted someone around who'd spent time in the big city. Sometimes he'd talk to her about New York—the traffic, neighborhoods, Broadway shows he'd seen, expensive restaurants where he'd dined. He never gave away much about his business there, though.

And, Sunny was glad to say, he never told her she was the sweetest thing in the MAX office.

She thought she'd be writing promotional copy for the travel agency, and there was some of that. Mostly, though, she tended the website, arranged accommodations and sightseeing opportunities for prospective tourists, and dealt with the rare drop-in customer.

The operation struck her as a little underhanded—Ollie had a "select list" of B&Bs, tour operators, and local destinations that gave him kickbacks. But there were occasions, like tonight, when Sunny felt she was actually doing a good deed and helping people. Besides, it wasn't as if there were that many other ways to earn a living in a town the size of Kittery Harbor, and she didn't want to leech off her retired father.

The thought of Dad made her frown as the e-storm finally quieted down on her computer. He was responsible for getting his own dinner tonight, and he still wasn't reconciled to the realities of a post–heart attack diet. Even worse, there were too many accommodating widowed neighbor ladies who'd be only too glad to cook him a nice, tasty, artery-clogging meal.

Their cooking's probably why they are *widow ladies,* she thought sourly.

Would things have been different if Mom were still around? Unlikely. Dad had spent much of his working life on the road instead of at home, trucking rock salt all over New England. Sunny suspected that it was decades of diner cuisine which had finally caught up with him, not home cooking. And anyway, Mom's cooking had ceased to be a factor almost fifteen years ago, when Sunny was just finishing exam hell for her first semester at Boston University. In a cruelly ironic twist, while Dad was out delivering a load of road-clearing salt to Boston, Mom had gone off the road in Kittery Harbor, just before Sunny was to come home for the holidays, another fatal accident victim of what became known as the Christmas ice storm.

Sunny pushed away her wandering thoughts when she heard a tapping at the door. She rose from behind her desk to see a birdlike woman waving energetically at her through the glass.

Sunny unlocked the door and the woman bustled inside. "You're Mike Coolidge's daughter, aren't you?" she asked, standing so close she almost poked Sunny in the face with her oversized nose. "I don't know if you remember me. I'm Ada Spruance, and I need help."

Sunny had to bite the inside of her cheek to keep from saying something stupid. Ada Spruance certainly *did* need help. Standing face-to-face with her, Sunny didn't need the faint whiff of cat pee that emanated from the woman's clothes to remind her that Ada was famous—or infamous— around town as the local Cat Lady.

Sunny shifted a little to put some distance between herself and Ada. Maybe she was wrong about the cat pee. Maybe it was a dab of very spoiled cologne.

Yeah, right, her cynical reporter alter ego responded.

"Your boss, Mr. Barnstable, has been around a lot lately, suggesting ways to assist me with my financial problems," Ada said.

That got Sunny's attention. Ollie the Barnacle turning up in response to money troubles was not exactly a charitable reaction. More like a shark attracted to blood in the water.

"The problem is, all of his suggestions involve selling my house. But I thought maybe I could bring in some extra money by setting my place up as a bed and breakfast." Ada smiled hopefully. "What would I have to do to get listed with you?"

You'd probably have to start with a fumigator—and then maybe an exorcist, Sunny's hard-edged inner voice chimed in. Ada's big barn of a house with its scaly paint job served as a hostel for too many cats to count. She lived right around the corner from the home Sunny had grown up in, and though Ada had always taken in a few strays even back then, these days it was apparently something else. From what Sunny had heard, both Ada and her pets drove the nearby householders crazy. Sunny had witnessed her own dad curse his dotty neighbor up and down whenever he detected cat pee on the prized rosebushes her mom had planted around the house decades ago.

Aloud, Sunny tried to be more diplomatic. "I think you'd face more of a job than many of the people we represent." How to put it delicately? "Some travelers are allergic to house pets. Those that aren't might be willing to deal with a dog, or a cat, maybe two, but . . ."

Ada nodded. "I have more than that around the house," she said with massive understatement, then sighed, her hands fluttering. "It's just . . . I really need to bring some more money in, and—"

She broke off. "You've been very kind. Not like some of the people who live in this town." Ada hesitated for a moment. "Could I rely upon your kindness just a little more? I have this other problem, and I—I realize I have no one to discuss it with. The new neighbors think I'm some sort of mental case, and the old-timers, well, they don't speak with me anymore. I need some advice—some help—and it seems as though I have no one I can trust."

The image of Ada sitting alone in her house with only the cats for company made Sunny regret her uncharitable thoughts. "What's the trouble?" she asked.

Ada gave her an embarrassed smile. "It seems I've misplaced a lottery ticket . . ."

You start to sympathize with people, and this is what you get, Sunny's inner reporter scolded. She tried not to roll her eyes at this offbeat turn in the conversation. Before Ada could explain any more, they were interrupted by a hand slapping at the door.

Sunny looked over to find a guy wearing muddy jeans and the kind of undershirt known in some circles as a "wifebeater," teetering under an enormous bag of . . . dry cat food?

"Mr. Judson in the store orders in bulk for me, and once a week my son picks up our supplies," Ada explained, noticing the look of confusion on Sunny's face.

It took Sunny a moment to recognize the guy under the cat food as Ada's son, Gordie Spruance. As a kid, she remembered a somewhat more mainstream Ada hopping like a sparrow around her big, slow-moving, egg-shaped son. Gordie was about five years older and had about fifty pounds on Sunny back then—and he'd had a tendency toward bullying that Sunny had curbed with a sharp knee where he'd least expected it.

Well, he's lost weight, she found herself thinking. *Maybe a little too much.*

The arms and chest revealed under the straps of his un-

dershirt were more stringy than scrawny. He'd inherited his
mother's oversized nose, but the skin of his face seemed
pulled overly tight to cover that hooter. And the inflamed
acne would have been more at home on a teenager's cheeks
than those of a guy pushing forty.

Gordie edged the door open with his foot. "Ma," he
called, drawing out the word to end with a bit of a whine.
After that one word, and without waiting for a response,
he turned to a rusty tan pickup parked down the block and
manhandled his heavy load toward the tarp-covered
truck bed.

As he moved to wrestle the big bag into place, a low,
long gray form came slinking out of the darkness and
started twining around Gordie's ankles.

Ada started in surprise at the sight of the cat. "Shadow!
What are you doing all the way over here?"

She gave Sunny the sort of look parents might use while
describing a rambunctious child. "Ever since he turned up
at the house, I've called him that because of his color. He's
a bit of a traveler. I never know where I'll run into him
around town."

Sunny said nothing, watching Gordie aim a surrepti-
tious kick at the cat as soon as his mother wasn't looking.
Shadow, however, seemed to expect the move. The cat
dodged without even seeming to try, prowling off as Gordie, thrown off balance, staggered around under the weight
of the industrial-sized feed package.

"Careful, Gordie," Ada called, having completely
missed the reason behind why her son was dancing down
the street trying not to lose his load or his footing.

The huge bag of cat food looked to weigh almost as

much as Gordie did, but after a brief struggle he managed to get his unwieldy burden stowed away in the pickup.

Ada Spruance stood in silence as her son shuffled toward the front of the truck, jerking his head at her in a "come on" gesture. But as Gordie stood with his back turned, putting his key in the lock, words came in a rush from the Cat Lady. "I've been playing that Powerball lottery ever since they picked it up for Maine," she said, "twice a week for years now, the same six numbers. I need someone to help find my lost ticket."

Sunny's dad threw an occasional dollar at the lottery—usually when the prize got into the nine-figure bracket—and he was always losing his tickets, too. Sunny forced herself not to sigh. A deep inhale didn't seem like a good idea with the Cat Lady standing so close by.

"I didn't even realize I had a winner until I was spreading some old newspaper around the litter boxes today," she explained. "When I realized those were my numbers, I started looking. I have to find it quickly, you see. Two weeks from tomorrow, a year will have gone by," Ada continued, "and after that, the ticket's no good anymore. So I've got to turn it up soon." She shot a pleading glance at Sunny.

"It's not a *really* big winner," she went on. "I'm not sure what it's worth anymore—something like six or eight million dollars."

2

Well, that shut up the snarky voice in the back of Sunny's head. She stood there, stunned, as the Cat Lady bustled toward the door after her son.

But Sunny managed to get her wits together and sprint to the door before Ada Spruance got into the cab of Gordie's pickup.

"If you'd like some help, I could . . . inspect the premises," she called out.

Ada picked up on the offer under Sunny's words, and her eyes looked grateful as she nodded. "Yes . . . yes, that would be very helpful. Do you think you could do it this Saturday?"

Sunny wasn't exactly filled with delight at the thought of spending her weekend discovering just how many byproducts a horde of cats could leave around a house, but she'd already promised to help, so she nodded. "Saturday should be fine. Would you be up at, say, eight-thirty?" Maybe that way she could still salvage a little personal time for Saturday afternoon.

Ada nodded back and smiled brightly, then boarded the pickup, which started up with a jerk and then roared off as she waved good-bye to Sunny.

Sunny returned to her monitor and spent another half hour making sure her stranded travelers all landed at their respective B&Bs. Then she rose, stretched, turned off the computer, got her coat, doused the lights, and closed the office. Sunny stepped out into full darkness. Although the weather had been remarkably mild, the days were getting noticeably shorter this far into September.

With the front door locked behind her, she shot her usual remorseful glance at the metallic blue Mustang parked at the curb. It had been her first new car, perfect for a single reporter in New York City. But it had rear-wheel drive, which didn't go well with road conditions in a Maine winter. The proof showed on the driver's-side fender, seriously banged in and roughly pulled out. Every time she opened the door, metal screeched against metal as if the car were in pain.

For the umpteenth time since coming back to Kittery Harbor, Sunny debated the notion of getting a new set of wheels. The calculations came down to the same disheartening conclusion. With the pittance she was getting from Ollie the Barnacle, she couldn't afford anything but a used clunker, which would just mean inheriting someone else's problem.

She got behind the wheel and sat for a moment, frowning. Sure, finances and hard logic played a part in her decision against replacing her car. But the biggest argument was emotional. If she got rid of the Mustang, she'd be admitting she wasn't going back to the big city, that she'd accepted being back in Kittery Harbor long term.

Not that there's all that much to rush back to at this point, Sunny thought. *No job, a busted relationship with the guy who wound up firing me . . . Holy crow, what's that?!*

But it wasn't a crow that leaped onto the hood of her car. It was a cat, a long-bodied, lean gray cat—Ada Spruance's wanderer . . . Shadow?

He walked straight up to the windshield, close enough that Sunny could see the tiger stripes hidden in his gray coat, and rested his right forepaw on the glass, as if testing how solid it was.

"Get away from there, you crazy cat!" Sunny raised her arms and began making shooing gestures.

The cat brought down his paw and stood watching her antics as if he'd just found something good on TV.

"Come on now, get off!" Sunny's temper rose as the cat continued to watch her with infuriating calm. She smacked the glass with her palm, hoping to startle him off.

Shadow raised a paw and smacked back.

He obviously knows I can't get at him through the windshield, Sunny thought. *So how the hell do I persuade him to go away?*

She put her thumb on the horn button and gave it a healthy blast. Shadow jumped up, but not away. He sat on the hood, giving Sunny a wide-eyed "Did you do that?" sort of look.

So much for that clever plan, Sunny thought. *I could be here all night, until I get a ticket for disturbing the peace, and* still *not get rid of this dopey animal.*

Her windshield wipers were not in the best of shape, and she shuddered to think how they'd look if a cat that size started playing with them. She stuck her key in the ignition and turned it, gunning the gas.

Shadow lay down as if he were preparing to enjoy a nice vibratory massage.

Sunny clicked the engine off. The damned cat was being annoying, but she couldn't just drive away with him on the hood. Yeah, he'd probably jump off, but what if he ended up under one of her wheels? She wouldn't want to feel responsible for any part of that.

Maybe, Sunny thought, *if I opened the window, I could sort of push him . . .* She instantly envisioned herself half out of the car, leaning as far as she could, while Shadow imperturbably positioned himself an inch or two out of her reach.

This guy's a comedian, Sunny reminded herself. *He thought it was funny to do figure-eights around Gordie's ankles while he carried that big bag of food.*

Still, she couldn't sit here all night until the cat tired of amusing himself.

With yet another sigh, Sunny undid her seat belt and heaved against her door, which opened with a screech. *I'll just have to get out there and move him.*

But when she went to do that, the hood was empty.

Sunny went to the far side of the car, then squatted down to look underneath.

No cat.

The noise of the door must have spooked him, she told herself.

She turned to get back in the car—and froze.

Sitting on the passenger seat, giving her another imperturbable look, was Shadow.

"Oh, come on!" Sunny said.

She made brushing motions, then beckoning ones, but the big cat didn't move.

She went around to the passenger-side door, opened it, and tried to cajole the cat out.

No way.

When she tried to pick him up, Shadow finally gave up his statue impersonation. He darted from between her hands and squeezed himself under the passenger seat.

Sunny foresaw a real battle trying to extricate him from beneath there. Shadow would probably rip up the floor mat—or maybe her arm.

"Fine, stay under there, you crazy critter." Sunny slammed the door shut and stomped around the car, already at work on the classified ad. *For sale, 2007 metallic blue Ford Mustang, feline passenger included.*

By the time Sunny got back to the driver's side, Shadow was back on the opposite seat again, sitting and watching her. He suddenly yawned, giving her a view of a pink tongue and surprisingly large, sharp teeth.

Sunny hesitated. Maybe she should get Animal Control. Shadow wasn't acting like a typical cat. Could he be sick? This wasn't exactly the country, but the woods weren't too far away. Raccoons and other wild animals had been known to turn up. What if Shadow had encountered one with rabies?

The cat stretched one forepaw onto the driver's seat and used the other to tap the steering wheel.

Well, I don't see any foam around his mouth, Sunny thought. With a shrug, she bent to get in.

Shadow immediately settled back on his seat as she started the car and headed home. As she drove, she chatted with the cat—it made a welcome change from talk radio. For his part, at least Shadow appeared to listen attentively.

"You know, most of the roads out here are old farm tracks—they sort of follow the lay of the land," Sunny told him. "It takes a little getting used to, after spending years living in a place with a grid plan like New York. Although there are parts of Brooklyn and Queens where you can really get lost. They've got these streets that curve around—crescents, they call them—"

She broke off. *I must really miss New York if I'm discussing it with a cat,* she thought ruefully.

They rolled on in silence until Sunny made the right onto her street, Wild Goose Drive, and pulled up in front of a shingled Cape-style house, painted white with green shutters. It had the kind of simple design that had made it easy for a much younger Sunny to draw pictures of "My House"—a central door flanked by two windows on the ground floor, gabled windows upstairs. The gable on the right was Sunny's bedroom. This had been the only home she knew until she went to college. Afterward she'd lived in a string of dorm rooms and apartments, but if she had to draw a picture of "Home," it wouldn't be all that different from the scrawls she'd made as a kid.

"We're here," Sunny announced as she opened her door, and Shadow followed her out. He stood for a moment, looking as if he were taking in the cylindrical wire cages filled with mulch, meant to protect the carefully trimmed rosebushes until spring. Since his retirement, her father had made a concerted effort to restore his wife's garden. Not even the heart attack had stopped him. Sunny had done the work of getting everything ready for winter under her dad's careful supervision.

"A word of warning," Sunny said to the cat. "Stay away from the foundation plantings." She shook her head and muttered to herself, "Like he's going to understand what I tell him."

After locking her car, she went up the walk with Shadow trailing behind. For a second, Sunny hesitated at the door. Shadow simply sat looking up at her with those curious gold-flecked eyes. *Well, he can't ask for a formal invitation,* she thought as she unlocked the door.

They entered the front hall, with a flight of stairs leading to the bedrooms. Sunny heard television noise off to the left in the living room. "Dad? I'm home."

Better not to mention her guest.

She poked a head through the open archway. Mike Coolidge sat on the couch watching some sort of sitcom, judging from the laugh track. His white hair rose in an unruly mass of curls—he was way past his usual time to get a trim. His face was on the pale side, the heart attack having robbed him of the high color Sunny remembered from days gone by. He'd also picked up a few wrinkles, partly as a result of losing some weight. But his blue eyes were as bright and piercing as ever when he turned to her. "So did Ollie Barnstable have you toting barges or lifting bales?"

"I was helping a bunch of people with an unscheduled stopover at Pease," Sunny told him.

Mike grunted. He didn't like Ollie. "Make sure he knows about the extra hours you put in. At least next week's paycheck will be bigger than the one you got today—" He broke off at the expression on her face. "He did give you your pay, didn't he?"

Sunny shifted uncomfortably on her feet. "He wasn't in today."

Her dad scowled. "Been doing that a lot lately—usually when payday comes around."

"I'm sure he'll be in tomorrow," Sunny said.

"Yeah, or Friday, or whenever he feels like it. I don't know why you stick with that Barnstable boy. Ever since he came back to town, he's been strutting around like God's gift to the local economy."

Why do I stay at MAX? Sunny silently responded. *Because given the state of the local economy, there aren't any other jobs out there. And I'm too old to work behind a soda fountain anymore.*

She shook her head noncommittally. "Did you have dinner?" she asked.

"Made myself a sandwich," Mike said.

Sunny went back to the hall and down to the kitchen, this time accompanied by Shadow. "Dad!" she called when she opened the refrigerator. "You ate *all* the turkey and cheese?" She glanced in the trash bin. "And all the mayo?"

She'd carefully shopped around for the best low-fat, low-sodium stuff she could find. But that wouldn't help much if her father ate several days' worth of supplies in one sitting. "It's only Tuesday. I didn't expect we'd need to restock until Friday!"

"I must be going deaf." Mike's voice grew louder as he padded toward the kitchen. "Shouldn't there be a siren to announce that the food police have arrived?"

He arrived at the kitchen doorway, stopping in his tracks when Shadow poked his head around Sunny's ankles to give him an inquisitive stare. "What's that?" Mike's blue eyes sparked with annoyance as he glared at Sunny, just as they had in about a million disciplinary encounters over the years. "And don't act smart, telling me it's a cat. What's it doing here?"

"He followed me home," Sunny ventured. That at least got a blink out of her dad, breaking his blue laser stare of death. The glare didn't seem to work on Shadow. He leaned down and licked his shoulder. Having seen the cat annoy Gordie Spruance—and play "catch me if you can" with her in the car—Sunny suspected Shadow was acting a little too innocent.

She told her dad how Shadow had appeared on the hood of her car and then wrangled himself a seat inside. The cat didn't show much interest in hearing about his exploits. He just sat quietly, facing the refrigerator, occasionally flicking his whiskers.

"Probably one of the strays that are always coming over here to do their business in the plantings—especially under my window." Dad aimed an unfriendly look at Shadow. "So what do you figure on doing with this fool animal?"

"Ada Spruance said he's a bit of a wanderer," Sunny

replied, hoping to smooth things over. "He'll probably just stay for the night and be on his way."

"And why were you talking to the crazy Cat Lady in the first place?" Mike wanted to know.

"She came into the office this evening," Sunny began.

Mike regained a little color as he listened to her story—*not necessarily a healthy sign,* Sunny thought.

"That dingbat thinks she has a winning lottery ticket? And you're going to search that cathouse of hers for it?" He shook his head, definitely unhappy. "Better wear the oldest clothes you can find—stuff you can burn in the backyard when you get back here."

"I thought you'd be more against it," Sunny admitted.

"You already told her you'd do it," her dad replied. "And you should be as good as your word." That was a real, strict-construction Kittery Harbor answer. But his voice held a definite "you'll be sorry" tone as he spoke.

"Does Gordie still live over there with his mother?" she asked.

Mike's shock of white curls bobbed as he shook his head. "He moved out when the cats began moving in. And then for a while he was a guest of the county, some sort of thing about missing car parts."

After taking in that information, Sunny thought for a moment. "In that case, there's a phone call I'd better make. Then I'll come out and check your meds."

Mike turned around and headed back to the living room, muttering something about the "pill police."

Sunny went to the phone extension on the kitchen wall, paused for a second, and then went to the cabinets. She took down a can of tuna, got the opener, and spooned half the contents of the can onto a small saucer. Shadow didn't even come close to the food until she'd deposited it on the floor and stepped away.

"Just remember, there's no litter box in here," she warned the cat as he investigated the plate of fish. "And you heard what Dad said about the garden."

While Shadow went to work on the tuna, Sunny stood frowning at the telephone as she recalled what she'd heard from Ada Spruance—and what she'd seen. Finally, she went up to her room and dialed the number for the *Harbor Crier.* Ken Howell was still in his office—he seemed to spend most of his time there, from what Sunny could tell.

"What do you want?" he demanded as soon as Sunny identified herself.

"A polite greeting would be a good start," she shot back. "Listen, I heard something that might turn out to be a good human-interest story." She told him about Ada Spruance's errant ticket, adding, "Ada mentioned that the expiration date is coming close. So there's a suspense element, too."

"And I suppose *you* want to write this . . . burning news story?"

Sunny was surprised that the editor's words even came through, what with all the suspicion clogging the phone line.

"No, I'm handing it to you to run with," she told him virtuously. "Check the facts. I just thought it could be a good piece for the paper."

"If Ada won an amount like you're saying, maybe she'll move that menagerie of hers out of town," Howell said sourly. "A lot of people would consider that good news."

But it won't be good news if somebody—like skeevy

Gordie—has glommed on to the ticket, hoping to cash it in quietly right at the deadline, Sunny thought. *A little publicity might lead to the ticket mysteriously reappearing, and save me from having to search through the Cathouse from Hell.*

*

Shadow poked his head into the room, listening to the Young One talk. He'd followed her up the stairs, eager to explore the new house. It was much cleaner than the last house he'd stayed in—the dust in most of those rooms had been so thick, it made all the cats there sneeze.

He'd already amused himself a little, skidding along the bright, shiny floors. But when the Young One went upstairs, he'd decided to tag along. Still, he kept in the hallway, barely poking a nose in wherever he found an open door. Some of the smells—especially from the room where the Young One was—were pretty interesting.

Even so, Shadow didn't go in. He'd discovered early on that some of these two-legged people had some odd ideas about privacy. And he was leery about following her into a space where a slammed door could leave him trapped in a small area. He hated the idea of being a prisoner; worse, a cat could get hurt if he didn't have space to run from danger.

Not that this one seemed dangerous. But harsh experience had taught him to be careful. He'd been in houses where seeming kindness had abruptly turned into kicks and curses—usually from males when the female wasn't around. When that happened, Shadow hadn't stayed around for any second helpings.

But for all his wariness, he couldn't help himself when

he saw the young woman get into her car. He'd leaped on the front of the thing to play with her. He'd taken a big chance, letting himself get locked up in that go-fast thing, especially after the young woman had tried to shoo him away. But something deep told him the time was right, and after watching from afar for so many days, he couldn't resist the urge to come a bit closer. And he'd been right. She'd spoken to him gently, taken him to this nice place, and even fed him despite the objections of an Old One who apparently lived here, too.

A male Old One—that would take some thinking about. Males could be dangerous, very free with their fists and their feet. But Shadow smelled illness on this one. Between that and the male's age, it wouldn't be too hard to dodge whatever he came up with.

Almost all the older two-legs that Shadow had lived with were females, like the one in the place full of other cats. She was a needy one, always clutching at her four-legged companions, petting and cooing at them. It was more than a self-respecting cat could stand, although some of the horde in that house put up with it to get treats.

They might as well be dogs, wagging their tails for a biscuit, Shadow thought with disdain.

But this two-leg hadn't been overeager to put her hands on Shadow's fur. She'd just been nice—and maybe a little bit lonely. Shadow could understand that.

It had taken all of Shadow's bravery to make the approach to the Young One. And so far, this had turned out to be a Good Place.

He took another deep, appreciative sniff in the doorway. A Good Place, indeed.

*

Sunny smiled as she came out of her room and found a gray-furred shape lurking in the hallway, his stripes making him almost blend into the shadows.

"What have you been up to?" she asked, bending and extending a tentative hand toward the cat, an overture which he smoothly sidestepped.

"Okay," Sunny said, standing up and heading back down the stairs, where she started rooting around in the front hall closet.

Mike emerged from the living room. "What are you up to now?"

"Looking for something that Shadow can sleep on," she replied.

"What, the floor's not good enough for him?" Mike shot a grumpy look from Sunny to the cat who sat at their feet, looking into the closet with interest.

"I read somewhere that cats should sleep a little bit up from the floor so they won't be in drafts." Sunny didn't mention that the "somewhere" was the Internet and that she'd just looked it up now. "I seem to remember an old pillow in here . . ." She got on tiptoe to rummage on an upper shelf.

"That's for guests!" Mike objected, but he shut up when Sunny brought down the pillow in question. It was lumpy and misshapen, and it boasted a tasteful collection of yellowish sweat stains.

"Looks better in a nice pillowcase," Mike mumbled.

"Well, I think it's fine for this particular guest just the way it is." Sunny tossed the pillow to the ground, and Shadow immediately climbed on, sniffing.

"Now what?" Mike demanded as Sunny began rattling hangers. She unzipped a plastic bag and pulled out an old bottle green raincoat. With a few brisk movements, she removed the raincoat's fake-fur lining.

Mike's face got a little pink. "What are you doing? That's a good coat!"

"Dad, when's the last time you wore it?" Sunny asked.

He humphed for a second, then said, "I've been waiting for it to come back into style."

"For the last thirty years, the only people who've worn this kind of coat were flashers," Sunny told him.

Shadow instantly abandoned the pillow, reaching up with a paw to bat at a dangling sleeve. Sunny returned the coat to the closet and brought both lining and pillow into the living room. Wrapping the pillow in the fake fur, she arranged it in a quiet corner.

Shadow crouched low, then sprang onto the pillow, kneading it with his forepaws and then rolling on the fake fur.

"He likes it," Sunny said in satisfaction, then glanced at her dad. "It's only for a night," she said with an apologetic grin.

"Looks to me as if you're making our house way too attractive to this stray." Ignoring Shadow's apparent ecstasies on the pillow, he returned to his couch and the program playing on the TV.

*

Shadow rolled until he lay facedown on the pillow, inhaling deeply. Warring scents fought for his attention, some of them old and faint, others more recent. He smelled cedar most strongly, and under that, the scent of the Old One without the taint of illness. The aromas of many heads wafted up from the pillow, and then there was just a trace of the Young One that teased his nostrils.

Most of all, he enjoyed the sensation of being caressed by the fake fur. When he closed his eyes, the sensation brought up his very earliest memories of his mother.

Shadow had been taken from his mother just after he'd been weaned. He'd found himself on the street as little more than a kitten, big for his age . . . but alone. For just a moment, he could lean against the soft fur and remember what it was to be loved.

He snuggled down into the fur. It might not be real, but it was very, very comforting.

3

Mike's dire warnings turned out to be groundless. When Sunny let Shadow out into the backyard the next morning to do his business, the cat didn't come back.

At breakfast, Sunny's father breathed a loud sigh of relief. "I guess we can burn that," he said, gesturing toward the living room and the improvised bed.

"I'd like to keep it around," she said. "He might turn up for another visit."

But over the next few days, Sunny didn't get a return appearance of her gray-furred hitchhiker, although she caught occasional glimpses of a feline figure from her office window and in the neighborhood.

"Cats on the brain," she told herself sternly.

But if she had struck out with Shadow, Sunny hit a home run when it came to publicity for Ada Spruance and her lottery ticket—far more than she'd expected. Ken Howell had led with the story when the *Harbor Crier* made its weekly appearance on Thursday, available for free all over town.

And the story had appeared at the end of a slow news week. The Portsmouth paper had picked it up on Friday, along with all the local network affiliates. Ada's ticket couldn't have become more famous.

But Ada herself hadn't called with any good news.

So when Saturday morning came, Sunny found herself staring at a bleary-eyed image of herself in the mirror. Once upon a time, that look would have been the result of hearty partying. These days, though, it came more from insomnia, checking the bedside clock at least once an hour from two a.m. onward.

But other than puffy eyelids and the beginnings of dark circles, Sunny had to admit she was looking pretty good these days. Sharing her dad's low-sodium, low-fat, and low-sugar diet had honed away a bit of pudge and enhanced her cheekbones. While she didn't have Mike's piercing gaze, her eyes were wide and blue. Her brown hair had a generous helping of her dad's curls and a hint of her mom's auburn coloring. As she pulled her hair back and into a scrunchie, though, Sunny grimaced. She really had to get this mane cut—but she'd yet to find a local stylist who could deal with her wild hair.

Well, no sense worrying about that right now, she thought, tucking her unruly curls under a battered baseball cap. Sunny gave a rueful smile at the rest of her ensemble—a stained long-sleeved T-shirt, a pair of rubber boots she'd dug up from the basement, and her oldest jeans.

A pair of heavy-gauge rubber gloves dangled from her back pocket.

All set to go Dumpster diving, she decided and quietly headed downstairs, leaving her dad to sleep undisturbed. She went out the front door and walked along the street. Ada's house was only around the corner and a few blocks away. Wild Goose Drive was quiet at almost half-past eight. The real early risers were long up and headed off to whatever Saturday activities they intended to do. The rest of the neighborhood seemed to be still in bed.

She passed only a single pedestrian—Mrs. Parker, one of the local widows, out power walking. Sunny gave the older woman a friendly nod, even as she inwardly cringed at the look Mrs. Parker gave her cleaning getup. Then she got a little annoyed. *If she'd gotten her husband to power walk, maybe he'd still be around and she wouldn't be chasing after my dad.*

Reaching the corner, Sunny took a quick right, walked two more blocks, and then crossed the street. Almost there. The Spruance place, a large Colonial Revival, had been the finest on the block in its day. Now it had a curiously mottled appearance, with patches of silvery wood revealing where paint had flaked off the siding and darker stains suggesting the beginnings of mold. Knee-high grass fought an infestation of weeds in the unkempt yard.

As Sunny came up the cracked walkway, she saw the undergrowth shaking in something's wake.

Please let that be a cat, she prayed. *It's still too early to deal with wildlife.*

The mover and shaker popped out ahead of her—Shadow!

"Where did you get to?" She bent to pet the cat, only to see him glide back into the strawlike growth. "You eat our tuna and then just disappear. Or do you just like Ada's dry food better?"

She turned to the scabby-looking door, trying not to think of the alternate theory she'd developed, where Dad had trapped the cat and ejected him from the house.

The doorbell was a tarnished mass that stained the wood around it. Sunny knocked on the center panel, wondering if she should put her gloves on right away.

No answer.

She knocked again, louder, calling Ada's name.

The only response was a faint "meow" from inside.

Sunny tried to peek through the dirty glass of the living room window. She jumped back, nearly tripping among the weeds, when she came face-to-face with a golden calico cat peering out and making a mournful noise.

"Maybe she's in the back," Sunny told herself. She worked her way over to the driveway and around the house, discovering she had an escort again. Shadow had reappeared, trailing about a foot behind her.

The backyard was just as poorly maintained as the front. Sunny found a few pebbles and tossed them at the kitchen window, calling Ada's name.

Nothing, except more meowing—louder meowing, too, as if several cats had taken up the call.

"I don't suppose you know where she is," Sunny asked Shadow, who stared unblinkingly up at her. She was torn between annoyance at being stood up after dragging herself up early and worry for the older woman—not to mention a mild case of the creeps from all the cat noises filtering out from the kitchen. Cursing the strict New England up-bringing that wouldn't let her take the easy way out (like leaving after she'd promised to show up and help), Sunny approached the only other way into the house—the slant-ing cellar doors whose hinges had rusted in the open posi-tion.

The aromas wafting up from that hole in the ground were anything but inviting. Sunny found herself thinking of those kitty-litter ads that boasted about their product's ability to hide the presence of multiple cats.

Obviously Ada Spruance wasn't using that particular brand.

Sunny brought her rubber boot down on the first step—and had to restrain herself from kicking out with the other as Shadow now planted himself underfoot. He added his voice to the meowing chorus, but it managed to sound more like a warning than a hungry complaint. He rose up until his paws were at knee level, trying to stop her even as she carefully stepped around him to descend another step. Still, he kept making unhappy noises.

She pulled on her gloves, held her breath, and worked her way down the rest of the stairs. They were damp and a bit spongy. The only light came from the doorway behind her. Sunny blinked a few times, trying to accustom her eyes to the dimness.

A shaft of stronger light came in as a cloud moved off the sun.

Sunny gasped, then coughed at the almost solid stink that attacked her throat and nose. Her eyes watered, but she definitely saw something at the foot of the other stair-way in the cellar—the stairs that led up to the kitchen.

It was too big to be a cat.

And anyway, she'd never heard of a cat going around in a worn, flowered housecoat.

*

Shadow watched warily as the young woman made her way to the huddled figure on the cellar floor. He'd tried to stop her. Now he crouched low, his ears instinctively going back. From his experience, these two-leggity types made a lot of noise when they came across dead things.

This young woman surprised him. She got close enough for a good look at the Old One—the Dead One, Shadow corrected himself—took a single, deep breath, coughed, and then quickly headed back up the stairs.

Shadow followed her, opening his jaws wide to let the rank, green smells of the backyard wash away the scent of old decay—and worse—lingering in his mouth and nose.

The Young One didn't stop to enjoy the change. She dug out one of those strange, bright things that humans liked to talk into and spoke quickly in a high, excited voice.

The Dead One had one of those gadgets, but it was heavy and clunky, mounted high on the kitchen wall, a clumsy place to leap at.

But the Young One's talking-thing was small enough to fit in her hand—cat sized. Shadow's paw itched at the idea of getting that gleaming gadget on a nice floor—like the shiny floor in the Young One's kitchen, so good for sliding along—and giving it a good bat . . .

A sharp click got Shadow's attention. The woman had

finished talking, hiding away that interesting toy. Now she paced back and forth in the yard, overgrown grass stalks lashing against her shins.

Was she annoyed? Without seeing a tail, he didn't have enough information to be sure—and Shadow wasn't about to risk a kick by coming closer to see her response.

Instead, he stretched low and closed his eyes, enjoying the sunshine. But the quiet didn't last. Long before Shadow managed to drift off into a nap, he found himself raising his head. A car was coming—one that didn't belong here.

*

Sunny stopped short as a furry gray form zipped across her path, almost over her toes. She followed Shadow to the corner of the house, where he peered around.

By the time she joined him, she could see what had attracted the cat: a dusty black pickup truck turned onto the weed-choked driveway and came to a stop. The driver's door opened, and a tall, rangy guy in jeans and a denim jacket got out.

One of creepy Gordie's creepy friends? Sunny suddenly became very away that this guy was standing between her and the street. She narrowed her eyes. What was that bulge on one side of his jacket—a gun?

She took a step back when the stranger's hand came up, but it went into his breast pocket, extracting a leather case. He flipped it open to reveal a badge.

"Will Price, town constable," he said. "You're the person who called 911?"

Sunny nodded, gesturing toward the backyard and the

Claire Donally

cellar door. "Ada—Mrs. Spruance—asked me to come over. When she didn't answer the door, I went around this way and found—" She broke off. "Her neck—" With that, she ran out of words and just pointed.

The cop went past her and down the stairs. A moment later, he came back up again. "That can't have been very nice to find." He took a notebook from the other pocket in his denim jacket. "Why don't you tell me the whole story, Ms.—?"

"Coolidge—Sonata Coolidge. You can call me Sunny." She filled in the blanks. "Ada Spruance came to the MAX office—I work for the Maine Adventure X-perience." She added, relating her meeting with the Cat Lady at the MAX office and their conversation about Ada's lottery ticket problem.

The cop frowned in disbelief at her story. "Six to eight million dollars? I figured the local gossip mill had just pumped up the prize money."

"That's the amount Ada said," Sunny replied. "I never saw it. The thing was missing. But it seems kind of—" She bit off the word "convenient" and substituted "weird" instead.

She couldn't help noticing that this guy was pretty good-looking, in a serious, kind of poker-faced way. His face was long, with a strong nose and a sensitive-looking mouth—at least it would be if he didn't keep it pursed so tightly. He had odd eyes, kind of grayish with light brown flecks. Actually they reminded her a little of Shadow's.

Sunny looked down to find the cat at her feet, directing an unblinking gaze up at the cop. Kind of the same gaze the cop was giving her.

"It's just that I was a little afraid for Ada—you know, maybe someone was trying to take advantage of her somehow. So I talked to Ken Howell at the *Crier*. He ran a story about it, and it got picked up on TV."

She paused for breath . . . and an interior wake-up call. She'd conducted enough interviews to know the tricks. The silent approach could be a potent weapon, inducing a subject to spill his or her guts.

Well, it sure worked like gangbusters on me, Sunny thought. *Stop. Let him ask a question.*

Even so, she couldn't help the words from coming out. "It was an accident, wasn't it?"

"I'd like to think so if I were you." Those lips she'd been admiring turned into a frown. "Especially if I'd helped arrange it so that every lowlife for a hundred miles around knew that a frail old lady was sitting on a huge pile of cash."

"B-but I was trying to help her—protect her!" Sunny sputtered. She didn't get any further because another car pulled into the driveway: an official white sheriff's cruiser.

Sunny recognized Sheriff Frank Nesbit before he even got out of the car. Over the years, his face had gotten rounder and his mustache grayer as he appeared on billboards with each election cycle, always over the same slogan: "Keeping Elmet County Safe."

As the sheriff came toward them, however, he wasn't wearing his avuncular election-year smile.

"Aren't you supposed to be off duty, Constable Price?" Nesbit asked. "I hope you're not trying to angle your way into some overtime pay."

Price shrugged. "This is Ben Semple's shift. Somehow his patrols always take him to the other end of town, where he nails speeders off by outlet-land. Guess Ben's just very diligent about enhancing road safety—and county revenue. Problem is, that leaves coverage pretty thin around these parts. You can see how long it takes to get here from the county seat." He looked blandly at the sheriff. "And how was the traffic coming from Levett, sir?"

"Not too bad—especially since this didn't sound like a lights-and-sirens job to me," Nesbit replied. "The 911 call reported an accident, not a crime. Even so, I beat the ambulance here."

The sheriff shifted gears into constituent mode as he turned to Sunny. "And you must be the young lady who called."

When he heard Sunny's name, his smile became a bit more personal. "Mike Coolidge's daughter? I heard you'd come up from New York to take care of him. The old bandit's doing all right, isn't he? Good. Now, what happened here?"

Sunny explained about Ada Spruance's ticket and their date to search the house.

Nesbit shook his head. "Going from an enormous windfall to a fatal fall down the stairs. Very—what do you call it?—ironic."

"There's still a question about that," Price piped up. "Ms. Coolidge suspected the winning ticket might have been stolen, so she attempted to head off the culprit with a good glare of publicity."

"That's right—the wife mentioned seeing something about a ticket on the evening news."

Nesbit's smile at the memory faded as Price went on. "Most likely so did every felon within broadcast range."

"Is there any evidence of forced entry?" the sheriff asked in a clipped voice.

"None visible," Price admitted. But he directed his gaze to the hinges on the cellar door, rusted in the open position.

Not much breaking required to break and enter here, Sunny had to admit, looking back at the constable. *I thought he was just giving me a hard time about the possibility of a crime. But he's making a case even though his boss doesn't want to hear about it.*

In the meantime, Sheriff Nesbit went down the cellar steps and returned a moment later. "Obvious accident," he said flatly. "The door to the pantry upstairs is open. Ada was an older woman. The stairs are steep. It would be easy even for a young person up there to lose her balance." He headed for the police cruiser. "I'll call in to make sure the remains are picked up—"

He broke off in midsentence as a furry form burst out of the overgrown grass and ran across the driveway. "And then I'll call Animal Control. They'll have their hands full collecting all these fleabags."

Nesbit gave Price a thin smile. "I'll leave you in charge of the scene until they arrive, Constable." From the look on the sheriff's face, Sunny guessed Price would have a long, uphill struggle trying to get that approved as overtime.

As the cruiser pulled away, Sunny glanced down at her feet. Shadow remained where he was, taking everything in.

"So the cats will be hauled off to a shelter?" she asked.

"Do you know if it's humane—nonkill or whatever they call it?"

Price just looked at her. "That sounds like a very New York City idea," he said. "Out here in the sticks, the budget goes for animal control, not animal rights."

Sunny was never sure whether it was a Maine thing in general or a Kittery Harbor thing in particular, that ingrained, clannish belief that local ways were always superior to any idea an outsider might have.

It especially stung since he was treating Sunny like one of those outsiders.

"Well, maybe it seems like an outlandish notion around here, but I don't like the idea of killing off anything that happens to get in my way, whether that means old folks— or even cats."

Ignoring the cop's startled look, she bent to scoop up Shadow and storm off. But the cat undercut her dramatic exit by somehow evading her arms. Feeling foolish, she straightened again with a glare. "Unless you need anything more from me?"

Constable Price shook his head, raising his hands almost defensively. "Don't think so, ma'am. I'll just be here guarding the . . . accident scene."

Sunny started on her way home. The neighborhood was getting a bit busier, people gearing up for their Saturday activities.

She passed a family loading up their station wagon for some sort of shopping trip and got a laugh from a little girl. "Look, Mommy."

Sunny glanced down. Her outfit was a bit on the

scroungy side, but not that far out of the ordinary. Unless she'd managed to step in something cat related.

The girl's mother smiled, too, but she wasn't looking at Sunny. She was looking behind her. Sunny glanced over her shoulder. About six paces from her heels, Shadow sat on the pavement, apparently looking at nothing in particular.

Sunny started walking again. The girl giggled. Sunny turned to find Shadow still seated—and still about six paces behind her, his tail wrapped around his feet.

Taking three more steps, Sunny suddenly whirled on him again. Somehow, Shadow was still six paces behind her, still sitting. Except now, he twisted his own gaze around behind him, as if wondering what Sunny was looking at.

The little girl laughed even harder.

Sighing, Sunny resumed her walk, ignoring any chuckles she heard from her neighbors. *Stupid cat wouldn't let me pick him up, but he trails along behind me,* she thought. *Maybe Shadow is a good name for him.*

She arrived home and held the door while Shadow walked in as if he owned the place. "Guess you're better off here than dodging nets or whatever the animal control people have in store for you," she told the cat.

"That you, Sunny?" Her dad's voice came from the living room. She walked in to find him sitting on the couch with Mrs. Martinson, one of the widowed neighbor ladies. "Thought you'd be busy all morning."

Mike was talking a bit fast. Sunny quickly realized that wasn't because she'd walked in to find him entertaining a lady friend. Her dad was trying to brush sugary crumbs off his sweater.

"Nice to see you, Mrs. Martinson. Did you bring some of your famous coffee cake?" The words came out a bit sharper than Sunny meant them to.

"Sorry, dear, no." Helena Martinson didn't even turn a perfectly coiffed hair as she lied to Sunny. But then, the older woman had always shown a remarkable coolness in any social situation. Back when Sunny was in high school, Mrs. Martinson had been the hot mom all the boys lusted after. And even now, Sunny had to admit that her neighbor still looked pretty darned good. A well-cut pantsuit showed off her trim figure. Her pageboy hairstyle perfectly framed her delicate features, and somehow the silver threads among the gold had simply turned her into more of a platinum blonde.

Mrs. Martinson gave Sunny a bland smile, but Mike had a nervous grin—he hadn't succeeded in getting rid of all the evidence of his illicit cake eating. Then his expression turned to a thunderous scowl when Shadow walked into the room. "What is that thing doing back?"

Shadow continued to the pool of light from the window and curled up.

Sunny paused for a moment, not sure where to begin. "I guess he's going to be living here, because he doesn't have a home anymore," she finally said. "Ada Spruance is dead."

Mike looked ready to dispute the idea of Shadow moving in, but Helena Martinson seized control of the conversation. "Oh, my!" She perched forward on her seat, her doll-like face alight with avid curiosity. "What happened, dear?"

No doubt she's taking mental notes for the neighborhood gossip society, Sunny thought. "I found her as soon as I arrived," she said aloud.

"Lucky thing you went over there." Mike shot a dirty look at Shadow. "Those animals have no respect. By din-din time, they'd have been all over her."

Shadow looked up and blinked at him.

"Don't go looking at me like I'm some kind of kitty buffet, you damned beast!"

Shadow rested his head back on his paws, closing his eyes.

Before Mike could make some other sarcastic remark, Mrs. Martinson said, "Poor Ada. I guess I was one of the last people in the neighborhood on speaking terms with her. Ada's house is just down the block a bit from mine and across the street."

"I spoke to her just last week," Mike grumbled, "after one of her menagerie mistook my roses for a litter box."

"You shouted at her, you mean," Mrs. Martinson replied.

"Sheriff Nesbit says hello, by the way," Sunny said, hoping to change the subject.

Mike grunted. "He actually came down from Levett? A sure sign election time is just around the corner."

"Actually, a town constable came first," Sunny told her dad. "He didn't seem to get along with the sheriff."

"Sounds like Will Price." Mike grinned. "The constables are supposed to report to the sheriff's office, but Alderman Chase slipped Will in to annoy Frank Nesbit."

Even after spending the better part of a year back in town, Sunny still didn't have a handle on all the local politics. "Well, it seems to be working. What's the problem between them?"

"Who was the sheriff before Frank got in?" Mike nudged her.

Sunny called on fuzzy memories of classroom visits from grammar school. "Sheriff Price. Oh. His son?"

"Stu Price was a good lawman." Mike shook his head. "He made a mistake on one big case, and Frank just about ran him out of town."

"Died just a couple of months after the election. Car accident." Mrs. Martinson pursed her lips. "Or so they say."

"Will left town—joined the state police way up north, and then wound up on the force over in Portsmouth," Mike said. "But Chase persuaded him to come back to this side of the river. A lot of people, businessmen like Zack Judson over at the market and Ken Howell at the *Crier*, are getting sick of how Nesbit preaches about keeping Elmet safe while cooking the crime statistics. Assaults magically become harassment, or cases get pushed to other jurisdictions."

"I didn't realize you were so plugged in, Dad," Sunny said.

Mike shrugged. "Folks talk to me. I'm around here all day with not much else to do."

Mrs. Martinson cleared her throat. "Do you know how Ada . . . passed on?" Her sidewise glance at Mike showed the war between her curiosity and her fear of upsetting Sunny's dad. "I know she'd been complaining about chest pains recently."

"It was a fall," Sunny said quickly, unwilling to get into

a discussion about cardiac care. "She must have been going down into the cellar from the kitchen pantry—"

"Oh, no, that's impossible," Mrs. Martinson interrupted, drawing herself up from her perch on the couch to her full diminutive height. "Ada was deathly afraid of those stairs. She never used them."

4

"**Well, not necessarily** never, I guess," Mike tried to joke.

But Mrs. Martinson remained very straight on the edge of the couch, quietly insistent. "Ada almost had a fall on those stairs years ago. I think Gordon Senior was still with us. Ever since that, whenever she had to go into the cellar, she went down through the door in the backyard." She looked at Sunny. "Why do you think the cellar door hinges are rusted open?"

Sunny gave the neighbor lady a sharp look. "How do you know about that?"

"Besides you, I'm probably the only other person in the neighborhood who's been back there in heaven knows how long," Mrs. Martinson replied. "I've been in her kitchen, too. The last time Ada painted, Clinton was president. And the door to the cellar was painted shut."

Sunny shut her eyes for a moment, replaying the wait while Sheriff Nesbit went down into the cellar. "I don't think he was in there long enough to have gone up the stairs," she finally said.

Mike grunted. "Sounds to me like maybe old Frank was a bit too quick to downgrade this particular crime scene, as usual."

"It's not even a crime scene," Sunny told him. "According to the sheriff, Ada's death is just an accident."

"Maybe we should try and show him differently," Mike suggested.

Sunny gave him a look. *We?* "Nice thought, Dad," she said aloud. "But I don't have any standing to conduct an investigation."

"Well, maybe we can change that, too." Mike reached for the telephone. "After I talk to the alderman and some other people."

*

Her dad's telephone politicking took a little while, but early that afternoon Sunny found herself driving downtown. Most of Kittery Harbor was pretty spacious—for instance, the houses in Sunny's neighborhood were built on good-sized lots, with plenty of trees and shrubbery around. But the old part of town seemed crammed in around the cove that served as a harbor, the buildings shouldering against one another along crooked streets, some of which were still set with cobblestones. Sunny ended up parking her car a few blocks from her destination to avoid the crowding—there were just too many tourists around, enjoying a Saturday afternoon ramble around the historic structures.

Almost every building in the county showed some influence from old New England Colonial architecture—even if, nowadays, the clapboard siding was made out of plastic instead of spruce. But downtown, these buildings were the real thing. They might look more weather-beaten and worn than the imitations on the outskirts of town, but, where they hadn't been messed with, they also showed that old-time craftsmanship.

That didn't necessarily mean they were prettier, though. The building that housed the offices of the *Harbor Crier* looked more like a barn than anything else, and inside, the place smelled strongly of printer's ink and looked more like a print shop than a newspaper office. Ken Howell's desk was tucked in a corner of a room where generations of printing technology sat on planked pine floorboards. In the far corner there was even a handpress of the type that usually turned up in old Western movies.

Ken's storklike form was somehow folded onto a battered old stenographer's chair in front of an even older desk, a tall, pine, pigeonholed affair that would have looked more at home in a nineteenth-century counting house or a production of *A Christmas Carol*. Though, of course, the computer terminal might come off a bit anachronistic.

Ken stood up, a living Yankee stereotype, a gaunt, fleshless hawk face frowning over a long, lanky body. His flinty blue eyes didn't exactly impress Sunny as welcoming. "Your father and Zack Judson both pestered me into seeing you. Since Judson's Market is a printing customer, I'm giving you five minutes. Then I've got a shopping circular to get out—something practical to pay the bills."

"You must have heard that Ada Spruance is dead," Sunny began.

Howell nodded. "A fall. Tough for an old woman living alone, pretty much shunned by her neighbors."

"The problem is, Helena Martinson says Ada never used the stairs she's supposed to have fallen down, that she always avoided them."

The editor listened closely as Sunny explained Mrs. Martinson's objections. "Dad says Sheriff Nesbit has a habit of pushing reported crimes down the scale to protect his image, and this time he may have gone too far."

Howell's frown went from antagonistic to thoughtful. "You really think a crime occurred?"

"To be honest, I don't know." Sunny spread her hands. "But I do know there was supposed to be a winning lottery ticket on the premises, and I went and plastered the fact all over the local media. So if something did happen, I kind of feel responsible."

Howell sat in frowning silence for a moment, then expelled a long puff of air. "That would make two of us—although I don't usually consider myself as local media."

His pale blue eyes shot a sharp glance at Sunny. "So you want to use the paper as cover to investigate the situation? You're not trying to worm your way onto the staff? This won't be a paying job, and it certainly won't be like working for a big operation like the *Standard*. Don't expect people to pay much attention to the power of the press. You get that, right?"

"I understand," Sunny told him. "And I appreciate the favor. It can't have been easy for you to agree to this—not with Ollie Barnstable as a partner. I understand he's got a lot of political connections up in Levett, including the sheriff."

"I don't like that Levett crowd, especially Nesbit. And Barnstable is only a junior partner," Howell corrected. He glanced over to the ancient crank-operated press in the corner. "My great-grandfather started the *Crier* because he wanted to write about abolishing slavery. We celebrated a century and a half of service a few years ago. I'm not having this paper go down on my watch—that's why I took Barnstable's money. But he doesn't dictate editorial policy. So go ahead and investigate." He sighed. "But try not to go tramping on a lot of people's toes."

*

Armed with an official press pass from the *Harbor Crier*, Sunny drove back to the Spruance place. When she pulled into the cracked driveway, she found Gordie's rusty tan pickup parked at the end—and Will Price's dusty black one pulling in behind her.

She forced her door open and got out of her Mustang as Will stepped down from the running board on his truck. "If I had known you were coming, I'd have stayed after the animal control people left," he began, then raised his hands at the look on her face. "Ken Howell told me you were coming over here—and why. He asked if I'd come along with you, and frankly, I'd like a look at that painted-over door you mentioned to him."

"What is this," she asked in confusion, "the Kittery Harbor Underground Resistance?"

Will shrugged. "There are a lot of people around here who aren't happy with the way things are run up in Levett."

"And I suppose you're especially unhappy with Sheriff Nesbit."

"The guy's a politician, not a cop," Will said, his voice going flat. "My dad caught the first murder around here in I don't know how many years." He paused for a second. "The last, too, unless we end up counting this one. Anyway, he investigated, found a guy, made a case, and the prosecutor got a conviction. Then the real guy got caught on a completely unrelated charge and confessed—right before the election. Nesbit crucified my father."

"I understand he died soon afterward."

Will gave a tight nod. "Car crash."

"I know how that feels," Sunny said. "I lost my mom in a crash, too. The big Christmas ice storm."

"It can be hard to get over." He shook himself, as if physically trying to change the subject. "Let's take a look inside."

Will paused for a second, drawing a small jar of salve from his pocket. He scooped a little on his finger and then dabbed it under his nose. Sunny caught the pungent scent of menthol. "Are you allergic to overgrown grass?" she asked.

The constable shook his head. "This stuff cuts bad smells, and I'm sure we're going to find some in there." He offered her the jar. "Try it. I've seen guys use it when they had to check out overripe corpses."

"Great," Sunny muttered, dabbing a little salve in place. "Now I'm going to have morbid associations whenever I have a cold."

They went around to the backyard, peering into the darkness beyond the cellar door. "Gordon?" Sunny called. "You in there?"

A screech almost as loud as the one from her damaged car door came in answer. Then hurried footsteps pattered down the cellar stairs, and Gordie Spruance came into view. He wore old jeans, a flannel shirt buttoned all the way up to the neck, a watch cap, and a surgical mask.

Well, there goes our chance of checking out the pantry door, Sunny thought. That could get chalked up just as bad luck. But as her eyes got used to the dimness, she saw black garbage bags piled up around the spot where Ada Spruance had fallen. *Well, if it was a crime scene, it's certainly all disassembled now.* Sunny remembered the suspicion that had led her to publicize the winning lottery ticket in the first place. *Either very convenient—or very clever.*

Right now, though, Gordie didn't look very clever. Red-rimmed eyes stared at Sunny for a moment. "Oh. Sunny, right? Mom said you'd be coming over to help her. But—"

"I know," Sunny put in gently. "I'm the one who found her this morning."

"Sorry for your loss," Will added.

"We just thought we'd come by and . . . see how you were doing," Sunny improvised. "Seemed like the neighborly thing to do."

"It's just a big mess." Gordie made a helpless gesture, his eyes darting around at the garbage bags. "Even worse than it was when I left." He looked at Sunny. "I had to move out—I'm allergic to the damn cats."

So we don't know if those red eyes are due to grief or cat dander, she thought.

"Come up and see." Gordie abruptly turned and headed upstairs.

The steps up to the pantry were steep and thick with disturbed dust. Will used Sunny for cover, trying to get a good look at them in the gloom. Sunny wasn't exactly sure what sort of marks a falling body would make on such a coating. She imagined a person tumbling down the steep stairway would pretty much leave traces on every step. Here it seemed that the dust was very disturbed at the bottom, but the higher she got, the more there seemed to be just scuffed foot marks. So either poor Ada had gone more than halfway down the stairs she never used and attempted a swan dive . . . or been thrown some distance before actually hitting the treads.

At the top of the stairway, Will Price directed a significant look at the pile of paint chips on the floor beneath the door leading into the kitchen pantry. Clearly the door had only recently been forced open.

But did that happen when Ada went through—or when Gordie did? Sunny wondered.

The door screeched open, and they moved through a skinny, shelf-lined space into the kitchen itself. While the appliances were old, they looked reasonably well kept: the stovetop was clean, as was a small tray table and chair by the window where Ada had apparently taken her meals, at the edge of a lighter spot on the linoleum where a larger kitchen table must once have stood. The remaining open space had been used to create a sort of feeding station for the cats. At least a dozen metal bowls of dry food and fresh water stood in a row along the wall.

Will stepped over to the open kitchen cabinets, eyeing the empty shelves, their contents stacked on the counter.

Gordie pointed to the piles. "It's mostly soup and canned cat food. I've read about old folks living on that stuff—you don't think Mom was, do you?" He shook his head, not waiting for a response. "It's just that I know she was pretty hard up lately."

He led the way into the living room. Clearly, Ada *had* done some housekeeping in the areas she'd used—or maybe that she could see. A small island of orderliness surrounded the overstuffed chair and ottoman with the reading light behind, and the television. The rest was given over to dust, the furniture shaggy with cat hair. Gordie must have been busy in here, too. Half of the couch looked almost normal, a vacuum cleaner leaning against it.

Gordie gave the machine a kick. "Damn thing clogged up." He ran his forearm in front of his face, muffling a cough. "It's even worse upstairs. Except for her room, the cats took over everywhere. You can't believe the stink up there."

Worse than this? Sunny wondered. Even here, where at least some effort had been made, she couldn't mistake the sharp, pungent reek of cat pee making itself known through her protective menthol salve. Will didn't seem fazed by the assorted stinks, but she didn't even want to think about where that other odor of decay she smelled might be coming from.

Sunny suddenly found herself wishing she had a mask, too.

"I dunno what I'm going to do." Gordie's eyes darted around the room, then settled on Sunny again—now an unfriendly gaze. "Your boss from that tour place, Barnstable? He came by—I guess one of his big-shot pals called him with the news. I see him all the time, driving around here in that stupid Land Rover of his like he's some big-game hunter. 'Cept what he's hunting for is houses he can snap up for chump change. He's been oozing around Mom for I don't know how long, saying he wanted to 'help.' Now that she's dead, he tells me that all of a sudden the place is worth less than half of what he'd been offering her."

Sunny raised her hands in a "what can you do?" kind of gesture. Ollie the Barnacle wasn't one to let finer feelings—or any emotion at all, for that matter—get in the way of potential business.

"I may have to accept it anyway. Gotta pay off—" Gordie suddenly broke off, glancing over at Will Price as if just realizing the town constable was there. "So, you were going to help Mom look for that ticket," Gordie said, changing the subject and concentrating on Sunny. "Did she have any ideas about where it might be?"

Well, here was a development Sunny hadn't expected. If Gordie was after the ticket, she'd have thought he'd have gotten hold of it before doing anything to his mother. *Unless,* she thought, *this is the setup for a miraculous discovery just before the damned thing would have expired.*

"Sorry, Gordie," she said. "Your mom had no clue. That's why she was asking for help."

"So what now?" Gordie strode over and flung open the heavy drapes over the front window, revealing grimy glass—and a very startled cat who'd apparently evaded Animal Control by hiding out there.

Shadow? Sunny thought. Then her eyes adjusted to the brighter light and she could see the white markings on the gray coat. This cat was smaller than Shadow, too.

Blinking in the sunlight, Gordie didn't make out the cat at first. When he did, he recoiled almost like a vampire confronting a cross.

"I thought they got rid of all of you!" He reached out to roughly grab the cat, who lashed out with his claws. Gordie drew back with a yelp, instinctively putting his wounded hand to his mouth, forgetting about his face mask—and only succeeding in smearing blood on it.

The cat went for altitude, swarming up the heavy velvet drapes and releasing clouds of dust into the air. He'd gotten just about level with Gordie's head before the man managed to latch on to the spotted gray body.

"Gotcha, ya little—" He tried to pull the cat loose, but his captive dug in his claws and held on for dear life. "Come on!" Gordon gave a mighty heave . . . and brought down the cat, the drapes, the curtain rod, and even the brackets that held it to the wall—all in an even bigger cloud of dust and plaster.

Alternate sneezes and disconsolate yowls came from under the downed curtains, which humped up as the cat tried to escape the heavy folds.

Gordie lay on his back, wheezing and hacking.

"Are you all right?" Will Price asked.

"By bask iz fudd uv stodt," Gordie hoarsely replied.

"What?" Sunny asked.

"His mask is full of—" Will broke off, shaking his head. "You don't want to know."

The cat finally appeared from under the fallen velvet, streaking across the living room and up the stairs.

Sunny and Will got Gordon back into the kitchen and helped clean him up. Gordie took off his sodden mask and threw it away. As soon as he did, he began sneezing. Sunny pressed a dish towel into service, soaking it in hot water and using some dish detergent to clean his scratches. Then she switched to cold water to bring the bleeding down. Will Price stepped out to his truck and returned with a small first-aid kit.

Gordie was almost pathetically grateful. "Aw, man . . . jeez, thanks," he said yet again, punctuating his barely coherent words by sneezing into several sheets of paper towel clutched in his uninjured hand. "You're really good, coming over to help my mom. Most of the neighbors around here wouldn't care whether she lived or died."

"People got into fights with her," Sunny said.

"The damn cats got Mom into fights," Gordie corrected. "A bunch of chicken farmers way out—" He gestured vaguely toward the town line with his wad of towels and then down at them. "What was their name? Towle? No, those were the people with the dog. Ellsworth, that was it."

He sat like a little kid as Sunny squeezed some antibiotic cream on the scratches, then covered the whole thing with a gauze pad and some tape. "And then there's the big boss lady of the neighborhood, Mrs. Yarborough. She told

Mom she wanted this place bulldozed." He sneezed, hawked, and spat in the sink. "Not to mention that lousy Barnstable pretending to make nice—and then showing what a turd he really is."

"I think you'd better take it easy," Sunny told him, rinsing the sink.

"Or at least get yourself thicker gloves before you tackle the upstairs," Will added, trying to keep a straight face.

Gordie cast a worried glance around. "You don't think there are more of them, do you?"

"Just be careful," Sunny said as she and Will decided it would be best to say good-bye and left through the front door. As they went around to the driveway, the constable glanced sidelong at Sunny. "Very impressive, the amount of information you pumped out of him while playing Florence Nightingale."

"Well, now we know that Ada had at least three ongoing disputes in the neighborhood," Sunny replied. "Four, if you count Ollie Barnstable."

"Just the kind of false trails a trained investigator might expect from the prime suspect—if this were an actual crime."

"We certainly didn't find any proof, one way or the other," Sunny admitted. "Especially with the way Gordie's been all over the place." She looked at the constable. "But is that enough to promote him to prime suspect?"

He stopped in his tracks, staring at her. "I don't know how far you're going to get in this investigation if you didn't even notice that Gordon Spruance is a tweaker."

5

"What?" Sunny turned around to look at Will Price. He definitely had his cop face on, grim and dead serious.

"You know—meth? Crystal meth? Methamphetamine? He's using the stuff."

"How do you know?" Sunny asked.

"How could I not?" Will burst out, then quickly turned to check the windows. All the ones on this side stood closed and curtained.

Still, he lowered his voice. "It's a classic case—his eyes darting around all over the place, several tasks started and left half finished, impulsive actions. It's not often you see a guy Gordie's age with acne, unless the person is a meth user. He had a strong reaction to light in his face—and even you must've noticed the paranoia." Will gave her a measuring look. "Something tells me your newspaper career didn't involve much work on the crime beat."

"I was a general-assignment reporter," Sunny told him. "I handled whatever came my way." She stalked over to her Mustang, but hesitated with her hand on the door. "Okay, maybe I'm overreacting, but it's just hard to wrap my head around. I could accept the idea of drug addicts in New York. But here? Gordie Spruance? He got left back a couple of times, so he was still going to high school when I started—not that I was friendly with the guy. But I still remember when people started calling him 'Gordo,' and how at first he was happy to have a new nickname."

"I sense a 'but' coming up here," Will said.

"It was a stupid joke out of Introductory Español— 'Gordo' is like the Spanish version of 'Fatso.'"

"With a high school career like that—and a mom like Ada—I'm surprised he didn't start taking drugs a lot earlier," Will joked.

Sunny laughed, then got serious again. "Do you really think he could have killed his mother?"

Will looked at her, a hint of humanity stealing out from behind his stern cop face. "What do you think?"

"I suspected that he might have stolen Ada's lottery ticket," she admitted. "That's why I tried to get some coverage about the story."

"Most tweakers get in trouble stealing money to support their habits." Will had returned to his cold, professional form. "And they don't have much impulse control. If the mother caught him with the ticket—" He shrugged. "Anything might be possible."

"Still," Sunny said, "drugs, in Kittery Harbor?"

"They turn up in tonier—and stranger—places than this." Will grimaced. "Not that Frank Nesbit would believe it."

Sunny laughed. "The See-No-Evil Sheriff."

"Not blind—selective," Will replied. "He can see lots of evils when they're the kind that result in fines to fill the county coffers."

"Is that what they mean when they talk about making crime pay?" Sunny asked.

"As I'm sure you've heard often enough in your career: no comment." Will tried to contain a wince at the noise as Sunny wrestled her damaged door open. "I still have some connections on the Portsmouth PD. I can check in and get an idea about the local meth situation—and whether Gordie Spruance has ever turned up on their radar."

"I'll follow up on the neighborhood end of things," Sunny said.

"Sure, though somehow, I don't think Ada Spruance got killed in a dispute over petunias," Will said over his shoulder as he went to his pickup.

"From what little Gordie had to say, I think it'll turn out to be a bit more serious than that," Sunny agreed. "Though don't dismiss flowers so easily. There've been a couple of times I was afraid Dad would have a relapse when he found her cats had peed on his roses."

With that, Will pulled out of the driveway, and Sunny headed home, mulling possible suspects the whole way.

Lots of people—including even her dad—had had beefs with Ada Spruance. But Gordie had mentioned the names of three people who might be more seriously involved. The top slot on Sunny's mental list was filled by Veronica Yarborough, head of the homeowners' association. Sunny had met her a couple of times, since her dad was a member of the board. Each time, Veronica had given the impression of bestowing a great favor just by visiting their house. If being not very nice was a character trait of cold-blooded killers, Veronica Yarborough would fit the profile nicely. But Sunny would have to look into all of them and not let her personal feelings prejudice her against Veronica.

At least, not very much.

*

As she came up the walk to her front door, Sunny spotted Shadow kicking dirt near one of her father's rosebushes.

Guess it would make sense for him to do his business where the ground has already been dug up, Sunny thought, *but I don't think Dad will appreciate the extra fertilizer.*

She went inside to make a list of the things Shadow would need if he was going to stay. Kitty litter and a litter box, a proper cat bed, food—he couldn't keep eating their tuna, after all. Closing her eyes, Sunny tried to remember the brand name on the cans she'd seen in Ada Spruance's kitchen.

She opened her eyes and went back to her list. This was probably going to cost a bit. But maybe that was a good thing. It would make it clear to her dad that she intended for Shadow to stay.

Mike Coolidge was not happy when Sunny returned with a big bag of pet purchases, but even his laser glare of disapproval didn't make Sunny back down. "I said Shadow would be staying with us, at least till we find him a decent place to live," she told him in no uncertain terms.

Shadow himself turned out to have some strong opinions. When Sunny arranged his new pet bed, he ran to recover the fake-fur coat lining from the pillow he'd slept on previously, clamping it in his jaws and dragging it to Sunny, who placed the ratty thing over the new bed's fleece lining.

Sunny shook her head. "Whatever floats your boat." Then she turned to her father. "Do you have Veronica Yarborough's phone number?"

"It's in the phone book in the kitchen drawer," Mike told her. "Look under S for 'snooty.' "

*

Even for a Sunday afternoon, the neighborhood was quiet as Sunny walked to her appointment with Veronica Yarborough late the next day. She'd felt lucky to wedge her way into Veronica's very full social calendar.

Apparently everyone had decided to do their weekend yard work the day before, so Sunny walked through empty streets, with the occasional burst of football-related crowd roar coming through open windows. She arrived at her destination purposely early and stood for a moment, taking in the shiny white clapboard house with its columned front porch and third-floor dormer windows. Twenty-five years ago it had been the Leister place, home of the blondest and most popular girl in her grammar school class. How many times had Sunny walked up that drive in her best dress and party manners, just because all of the golden girl's classmates had been invited? And she hadn't even liked Jane Leister, damn it.

When Sunny was a kid, the house had engraved itself

in her memory under the heading "Stately Home." Certainly it was the most expensive place in the neighborhood, more suited to the upper-class enclave of Piney Brook. It stood out among the more modest houses in the surrounding blocks, but in a more graceful way than some of the McMansions that had popped up in recent years. Those looked just plain ugly.

Now Sunny found herself walking up to the front door yet again, dressed in a good suit from her reporting days. From the front, the place didn't seem to have changed at all. A quizzical smile tugged at Sunny's lips. *Funny how some places stick with you,* she thought.

Veronica Yarborough opened the dove gray door. The Icelandic wool sweater the president of the homeowners' association was wearing probably could have paid for Sunny's good suit three times over. Well, at least she wasn't a blonde, just an elegantly tall brunette with a frost of silver in her hair.

"Ms. Coolidge, how nice to see you." Veronica sounded about as chummy as the queen of England greeting a commoner upon whom she was about to bestow a medal.

Not for the first time, Sunny found herself wondering how this woman had elbowed her way to power in the homeowners' association. Not only was she an outsider, she was a pushy outsider. That was the way Sunny's dad had described Veronica when she'd first arrived a few years ago. When Sunny had called up from New York, Mike always had a funny story about the bossy new neighbor, telling everyone how things ought to be run in the association.

But maybe, just as the sea wore away the rocks on the

Maine coast, it was Veronica's relentless pushing that had brought her to the position of the neighborhood's queen bee.

And as such, Veronica did her best gracious-host impersonation. "Why don't we step into the family room?"

The living room Sunny remembered had become a formal parlor, and a very grand mahogany table now dominated the dining room, with a silk runner and a crystal bowl of flowers in the middle. Beyond that, however, was all new territory. The old rear wall of the house had been moved back a good fifteen feet, enlarging the old kitchen, adding a breakfast nook, and creating a large, airy space that housed leather couches, reclining chairs, a wall-mounted entertainment center, and a fireplace. French doors gave a view of a carefully rustic garden centered around a pool that Sunny didn't remember, either. With its varnished wood and pale peach paint on the walls, the whole place seemed more northern California than southern Maine.

"Very impressive," she said.

"Thank you." Veronica took in her surroundings with a smug smile. "We had considerable work done before moving in."

She gestured toward one of the couches. "Welcome to the neighborhood," she said, then fluted a laugh. "Or rather, welcome *back* to the neighborhood, considering you've lived here before."

Sunny managed an equally insincere smile. "Yes, we even met a couple of times."

Veronica didn't quite know how to answer that. Stepping over to the counter separating the seating space from the kitchen, she asked, "May I offer you a sparkling water?"

When Sunny said yes, Veronica took a bottle from the built-in refrigerator and poured them both wineglasses of bubbly water—an expensive, imported brand, of course. No generic seltzer from outlet-land here.

"I understand you're doing a story for the *Harbor Crier*," Veronica said.

Still smiling, Sunny nodded. She hadn't mentioned exactly what the story was about, and she wasn't about to open her mouth now. Sometimes letting an interviewee take the lead could result in more interesting revelations than the tightest interrogation.

"As you know, this is an older homeowners' association," Veronica began.

The neighborhood had been developed a good fifty years before, starting with the construction of what folks in town still called the New Stores.

"Over the years, the association has had its responsibilities eroded as the township took over various services like street lighting and some of the formerly private roads. I'm afraid this also led to a certain . . . withering . . . of our regulatory ability."

"That must have come as something of a shock when you joined the board." Sunny did her best to sound sympathetic. She had to wonder how the Yarboroughs had bought an expensive house and sunk big bucks into this extension without being aware of the growing cat menagerie just blocks away. Didn't they ever drive around the neighborhood? Aloud, she asked, "Is that part of the problem you faced with Ada Spruance?"

For just a moment, the mask of gracious living fell away from Veronica Yarborough's face, exposing the frosty, ruthless woman who had conquered her little empire. "If I'd had my way, we'd have surrounded the Spruance place with a twenty-foot-tall fence and prayed for rain." With an effort, she moderated her tone. "Not to speak ill of the dead, of course, but that woman had no right to be operating a—a shelter for stray cats in the middle of a residential neighborhood."

From Veronica's tone, Ada might as well have been running a cathouse instead of a cat shelter.

"And the board has been very lax," Veronica complained. "I've recommended punitive action—levying fines, for example. But even your father—despite his personal problems with Mrs. Spruance—wouldn't live up to his responsibilities, I'm sorry to say."

Good for Dad, Sunny thought. Except for a sprinkling of newcomers, most of the houses in the neighborhood were still owned by the "original settlers," as they called themselves, or by their children. While Sunny could feel a little impatience when that close-knit feeling exhibited itself negatively as clannishness, she also shared their background. This was her home, and it was the Spruances', too. Ada and Gordon Spruance—Gordon Senior—had bought their house as newlyweds. They'd raised a family, and Ada had grown old there. *And maybe a little odd, too,* Sunny privately admitted. But Ada had been a part of the community for decades. Where did Veronica Yarborough come off trying to change that?

"Perhaps Mrs. Spruance would have taken her lottery winnings and moved out, cats and all," Sunny suggested.

"More likely, she'd have thrown the money away on kitty caviar and lawyers to harass the association." Veronica moodily sipped her water. "The crazy old woman told me often enough that she intended to stay in that house until the day she died."

"Well, that is what happened, isn't it?" Sunny said brightly.

Veronica took another sip as she considered the implications. "There's a son, isn't there? Although he hasn't lived on the property in some time."

Sunny stayed silent, letting Veronica think aloud. "It might be possible to require him to make repairs—at least to paint the place. Certainly the board couldn't argue with that. The son might have roots in the community, but he's moved out. And the man has a criminal record, for heaven's sake. We might even be able to levy fines for noncompliance, make it too expensive to keep the property—"

"I understand Oliver Barnstable has already made an offer on it," Sunny said.

Veronica actually looked pleased. "The house could end up in worse hands. He's one of the more forward-thinking people in this town. The right sort of renovations could bring a much more suitable family into the neighborhood."

Yeah, you would think that, Sunny thought as she rose. "Well, I don't want to take up too much of your Sunday afternoon."

Veronica looked disconcerted. "I thought you were going to interview me."

"First meetings are generally for background." Sunny lied easily. "I think I have enough to start with. I'll be in touch if I have more questions later."

Frankly, Sunny had already heard enough from Veronica Yarborough. The woman hadn't just declared war on Ada, she'd shown herself equally willing to carry on the war to the next generation, harassing Gordie. The homeowners' association president definitely had a strong motive. Ada Spruance with a six-million-dollar war chest would have been a definite threat to Veronica's plans to make this part of Kittery Harbor safe for "more suitable" residents.

And now that threat was gone.

*

His belly low, Shadow advanced to the top of the coffee table, moving each paw as silently as possible. Not that the prey he was stalking was going anywhere. The thick book sat at the far end of the table, near where the Old One sat dozing.

A change in breathing made Shadow lift his head up. *The new Old One,* he corrected himself. This one was male, and much quicker to anger than the old Old One . . . the dead Old One.

But this Old One just made a couple of lip-smacking noises and sighed, drifting into deeper sleep.

Shadow resumed his project. He'd never really considered why things fell. There were times when he'd fallen, sometimes twisting desperately in midair to land on his feet. But why was that? Why didn't things stay as they were instead of tumbling down?

He got both his forepaws on the spine of the book, braced himself, pushed—and pushed again.

*

Sunny came home just in time to see Shadow shove the thick book off the living room coffee table. He leaned

~67~

over the edge as if fascinated by the falling object, letting out an odd meow of pleasure—more like a "Yow!"

Between that and the loud thump of the book hitting the floor, Mike Coolidge jerked awake. "Damned cat!"

Before he could say or do anything more, Shadow dodged backward, not afraid of Sunny's father but with a practiced wariness that made Sunny wonder about Shadow's history. As a stray, the cat had more than likely encountered the nasty side of human nature in the past.

Too bad I never had a chance to talk with Ada about Shadow before she died, Sunny said to herself. *But then, I thought I had all the time in the world to ask her questions.*

Shadow launched himself into a long leap, hitting the floor on the bounce and landing at Sunny's feet, where he immediately started twining around her ankles.

She laughed, and Mike directed a sour look both at her and the cat. "Made me lose my place," he grumbled. "Not that you care, with how he's sucking up to you, Sunny."

*

Shadow approached the New One—Sunny, she seemed to be called—and worked his way around her ankles, inhaling deeply, enjoying some of the new smells she brought into the house. He inhaled a hint of wax and fragrant wood smoke.

Much better than the last time she'd come in, reeking of the Dead One's house—and the Dead One's stinking son, whose unwashed clothing had been bad enough, but who also radiated traces of anger and fear. And beneath that, another odor, not only unpleasant but threatening. It wasn't just the stench of death; in his wanderings, Shadow had smelled plenty of dead things.

No, this smell was something deadly—toxic—that had led Shadow to name him the Stinky One.

6

The next afternoon, Sunny sat on one of the wharves in the harbor, eating lunch and staring at the sunlight on little rippling waves. Otherwise, there wasn't much of a wonderful panorama to enjoy. Seavey's Island and the naval shipyard blocked her view of deeper water. The town had installed benches at the head of each wharf for any footsore tourists enjoying the quaintness of the old downtown buildings. On a Monday, these piers were pretty much empty except for a few outdoor lunchers like Sunny, alone with her thoughts.

Shipbuilding made up an important piece of local history. Back in 1777, the sloop *Ranger* had been launched in these waters, sailing out under the command of John Paul Jones and into naval history.

Maybe that's my problem, Sunny thought. *I love this*

town, but I always thought of it as a place to come from, not a place to live. Dad is forever trying to get me to go out and meet people, but my friends—my real friends— have all left Kittery Harbor. To the people who stayed, I'm more a New Yorker than a local girl now.

She tossed the last crust from her sandwich onto the water, and a seagull wheeled to pounce on it.

I've been in a funk since I found out I was stuck up here—no, she corrected herself, *even before.*

As soon as she'd heard about her dad's heart attack, she'd headed back to Kittery Harbor immediately, using up her vacation time and then applying for a leave of absence. Taking care of her father had been the first priority, of course. But Sunny had also thought it might be a good idea to put some distance between herself and the editor she'd been dating—the married editor. Although Randall had been separated from his wife for more than a year before Sunny started going out with him, he was obviously very conflicted on the idea of a divorce. Sunny believed both of them had to figure out exactly what their feelings were, and this would be an excellent opportunity to do that.

Well, absence hadn't made Randall's heart grow fonder. As the situation on the *Standard* got worse and he found his own job threatened, he'd plumped for family values and sent Sunny a severance notice.

Speaking of which, Sunny thought, *I'd better get back to work before Ollie the Barnacle gets the same idea.*

She headed back through the crooked, Colonial era streets and then through the newer, more open part of town, passing city hall and the big brick library. After a quick glance at her watch, she lengthened her stride along the final long blocks to the New Stores.

Unlocking the door, she stepped into the MAX office and immediately checked the answering machine. Nothing critical there. Sunny settled behind her desk and switched on the computer. A couple of clicks on the mouse, and she'd brought up the project she'd been working on before lunch, marketing copy for the website.

Then she checked her e-mail. The first few items were just routine business. But after them came a string of e-mails from Ken Howell at the *Crier*.

Sunny sat for a moment, looking at her computer monitor.

She tried to concentrate on the marketing copy on the screen. This was supposed to be the good part of her job, the creative work that made up for the website maintenance and listing updates.

But now she had something a hell of a lot more interesting than that to think about. After she'd called him yesterday, Ken had promised to send over the *Crier*'s coverage of the two disputes she'd inquired about.

Sunny sighed, glanced around guiltily—although she knew no one else was in the office—and started downloading the files Ken Howell had e-mailed over. As each one came through, she found herself reading a new installment of a continuing saga to rival a soap opera.

Ada Spruance's friction with the neighborhood homeowners' association had essentially boiled down to an offense against Veronica Yarborough's esthetic sense—and her property values. That didn't exactly make for a front-page news story, even for a small weekly like the *Harbor Crier*.

Ada's other disputes, however, were precisely the stuff of small-town newspapers. The first wasn't a man-bites-dog story, but a dog-bites-cat one. One of Ada's feline residents had gotten mauled—and ultimately died—after a run-in with a neighbor's pit bull–Rottweiler mix.

The *Crier* tried to keep an impartial stance, but it was interesting to see how the community's sympathies had shifted. Initially, folks had been shocked by the attack, and Ada had threatened a lawsuit. But the Towles—Chuck and Leah, the owners of the dog—had a story to tell, too.

Although their dog had caught up with the cat in front of Ada's house, the chase had begun in the Towles' backyard. According to them, the cat had climbed over the fence and taunted the dog until he'd broken his tether and taken off in pursuit.

Howell hadn't sent just the news stories; he'd also sent the impassioned exchanges from the Letters to the Editor section. The situation had only gotten wilder with the second case.

Nate and Isabel Ellsworth ran a free-range chicken operation at the edge of town. They thought they were facing a fox problem—until they installed some video surveillance and discovered it was a cat that was raiding their stock.

When they checked the largest local collection of cats—the Spruance place—they found a chicken foot with their identifying tag on the ankle near the porch.

This pretty much swept Ada off the moral high ground.

Now she was the one with the predatory pet. Tempers ran so high that one local wag wrote to the editor suggesting that the cases be put together and adjudicated on one of those TV legal shows.

As far as Sunny could make out from the accounts, none of the situations ever got to court. Would that have changed if Ada Spruance had received a whopping infusion of lottery money?

She scrolled back through the various stories until she found a quote from the Ellsworths describing the chicken thief. Although they had a hard time telling from the night-vision images, it appeared to be a large black or gray cat.

Sunny bit her lip. *That couldn't be Shadow—could it?* she thought uneasily, then shook her head. Seemed like every time she saw a cat, she thought of Shadow.

The rattle of the front door opening gave her an instant's chance to click the computer mouse. By the time Oliver Barnstable stood beside her, the promo copy was back up on the screen.

"Hello, Ollie." Glancing up at him from her seated position was a bit like watching a partial eclipse. She had to look around his big, round belly to catch a glimpse of his florid face. He was a blazer and khakis kind of guy, with an expensive, wrinkled blue cotton shirt that strained around his overly ample middle.

"Keeping busy, Sunny?" he asked.

"There's always enough to do," she replied.

Especially considering the pitiful salary you're paying me, she added silently.

It was as if he'd read her thoughts. "It's just that I heard you've taken up a side job with Ken Howell. Hope that won't cause a conflict of interest."

"Conflict?" Sunny echoed.

"The way I hear it, you're trying to prove that Ada Spruance's fall was no accident. Since your job—your *main* job—is supposed to be promoting tourism, I'm wondering exactly how publicizing a murder around these parts would help to pack the customers into our accommodations."

For a brief second, Sunny wondered how it would feel to shove her keyboard right through his smug, fat face.

But she needed the job. So she braced herself for whatever Ollie the Barnacle had to say, but this was interrupted when the door rattled open again.

A man, tall and slim, stood silhouetted in the doorway. As he came inside, Sunny noticed his sharp features and rich tan. Yeah, "rich" would be the word for him. He wore thin-wale cords and some sort of car coat, black wool, very soft. Probably cashmere.

Ollie took in the vision as well, saying, "Welcome to the Maine Adventure X-perience," in his most genial tone. "We don't generally get walk-in traffic, but we're certainly ready to help you."

"Thanks very much." The man gave a small smile, barely moving his lips when he talked. And the way he spoke—was that some sort of accent? Sunny couldn't place it.

"I had some business in Portsmouth that concluded early, so I have a few days free. I'm told my family has some roots here, and I'd like to explore the area a bit."

"I'm sure Sunny can arrange something appropriate." Ollie looked at his watch, every inch the man of affairs. "You'll have to excuse me, Mr.—?"

"Richer," the elegant stranger supplied, giving the name a French pronunciation. "Roger Richer." The first name got more of an English treatment, but still came off sounding like "Razh-AIR." He also gave Ollie a slight bow instead of a handshake.

A little taken aback, Ollie nodded in response, said good-bye, and took off.

Sunny nodded toward the chair beside her desk. "Why don't you have a seat, Mr. Richer?"

"Please, call me Raj." He gave her another tight-lipped smile.

"Okay." Sunny brought up a new window on her monitor. "I guess the first order of business would be accommodations. I could book you a room"—she glanced again at that expensive coat—"or a suite at the Colonial Inn. It's probably the nicest place in the area."

"A hotel?" Raj looked a little disappointed. "I had hoped for something a little more—homelike."

"Ah." Sunny switched to her bed-and-breakfast database. Most B&Bs in the area catered to a more modest tourist crowd, but . . .

"Here's something," she said, double-checking that the listing hadn't been booked. "The Rowlandson estate. It's in Piney Brook, a very exclusive community. A cottage, usually for weekend guests, but it happens to be available. Single bedroom, a bath, and a working kitchen." She paused for a second. "The Rowlandsons won't actually be there—they're away on their yacht. I guess you'll have to cook for yourself, but you can use the amenities. Although it's kind of late in the season, they do have an enclosed pool. Would that be all right?"

Raj nodded. "That would fill the bill nicely." He reached into his coat and drew out a wallet that should have been as slim and elegant as the rest of him. The effect was somewhat spoiled by the batch of hundred-dollar bills packed into it. "What would the rate be?"

"We usually do payments by credit card," Sunny began, then shook her head. Their business was done online, and that was where their payments were processed. The office didn't have a credit card terminal. "But I suppose a cash deposit would be all right."

She got out the lockbox for petty cash, which also held the Rowlandsons' keys. Raj handed over a fat fee for five days, and Sunny tucked away the bills in the box. *That should warm Ollie's cold little heart,* she thought.

Returning to her keyboard, she printed out the directions to the estate and then maneuvered a few new windows onto her screen. "Richer. That's a French name, isn't it?"

Raj nodded.

"Is that the branch of the family you're tracing? We have a pretty active historical society here in town." A quick click on the mouse, and she added, "Most records are up in the county seat in Levett. They have some genealogical resources up there, too."

A little more computer digging, and she said, "If there's a Canadian connection, there are several French-Canadian heritage groups you could contact. Most of them are farther upstate, though."

"I am sure the local groups you have mentioned will do for a start," Raj said, his hands making little pushing-down gestures.

"Would you prefer I download all of this to your computer or phone?" Sunny asked.

That got another smile from Raj. "I have not embraced technology so enthusiastically, I'm afraid. The machines I use tend to be very simple."

The cell phone he took out of his pocket was a lot less high-end than the rest of his outfit.

"I could just print it out for you, if you prefer," Sunny offered.

"That would be excellent."

As the printer hummed, she asked, "Is there anything else you need? Tours? Local attractions?"

Raj shook his head.

"How about local transportation? Do you have your own car?" Sunny asked.

"I rented one in Portsmouth." He nodded out the window to a racing green Jaguar parked behind Sunny's Mustang.

"Very impressive," Sunny told him. "You're lucky it's still fall, though. I don't know how practical it might be for a Maine winter. My own car got in a little trouble when things were icy."

"I thought I saw some damage on that car." Raj pointed to her Mustang.

"That's the best I could do to fix it up." Sunny collected the papers from the printer and stood. "Luckily, I don't think you'll have to worry about that—unless you decide on a prolonged stay."

He smiled again, that curious, tight-lipped smile, and took the sheaf of papers. "Thank you, Sunny."

"You're welcome," she told him. "If you change your mind about the local attractions, or if you need anything else during your stay—well, we're here to help."

He thanked her again and gave another little bow, then left. Still, it was the highlight of her working day, and it charged up her batteries to tackle the promotion copy.

Then she got an e-mail from the company's Web server reporting a problem and spent hours trying to reconcile two applications that had suddenly decided not to play nicely with one another anymore.

On the bright side, Ollie didn't come back for a repeat browbeating session. Sunny took a chance and printed out hard copies of the stuff Ken Howell had sent her, stuffing them in an envelope.

After responding to several tourism information requests and processing a couple of visits, her eyes felt fatigued and her neck stiff.

That's what happens from sitting in the cheap seats, she thought, rolling back in her office chair. *This thing is barely one step up from the antique in Ken's office.*

Sunny shifted in her chair. Fat chance that Ollie the Barnacle would shell out to upgrade the office furniture, especially after he'd just chewed her out for conspiring to damage local tourism.

Well, he'll see I did my best to fill the coffers today, she thought as she locked up the office, stepped over to her trusty Mustang, and started the engine.

Sunny suddenly bit her lip. That was a lot of money in the cash box—more than she'd ever left in the office. She looked along the street, at the deepening evening shadows. Most of the businesses had already closed up. This wasn't like New York, where merchants pulled down metal shutters or gates. There was just an expanse of plate glass, a cheap drawer lock, and an antiquated lockbox between anybody out here and the money she'd collected today.

You're being silly, she scolded herself, *but it would be just my luck that tonight would be the night somebody tried something.* She left her car running and went back to the office, opened the door, unlocked her desk, scooped up the cash box, and headed back outside.

As she did, her car gave a loud *BANG!* She could see it shake for a second.

Wonderful—a backfire. Maybe she shouldn't try to stretch her dollars by buying cheap gas.

She went to open her car door again and stopped. Something was wrong with the steering wheel—or rather, with the plastic sheathing on the steering column. A good chunk was torn out of it.

Then she dragged her eyes from the damage inside to the damage to the top of her windshield—a spiderweb of cracks centering on a small, round hole.

A bullet hole.

7

Sunny didn't know how long she just stood there, staring with her mouth hanging open. The sound of a car pulling up behind her finally snapped her out of her trance.

She whirled around to see a midnight blue patrol car, the words "Kittery Harbor Police" in gold on the front doors. No flashing lights on top. And behind the wheel, grim faced as usual, was Constable Will Price.

"Why should I not be surprised to find you?" he said, getting out of the car. "Zack Judson called from his store, reporting a gunshot. Dispatch thought it was probably a backfire, but they sent me by to check things out."

Will's stern demeanor melted a little as he looked at her more closely. "Hey—Sunny? Are you all right?"

Sunny wordlessly pointed at the inside of her car and the windshield.

The constable did a double take when he spotted the bullet hole. But then he was back to business as usual.

He took Sunny's arm, almost dragging her over to Judson's Market two stores away. At the same time, he spoke rapidly into the microphone attached to his blue uniform, radioing for backup.

The next few minutes got pretty exciting as another blue town patrol car and two white cruisers from the sheriff's department came flying up, sirens blaring. The area filled with uniformed officers, redirecting traffic away from Sunny's car and trying to shoo away the onlookers who began to congregate.

Will had already pulled his car away from Sunny's. Now he pointed to her Mustang, talking to one of the deputies who seemed to be in charge. "Looks like something went off in there. The angle's all wrong for a bullet fired from the outside."

"Some kind of booby trap?" The deputy, a tall, lanky guy in a forest green uniform, frowned unhappily.

"Yeah—and we don't know what else might be in there." Will took the lead, approaching Sunny's car with a large flashlight. "There's something down by the gas pedal."

Sunny held her breath as he craned his neck, trying for a better look. "I think the panel is off the fuse box, and there's some kind of gizmo attached. I see wires—"

"You going in?" The lanky deputy swallowed audibly. Sunny saw his prominent Adam's apple bob up and down.

Will's hand went for the door handle, then hesitated. "I dunno, Fred. Maybe we should leave this for the professionals."

The deputy stood staring at him. "You mean the bomb squad?"

Will began backing away. "Unless you want to go poking around in there yourself."

Retreating to Judson's Market, the deputy began talking into his own radio.

Perhaps five minutes passed. Then another sheriff's department car came roaring up. It screeched to a stop, the door opened, and a red-faced Frank Nesbit emerged, dressed in a tuxedo.

Either he's going for the James Bond look this evening or he has some political dinner to attend, that irreverent voice inside Sunny's head suggested.

The sheriff took in the whole scene—the blocked road, the growing crowd—and flashed a baleful glance around the assembled lawmen. "What lamebrain's trying to call in the state police bomb squad?"

The lanky deputy suddenly took a giant step away from Will Price.

His movement caught Nesbit's attention. Now his generalized glare had a focus: Will.

"I should have known," Nesbit growled.

"There's some sort of device in there," the constable tried to report. "Apparently it set off a shot."

Nesbit stomped over to Sunny's Mustang, grabbed the door handle, and heaved on it. The door opened with its usual unearthly screech.

The law officers and the crowd of civilian rubberneckers that had gathered all cringed back. But the awful noise was all that happened.

Nesbit put out his hand, calling, "Flashlight!" When he

got one, he bent forward, peering at the floor in front of the driver's-side seat. Then the sheriff straightened up. "Looks like somebody wired in a circuit board with a bullet attached to it." He threw another aggravated look at Will. "A single shot. Nothing else."

"There's an urban legend like that," one of the deputies said. "From back in the old days, when cars used those cylindrical fuses. They were the same size as a .22 shell, so some goober who was short on fuses used a bullet to replace a burned-out fuse. Worked okay until an electric charge finally set the damned thing off. Caught him right in the—"

The guy suddenly paused when he realized the whole crowd on the street was listening. "Er—groin region," he finished lamely.

Nesbit in the meantime was looking fixedly at the Mustang, his lips set in a frown beneath his silver mustache. "This car looks familiar," he said. "Whose is it?"

Sheepishly, Sunny raised her hand. If the sheriff had been angry before, a picture of his face now could be used in the dictionary to illustrate the phrase "if looks could kill."

"You!" Nesbit visibly tried to restrain himself, but even so, his voice was overly loud when he spoke again. "Young lady, if you've—"

He broke off, looking over Sunny's shoulder. She turned to see that Ken Howell had appeared, scribbling frantically in a notebook.

He'd love for the sheriff to say something stupid on the record, Sunny realized.

"All right." Nesbit brought the volume down when he

spoke this time. "We're not sure what happened with this car, so we're impounding it for investigation. If, at the end of our review, we discover that this was in fact some sort of misguided publicity stunt, criminal charges will be filed." He glared at Sunny. "Count on it. It is a crime to waste police time."

He jerked a hand at the Mustang, and several of his deputies jumped to start securing the car. The other town constable quickly pulled his car away.

Sunny tried to speak, cleared her throat, and finally succeeded. "Excuse me," she said.

When nobody responded, she raised her voice. *"Ex-cuse me!"*

Nesbit was getting back into his car. He stopped, giving her a hostile look. "Yes, Ms. Coolidge?"

"If you're taking my car away, how am I supposed to get home?"

The sheriff directed a poisonous look at Will Price. "The motto of our force is 'To Serve and Protect Elmet County.' Since Constable Price is no longer busy trying to protect us from imaginary bombs, perhaps he wouldn't mind serving as your cab driver."

"Yes, sir," Will said, his face carefully blank. Sunny could only imagine what was going on behind that facade.

Nesbit jumped into his car and escaped before Ken Howell could ask any embarrassing questions. The sheriff's official vehicle roared off, followed by most of the deputies in theirs. Without the draw of the flashing lights, the small crowd quickly dispersed. The show was over.

Will and one of the deputies stayed until a tow truck came to collect Sunny's Mustang. Then the constable led the way to his patrol car. He surprised Sunny by opening the front passenger door for her.

"Trust me, you wouldn't want to try sitting in the rear seat. We do our best to clean things up, but there've been too many drunks back there—and you really don't want to know what they've been up to."

Sunny peered in at the seat he was offering.

"What? Did you expect it to be covered in hamburger wrappers or doughnut frosting?" Will asked.

"Okay, okay." Sunny got inside.

Will closed the door, entered on the driver's side, and picked up the radio microphone. "This is 243; 1000 has me on a 10-76 to—" He glanced over at Sunny. "What's your address?"

"Wild Goose Drive, number 23."

The constable relayed the address, put down the mike, and started the car.

"So this is Car 243?" Sunny asked. "I thought they used things like '1-Adam-12.'"

"You've been watching too many TV reruns," Will told her, but then he unbent a little. "It depends on the force. In this case, 243 refers to, well, me. All patrol officers get a number in the two hundreds."

"And the sheriff?"

"I mentioned him in that message—he's 1000." Will glanced over at her. "And before you ask, 10-76 means we're en route to your address."

Sunny was a little surprised that he was acting so human, explaining the police call signs.

"I guess I should apologize, Will," she said.

"Apologize? For what?" he asked, his eyes still on the road.

"I'm sorry you were the one who had to come and get involved with that whole brouhaha and listen to Sheriff Nesbit—"

"If there were any justice in the world, he'd have pulled that door open and blown himself up," Will replied with a lopsided grin. "You've got nothing to be sorry for— unless, of course, you really did place that dingus as a misguided attempt to get some publicity."

"I didn't—" Sunny's voice choked off, and her whole body began to quiver.

Will Price glanced over and then pulled his patrol car to the side of the road. "Hey, are you okay?" He took her hand. She could feel the warmth of his palm against her suddenly ice-cold fingers.

"Guess it finally caught up with me." The words came out in a queer, wobbly tone. "Somebody tried to kill me tonight."

"I forget that you're a civilian," Will said in a low, soothing voice. "It's like the first time someone shot at me. I was so angry, and yeah, scared, and determined to get the guy, so focused on the situation that a few milliseconds felt like an hour, and when it was all over, the whole thing sort of piled on top of me."

"And how did you feel then?"

Will shrugged. "Mostly, I felt afraid that I was going to throw up in front of the other guys," he confessed.

That shocked a laugh out of her.

"It didn't turn out to be all that dramatic in the final analysis. The shooter emptied his gun and forgot to bring more bullets. So I guess I didn't have a full-fledged case of PTSD—post-traumatic stress disorder," he said when he saw the question in her eyes.

"At least it wasn't PMS," Sunny joked weakly.

His left hand came over, giving a bracing rub to loosen the white-knuckled grip she'd maintained on his right. "So, come on, relax. As murder attempts go, this was pretty much a half-assed affair. With the trajectory the bullet took, it ended up killing your steering column and your windshield instead."

"So—what?" Sunny asked, trying to follow his line of reasoning. "This was meant as a warning?"

He looked at her face for a moment before answering. "I don't know," he finally admitted. "Peeking in through the window, I couldn't get a good view of the device, but it looked as if it had twisted around on its wires. Maybe the force of the bullet going off dislodged the base and made the shot fly wild." Will shrugged. "I'd give whoever designed the dingus top grades for conception, but a failing mark for execution."

Sunny fought to hold still as an involuntary shudder ran through her. "Don't use that word."

"Come on, Sunny, don't take it so hard. In a weird way, this whole crazy incident actually justifies us looking into the Spruance case."

"So it's a case now, instead of an accident?" Sunny said.

Will Price nodded. "Looks to me like someone's sure going to pretty extreme lengths to stop you from asking questions about Ada."

"But who even knows—" She stopped, remembering the nasty comments earlier in the day from Ollie the Barnacle.

"Probably half the county." Will flexed his right hand as Sunny finally released it. "Hell, even Nesbit knew. He was just about to call you on it before he realized there were witnesses all around."

Sunny nodded. "Ken Howell was behind me."

"So he had to content himself with that crack about publicity stunts." Will leaned back in his seat. "So, are you feeling better enough for us to go on?"

When Sunny nodded, he started the car.

"The only person I talked with who might have gotten suspicious was Veronica Yarborough," Sunny said as they passed a stand of maples, their shadows turning the evening dimness into solid black for a moment.

"Ah, yes, I can see the evil homeowners' association president sneaking off to her secret lair and getting out her floral chintz soldering gun so she could assemble an infernal device to do you in." Will laughed.

"And, of course, we spoke to Gordie Spruance," Sunny continued, deciding to ignore his mockery. "Did you hear anything about him from your friends in Portsmouth?"

He shook his head. "It's not just a simple case of peeking into a couple of files. They need to ask around among the guys on the squad and find out what hasn't gone down on paper."

"Is it worth looking into the other people Gordie told us about?"

Will shrugged. "Considering the way folks gossip around here, we pretty much have to expect that any of our suspects could have heard that you were asking around about Ada. So that's a possible motive. Wouldn't hurt to check on means, see if they have any guns registered. Then if the lab identifies the type of bullet in that booby trap, we can try for a match."

"Aha, the MOM theory—motive, opportunity, and means," Sunny said. "I've seen that turn up so many times on TV shows, I almost didn't expect to hear that from a real, live cop."

"If it actually happens in real life, can it still be a cliché?" Will asked with a grin. "Motive, opportunity, and means are actually part of the job. If you wanted to, you could cobble up a case against almost anybody. Take your boss, for instance. Gordie had some nasty things to say about Barnstable."

"Gordie and about half the town," Sunny scoffed.

"Yeah, but let's look at him through the eyes of an overzealous TV investigator," Will said. "Why was he hanging around Ada Spruance? I think we can dismiss a romantic motive."

"Ada herself told me he was trying to help with her financial troubles," Sunny said slowly.

"So he's taking up charity work?"

She shook her head. "Ollie Barnstable doesn't have a charitable bone in his body—well, maybe one. He did give me a job, after all."

"So why was he hanging around Ada?" Will pressed.

"It has to be the house," Sunny decided. "He offered Ada money for it, and after she died, Gordie said he cut back to half of what he'd offered before."

"So he's being a businessman. Or . . ." Will drew out the word, coming up with a new inspiration. "Maybe he's got money troubles. So he's working on the cheap, hoping to get the house at a rock-bottom price and then flip it. Or even better, he heard about the lottery ticket and hoped to get his hands on it."

"However short he may be on personality, Ollie has lots of money," Sunny said, shaking her head. "Not to mention fingers in more pies around here than we could count."

"Maybe that's it, though," Will suggested. "He's over-extended and short of cash. Even after taxes, six to eight million would give him a lot of liquidity."

"Fine, fine, I'll give you motive," Sunny admitted, laughing. "How about opportunity?"

Will shrugged behind the wheel. "Barnstable doesn't keep regular office hours, does he? I bet he comes and goes as he pleases."

Sunny considered Ollie the Barnacle's occasional office visits. "True," she granted.

"So how would he usually spend Saturday morning?"

"I'm not that close with the guy," Sunny protested, but then she shrugged. "Probably he'd be adorning his bed. He always talks about Saturdays as his 'me' time."

"In other words his schedule could be open for anything, up to and including murder." Will brought his voice down into the bass register to make the last words sound as threatening as possible.

Sunny laughed again. "You're making me afraid to go in to work tomorrow," she kidded. "I can hardly wait to see what you're going to do with means."

"That's the easiest," Will told her. "Ollie's a pretty big guy—"

"Mainly fat," Sunny put in.

But Will shook his head. "Most people don't realize that you need a fair amount of muscle to move that fat," he said, "so don't rule him out on that account."

He paused for a second. "I'll rephrase the comment. He's a pretty solid guy. If he tried to block Ada from running out of the pantry and she just bounced off him, the force could have been enough to send her through that door."

"No way!" Sunny laughed. They spent the rest of the ride arguing about the physics of murder.

When they reached Wild Goose Drive, Will coasted to a stop in front of Sunny's house. "Figured I'd try a discreet approach," he explained. "Some people get kind of upset seeing family members come home in a police car."

Sunny agreed. "Dad doesn't need a spike in his blood pressure right now."

"So what's your plan?"

Sunny patted the cash box in her lap. "First, I'm going to lock this away. We got a big advance from a client today. For the rest of the evening"—she pulled out the envelope full of printouts from her pocket—"I'm going to read through the *Crier* articles about Ada's local feuds again." She grimaced. "And I guess I'll have to figure out some sort of way to get in to work."

"Doesn't your dad have a car?" Will asked.

"His truck's been sitting in the garage since his heart attack. Dad's been afraid to drive, even though the doctor says he's okay," Sunny said. "I don't even know if the battery has held a charge after all this time."

"Even if he was worried about using it, you'd think he'd let you take it out every once in a while just to keep it going." Will paused for a moment, then added slyly, "On second thought, remembering how your driver's-side door looked . . ."

"Wow, thanks for the compliment, that makes me feel a whole lot better." But Sunny found herself smiling as she stepped out of the car.

She turned to wave, but Will Price was already on the radio, telling Dispatch that he was back on patrol.

Yeah, romance is in the air. I guess he'll be calling for a date real soon, Sunny's inner voice predicted sarcastically. *The first time I've hung out with a guy in I don't know how long, and I freak out and then spend most of the ride arguing with him.*

Of course, she reminded herself, this was business. They'd joined forces—or been joined by her dad and a bunch of would-be local politicos—to solve Ada Spruance's mysterious death. It wasn't supposed to be a social occasion.

Still, she couldn't help thinking, *it was nice when he held my hand.*

The police cruiser pulled away, and Sunny headed up the walk to her front door. She barely got it open before a gray streak, almost impossible to see in the dim hallway, rocketed out of the kitchen and came straight at her.

"What the—?" Sunny burst out.

*

Shadow watched the strange car pull up, but a familiar figure got out. He gave himself some running room and raced for the door before he even thought about it. But just as he was about to fling himself around her ankles, he leaped back.

Sunny didn't carry any new smells. All he breathed in was the same old scents from the place where she spent her days.

So why, under all that, should he catch a whiff of the poisonous reek that came off the Stinky One?

8

"Shadow, you startled me!" Sunny said.

But as quickly as the cat had started running, he stopped, seemingly in midair, almost as if he'd hit an invisible force field around her legs.

Shadow gave one sniff and then turned around, stalking majestically off, tail high, apparently with important business to attend to in the living room.

Am I supposed to interpret that greeting as a good or a bad thing? Sunny wondered. *If Shadow's going to stay around here, maybe I should invest in a book on cat psychology.*

She stuck her head in the living room to say hi. Her dad nodded vaguely, watching the news.

And another book on the psychology of invalid fathers,

she thought, heading down to the kitchen to start on supper.

As they sat down to eat, Sunny asked Mike about borrowing his truck the next day. A forkful of baked salmon halted on its way to his mouth. "What do you need the pickup for?"

Sunny gave him the edited version—heavily edited. "There was a little trouble when I left work. It looked as if somebody may have gotten into the car. The police are checking it out—"

"Why couldn't whoever it was have done you a favor and stolen the damned thing?" Mike interrupted. "You ought to get a new car, something better suited for conditions up here."

Okay, so he wasn't asking embarrassing questions about what exactly had happened to the Mustang, but this wasn't a great conversational alternative. "You're probably right, Dad, but right now I'd rather concentrate on getting a ride for work tomorrow. So is it okay for me to use the pickup?"

Mike shrugged. "The spare keys are in the kitchen drawer." He frowned. "But that truck hasn't been started since before I went into the hospital," he warned. "The battery may be kaput."

Sunny nodded. "So maybe I ought to check it out."

They finished dinner, then Sunny washed the plates while Mike dried. Afterward, he rummaged in the junk drawer until he came up with the spare keys. "Here you go. Good luck."

Sunny went into the garage. Mike's pickup was a dark maroon—he wasn't into flashy colors like red. Sunny climbed into the cab and settled herself behind the steering wheel. Inserting the key in the ignition, she twisted, ready to give it a little gas.

But all she got was a dry *click* instead of a deep rumble from the engine. She tried it again, hoping the engine might still turn over.

Nothing.

Exactly what I was afraid of, Sunny thought, shooting an exasperated look at the hood as if that might change the engine's mind. Sunny sighed. She knew her dad had a trickle charger somewhere; he always said it was a good investment, given the cold Maine winters.

But if the battery is that *far gone, it may not charge up even if I leave it overnight.*

She had a second problem, too. How was she going to find the stupid thing when the garage was filled with the belongings she'd cleaned out of her New York apartment? Piles of cardboard boxes loomed wherever she looked.

Then she caught a hint of movement in the dimness.

Perfect, she thought, *that's all I need—a raccoon taking up residence among everything I own.*

The intruder sailed gracefully to the top of a pile that looked like a step pyramid, and Sunny realized it wasn't a raccoon, it was Shadow.

I guess a cat would think this was a great jungle gym, she had to admit.

Shadow set his forepaws on the topmost box, bracing his back legs on the box beneath, and pushed.

At least he tried to.

"Good luck with that." Sunny jeered at him from inside

Claire Donally

the truck. "Those are boxes of books. Each one probably weighs twice as much as you do."

That didn't stop Shadow. He tried a shove, giving Sunny an impromptu physics demonstration. His action had an equal, opposite—and unfortunate—reaction. Shadow's back feet skidded out from under him, and he tumbled to the floor. Sunny rose up in her seat to see him twist in midair to land on all four feet. With a flick of his tail, he set off at a stately walk, as if to say, "Excellent, precisely as I planned."

Sunny laughed. "You got just what you deserved, smart-ass."

Hearing her, Shadow paused, glancing up. Then he launched himself in a smooth leap for the top of a long, thin box leaning against the wall. It should have put him on eye level with her. Unfortunately, his weight landing on top caused the bottom of the angled box to start sliding out. Shadow danced desperately to keep from falling again.

Sunny laughed at his antics, then abruptly stopped, recognizing the box. It held art prints from her former living room. She'd spent a fortune to have them framed professionally under glass. A fall wouldn't do them any good.

Yanking the door handle, Sunny barreled out of the truck and dashed for the box, managing to catch it with her foot before it fell flat.

Shadow watched with interest as she brought the box upright again; he sat perched with all four feet on the seat of the mountain bike hidden behind the box.

Sunny pulled the artwork box away. "I'd forgotten this was even here," she said, spotting the bike.

Shadow found it interesting. He dropped down to the floor, sniffed the wheels, and sneezed from the dust that furred up the spokes.

Back in the ancient days, B.C.—Before Car—Sunny used to bike over to the New Stores and her job at Barnstable's Sweet Shoppe.

"No reason I couldn't do it again," she said.

*

The next morning, Sunny found herself laboring up an incline that had somehow grown ridiculously steeper since her cycling days. Her calf muscles protested as she kept on pedaling. *Just a little farther,* she thought.

She reached the top of the hill and pulled over to the side of the road. It could have been worse. The sky was clear, and the air was crisp. She also had plenty of shade from the trees alongside the road. *Wouldn't want to do this in the heat of summer,* Sunny mused. *I'd have to wring myself out by the time I got to the office.*

Leaning against the handlebars, she glanced over her shoulder at the way she'd come. A lot of the tourist propaganda—er, marketing materials—she wrote and edited talked about the rocky coast of Maine, and certainly the view from the water could be quite picturesque. But the southern part of the state got pretty green during the summer. She looked back over a landscape of rolling hills, the homes getting sparser, and then farmland. This was harvest season. The trees were just beginning to show a little color.

Sunny turned to the path ahead. From here it was downhill all the way. The road curved along the contours of the hills, passing streets where the houses grew closer together until, as you got close to the harbor, you also encountered the crooked streets of the old downtown business district. Sunny's destination was at the edge of the built-up part of town, the so-called New Stores that had gone up when her dad was a kid.

She'd set out early enough to beat Kittery Harbor's version of the morning rush. Nobody had passed her as she'd pumped her way uphill. In fact, the only car she saw on the road was coming from the direction of town.

When it came closer, she recognized it as Raj Richer's racing green Jaguar. As Raj reached the crest, he apparently recognized her, too, and pulled the Jag over on the opposite side of the road.

The driver's-side window rolled down, and his thin face appeared. He pulled off a pair of expensive sunglasses and gave her one of his tight-lipped smiles.

"I have to congratulate you," he said. "That's a very healthy way to go to work."

"More like a necessary way," Sunny told him. At least she wasn't huffing and puffing as she spoke. "My car is out of commission, and my dad's truck is waiting for a tow due to . . . let's call it deferred maintenance." She patted the bicycle. "Good thing I still had this hanging around. Otherwise, I don't know how I'd be getting into town."

"I'd be glad to offer you a ride," Raj said. Then he broke off, shooting a look at the backseat.

No way, she knew, could she fold this big honking bike to fit back there. Even trying would shower dust and crud on those expensive leather seats.

Sunny gave him a wry smile. *If I'd known about the*

possibility of a lift, maybe I'd have paid more attention to shining up the old girl instead of just making sure the tires were filled.

"Thanks for the kind thought," she said. "But it's no big deal. It really is all downhill from here."

Another smile tugged at Raj's lips. "I hope you're only talking about the road, and not your day."

Sunny laughed. "Hopefully," she said. "How did you find your accommodations?"

"They were right where your directions said they'd be." Raj's eyes twinkled as his lips curved in a smile. "Joking aside, they're perfect. The guest house is well-appointed, and I've enjoyed the pool . . . and my privacy. I picked up some supplies at that market down the block from your office—that Mr. Judson gave me quite a cross-examination."

"He likes to get to know his customers," Sunny told Raj, while silently cursing Zack Judson as a nosy old so-and-so. She hoped he hadn't put Raj off from spending some more time around town. Not every tourist could afford the kind of rental the Rowlandsons were asking for their guest house.

As if reading her mind, Raj said, "He was most impressed when I told him where I was staying."

"It's one of the nicest places in town," Sunny said. "If I could afford it, *I'd* go there for my vacation."

Raj chuckled. "I'll have to take good care of it, then."

They said good-bye, and Sunny watched him head out into the country before she pushed off, rolling down into town.

Reaching the office, she checked her watch. Early—

good. Sunny unlocked the door and trundled the bike inside, behind her desk. First things first. She unslung the messenger's bag from over her shoulder, retrieved the cash box, and returned it to its usual drawer.

Then she took the bag into the bathroom. The dress code at MAX was pretty relaxed, so she could get away with jeans. But the faded Boston University sweatshirt she'd worn on the way here definitely wouldn't qualify as business casual. She took a moment to freshen up, then slipped on a gray T-shirt and a deep blue cotton sweater.

Sunny fluffed her shaggy mane, fretting yet again how long her hair was getting. Maybe Mrs. Martinson could suggest a hairdresser who could handle unruly curls. After a final look in the tiny mirror, she shrugged. "Ready as I'm going to be," she decided.

Getting behind her desk, she powered up the computer and began dealing with the morning's e-mails.

She fielded a couple of calls, organizing lodging for the people who knew what they wanted and tailoring some information packets to send to the people who didn't.

Ollie the Barnacle didn't darken the door. If he'd learned of her side venture with Ken Howell, Ollie certainly must have heard about the bullet incident that had knocked out her car. Maybe he'd decided that coming in to hassle her some more would be overkill when she'd almost been shot.

Oddly enough, Sunny found herself worrying about Ken. If Ollie had been nasty to her when he'd heard about the story, how had he treated Sunny's editor?

Barnstable was pretty tight with the county's movers and shakers up in Levett. By agreeing to twist their tails,

Howell had seriously annoyed his main investor. When it came down to it, Sunny could afford to follow this story—she could always get another job. Ken Howell had put his whole family heritage on the line.

While Ollie's absence made for a more pleasant work environment, it also caused a small problem—all that extra money in the cash box. Sunny finally solved that by stopping at the bank when she began her lunch break and making a deposit into the company account.

Then she took her sandwich to the wharves and again fed some crusts to the seagulls while communing with the wind and water. Sunny even did her bit for local tourism, guiding an elderly couple down the cobblestone street to the navigation museum and taking their photo at the entrance.

She was a little behind schedule when she got back to work, and her heart sank when she found a Land Rover parked in the street, the office door unlocked, and Ollie Barnstable sitting in her chair, shouting into his cell phone.

Well, there goes my string of good luck, Sunny told herself. *At least I didn't have anything incriminating up on my computer screen.*

Ollie's angry voice penetrated her thoughts. "I don't give a crap what your lawyer says. When I get my money, you'll get your money—"

He paused for a second, looking almost guilty, when he saw Sunny in the doorway. But he recovered himself quickly, snarling, "That's all I'm going to say on the matter."

Ollie slapped his phone shut so hard, Sunny feared he might break it. But she decided not to say anything. The look on her boss's face definitely didn't invite comment.

"Thought you'd be out to lunch longer," Ollie said gruffly, collecting papers off the desk and jamming them into a leather portfolio.

Sunny blinked. Ollie usually complained that she took too much time to eat.

Zipping up the portfolio, Ollie rose from the chair and headed for the door, tromping even more heavily than usual. Given his mood, Sunny found herself glad that he had nothing else to say.

Still, she found herself thinking back to the previous evening and Will's flight of fancy about motive, opportunity, and means.

Maybe Will wasn't so out there about one thing, she thought. *It sounds as if Ollie may be having money problems.*

She took her seat—a little warm from Ollie's bulk—and spent the afternoon updating the website. Then she tackled that pesky promo copy. Apparently, while her conscious mind had worried over her car troubles, Sunny's subconscious had been working on the writing problem overnight. Coming up with a whole new take, Sunny trashed her original draft and typed up a new one.

"Looks pretty good," she muttered, checking over her work one last time before attaching it to an e-mail and sending it to Ollie. Feeling virtuous, she breezed through several more items from her electronic in-box.

Then her string of small victories was broken by a phone call from her dad.

"Sal DiGillio picked up the truck and brought it to his station," Mike Coolidge reported. "But a bunch of other jobs came in. Sal says that the earliest he can have her back is tomorrow afternoon."

"I think I can live with another day of biking," Sunny told him. "Let's not worry about it."

Now the day was winding down, and Sunny could start thinking about heading home—barring some disaster deluging her with stranded tourists.

The phone rang.

Sunny picked it up. "Maine Adventure X-perience," she said in her most professional tone.

An unfamiliar female voice came over the line. "Sunny Coolidge, please."

"Speaking."

"This is Leah Towle."

Towle—the name was familiar. Wait a minute! She was one of the dog owners Ada Spruance had tangled with.

"I overheard someone in Judson's Market say that you're doing a piece in the *Crier* about Mrs. Spruance," the voice went on, as if reading her mind. "There's been a lot said back and forth in the paper. But my husband and I would like to talk to you in person, to give our side of the story."

"Of course," Sunny said, pleased at her good fortune. She'd wanted to get in touch with the Towles, and here they were, volunteering. "Could we say sometime this evening?"

They set a time, and Sunny put the phone down. *I don't know why they even worry about the paper,* she thought. *The grapevine works faster, and you can skip all the ads.*

9

The day finally ended. Sunny wheeled her bike out of the office and locked up. There was a little traffic on the street now. She may have beaten Kittery Harbor's rush hour that morning, but she couldn't wait it out now—she had that appointment with the Towles.

As she nosed into the stream of traffic, Sunny heard a heavy engine start up, like a giant clearing his throat. She shot a glance over her shoulder—her dad had been very careful with bike safety when he taught her to ride, showing her how to look in all directions without wobbling on her course. A metallic blue SUV with tinted windows, a Ford Explorer, rolled along behind her, its rumbling engine throttled down.

Maybe I should pull aside and let them pass, she thought.

But when she tried to, the big blue vehicle just slowed down.

Sunny shrugged. The SUV had New Hampshire plates. Maybe they were tourists looking for a place to park. She pedaled on for about a block until she saw an arm waving at her from a black pickup truck. As she rolled to a stop, Will Price stuck his head out the window, grinning.

"I'd gotten reports of this spectacle, but I had to see it with my own eyes," he said.

She took in the fact that he was in his own pickup and out of uniform. "Is this traffic stop official police business, Constable Price?" she teased.

His voice took on a professional pitch. "In point of fact, Maine highway safety regulations state that protective helmets must be worn by all cyclists—"

"Oh, come on," Sunny muttered.

"—under the age of sixteen," he finished, letting his stern cop facade melt under another grin.

"I don't know whether I should be flattered or worried for your eyesight," she told him.

"Look, I've got a little time before my shift starts," he said. "Why don't you stick that bike in the back and I'll give you a ride home?"

As she swung the mountain bike into the truck bed, Sunny glanced around, looking for that big Ford that had seemed to be following her. No trace—it must have turned off in search of a parking spot.

Guess I was just imagining things, Sunny thought, shaking her head. *Can't let that half-assed stunt with the bullet get to me.*

She went around to the passenger side of Will's truck,

put her foot on the running board, and boosted herself into the seat. "I guess I should thank you," she said. "I'm supposed to be seeing the Towles, and I'd have to pedal pretty fast to make it in time."

"Sticking on the job, huh?" He laughed. "Well, you'll be glad to hear that they won't meet you at the door with a gun—at least I didn't find one registered."

"No," Sunny said, "all they have is a killer dog."

"My research shows that Veronica Yarborough doesn't have a gun, either."

"No doubt she considers them too lower class." Sunny smiled. "If she had a problem with someone, she'd probably beat them to death with her moneybags. What about those farmers, the Ellsworths?"

"Now, they apparently did buy a rifle after they began having predator problems," Will reported. "Nate Ellsworth got a .308 caliber—a little heavy for your traditional varmint gun."

He paused for a second. "Of course, the bullet that messed up your car exited through the windshield—and nobody broke their necks looking for it. But we still have the bullet casing from that little dingus inside the car, and it's a .308—imagine that."

"I'll save thinking about that for after my visit with the Towles." Sunny rolled her window down. They were climbing up the hill, heading out of town. "Looks like you did your homework. Did your friends in Portsmouth come through with any information about Gordie Spruance?"

"They're aware of him," Will said. "His license plate

got taken down because his car turned up in some not-so-nice parts of town, and he's been spotted with some seriously dirty people."

"You mean he's been buying drugs?" Sunny's voice went flat. She hated to hear Will's suspicions verified.

"Maybe more than that." Will's face got grim. "I want to show you something."

He pulled the truck off the road and opened the console on the seat between them. "Gordie's been hanging out with a guy named Ron Shays, a.k.a. Rob O'Shea. He's a meth dealer with an interesting history."

Will pulled out a grainy photo printed on plain paper. "They e-mailed me this picture."

The image was obviously a mug shot, showing a guy with long, unkempt hair and a beard down to his chest. Actually, it wasn't so much a face as a set of pinched features poking through a wall of shaggy fur. Sunny got an impression of angry eyes set close together above a sharp nose. What really caught her attention was the man's mouth, set in a snarl that revealed several stained and snaggled teeth.

"Looks like a charmer." She shuddered.

"What amazes me is that he's found people to do business with him all over New England," Will said. "His business model is to find a virgin territory and open a lab using local contacts. They go in big, make some money, and then the partnership goes to hell—usually with the local partner ending up dead. And then Shays moves on to greener pastures."

"Better and better." Sunny gave the picture back. "And nobody's caught him yet?"

"He's been pretty smart so far, and he's kept moving out of jurisdictions before local law enforcement can pin him down. Lately he's been seen around Portsmouth, looking into business opportunities in the area."

And what would be better than Elmet County? Convenient to Portsmouth, a good-sized city right across the river, and guarded by a sheriff who seemed to think he could keep crime down by wishing it away.

"This doesn't sound good," Sunny said.

"Yeah. You could imagine what might happen if Gordie bragged about his mom's lottery ticket to this guy."

"Tell him you had money?" Sunny burst out. "I wouldn't want that character to know I owned a wallet."

"So if Shays put the squeeze on Gordie, and Gordie tried to steal that ticket . . ." Will didn't even have to finish.

But Sunny remembered the lost, frightened look in Gordie's eyes when he talked about his mother. "It looks bad," she admitted. "But I still want to get a look at the other people feuding with Ada Spruance."

Will shrugged. "Suit yourself. You're the one writing the story."

"Besides," Sunny went on, "how much of this stuff you're telling me could I use with attribution?"

Will sat silent for a moment. "None of it," he finally admitted. "If I had any kind of a solid case, I'd've already taken a chance and brought it to the district attorney."

"So instead, what you're doing is turning to me to stir the pot and see what floats up." Sunny shook her head. "This is supposed to be a news story. I can't just make unsubstantiated accusations about drug dealers hiding in the woodwork."

Will started the truck in glum silence and drove her home. As he pulled up on Wild Goose Drive, he said, "Guess it's my turn to say I'm sorry."

Sunny looked at him. "For what?"

"For getting you involved in this," Will said. "At first glance, I thought this would be a way to yank Frank Nesbit's chain about ignoring a possible suspicious death. But it's gotten a lot worse than I imagined."

"Let's say 'more complicated' instead of 'worse.'" Sunny shrugged. "And I'm the one who insisted the death was suspicious in the first place." She sighed. "I just wish I had some solid facts instead of rumor and conjecture and maybes."

"So you're staying with it?"

Sunny nodded. "I'm going to check on my dad, and then off to the Towles'."

She went into the house and stepped into the living room, stopping dead when she caught the scene on the sofa. Her father and Mrs. Martinson sat bolt upright, their hands stiffly at their sides. At least Sunny's dad didn't have powdered sugar all over his sweater. But Mrs. Martinson wasn't her usual self.

The normally imperturbable widow looked a little wild-eyed. Her hair was slightly mussed, her makeup smeared—

Oh, God, Sunny thought, *what have I walked into now?*

Whatever they'd been doing, Mike and his lady friend weren't doing it anymore. They hadn't even noticed Sunny entering the room, their gazes frozen on the floor, a bit to the left of the coffee table . . .

Where Shadow sat, his hindquarters down but his forelegs straight, his ears erect, the picture of interested attention.

Sunny couldn't help it. "What's going on, folks?"

That broke the spell. Helena Martinson patted desperately at her hair, stumbling over her words. "We—I—when I looked over, I saw him *watching* us."

Mike, on the other hand, silently worked his way from astonishment to embarrassment to fury. Thanks to Shadow, whatever Mike had hoped would happen wasn't going to. And that went double now that Sunny had turned up.

The glare he directed at Shadow should have left a charred ring on the rug where the cat used to be.

"Um. I'm just passing through. Only stopping off to get some stuff. Then I'll be heading out for a while." Sunny got out of there before she completely started babbling.

Shadow came over to give Sunny's shins a sniff, but he was obviously more interested in the couple on the couch.

Sunny headed up to her room to get her notebook, stopping for a second to check out her reflection in the mirror. *Maybe this isn't the time to ask Mrs. Martinson about hairdressers,* she decided.

She hadn't put her BU sweatshirt back on for cycling home, intending to change before going to the Towles'. Thanks to the lift from Will, she didn't have to do that.

"I'll just walk over there, take a nice, leisurely stroll," she told herself.

Right now, the sooner she got out of the house, the better.

*

The Towle house was newer than the Coolidge family home and definitely more upscale—though not as luxurious as Veronica Yarborough's mansion upgrade. Although the front lawn was open to the street, a head-high white fence—wood, not plastic—flanked the house and apparently ran the perimeter of the backyard. Sunny spotted a gate beside the garage.

When she came up to the front door and rang the bell, she heard deep woofing from around in back.

Probably the dog in question, she thought.

The door opened, and Sunny found herself looking at Leah Towle—looking *up* at Leah Towle.

At five feet, six inches, Sunny usually considered herself on the tall side for a woman. But Leah had to be up around six feet, easily. She had a face that was more pleasant than pretty, perhaps a little too broad—like her shoulders and her hips.

Leah tried to smile politely, asking, "Sunny?" But her face showed signs of sleeplessness and strain. "Thank you for coming." She led the way to a family room with a leather couch and armchairs. Good stuff, but not over-the-top.

Leah headed for the hallway, as if to call her husband, but then Chuck Towle came into the room. Leah might be tall, but Chuck still topped her by several inches. He had the look of a college jock running to seed—a bit of stomach straining over his belt, extra flesh softening the line of his chin. Apparently he was losing his hair, because he kept his head shaved—not the best look for him. His incipient jowls made his face bottom-heavy, tapering up to a sort of bullet-headed dome.

Chuck shook Sunny's hand in one of his big paws as Leah did the introductions.

"First of all, we both want to say how terrible it is that Mrs. Spruance died," he said. "I can't say we liked her—or her cats—but we certainly never wished her any harm."

"We can't say the same about her and Festus," Leah burst out.

"Festus?" Sunny asked.

"Our dog. He's a good dog, Sunny, but that woman said she hoped the judge would order him p-put to sleep." Leah's eyes filled with tears and her voice grew hoarse.

"Mrs. Spruance swore out a civil complaint that Festus was a dangerous dog," Chuck explained. "She also wanted to sue us."

"Everyone said how horrible he was." Anger crept into Leah's voice. "But they never took our side of the story seriously."

"How did the—um—incident happen?" Sunny asked cautiously.

Chuck nodded. "When we're at work, we keep Festus in the backyard, on a lead. There's shade from the trees if it gets too warm, and a doghouse for shelter."

"And we leave dry food and water for him," Leah added. "But then those cats began coming over."

"Teasing him," Chuck said.

"Terrorizing him," Leah corrected. "They'd hide until he was ready to do his business—then they'd pounce on him! I've actually seen them do it!" She quivered with indignation. "How would you react if someone kept jumping out at you every time you had to use the bathroom?"

Sunny could only shake her head, remembering how Shadow tried to trip up Gordie, and the cat's mania for knocking things over. *All I can say is, cats have a pretty strange sense of humor,* she thought.

"Finally this one cat, Patachou, or whatever she called him, ran across our yard and jumped up on the gate," Chuck said. "I guess poor Festus had had enough. He broke his leash and went right through the gate. I was just getting home and heard it all. I followed them as Festus chased the cat. Dunno how he managed to catch him, but he did, right outside the Spruance place."

His heavy shoulders lifted in a shrug. "I tried to get him off, but by then it was too late."

Leah blinked away more tears. "She let those cats go wandering around the neighborhood, getting into any dangerous things they pleased, but she blamed us! It's just not fair!"

Chuck tried to pat her shoulder, looking helpless. "We put up a bigger fence, and we've got special trainers coming to work with Festus. But he may end up muzzled, or confined to the house"—he broke off for a moment—"or we may have to give him away."

"He's a good dog," Leah insisted. "Let me show you."

She left the room, to return a few moments later with a large black and brown dog on a leash. He trotted in, spotted the new person, and approached.

But when he was just a couple of yards away, he stopped, sniffed, and began to growl.

Leah was mortified. "Bad Festus! What are you doing?"

The dog's tail went down and he looked around, whining.

Sunny had an awful suspicion. She twisted on the couch so that the rays of the setting sun fell on the front of her sweater. Yes, there they were, shining in the light—fine strands of grayish fur against the blue fabric. She thought back to when she'd been getting ready for work that morning. Shadow had jumped up on her bed, examining the stuff she placed there, including her T-shirt and sweater. She'd left him alone while she got her bag out of the closet. He'd probably taken the opportunity to roll on the soft cotton.

And Festus had caught a whiff of Shadow's scent.

That damned cat's trying to get me killed, she thought.

"I'm sorry, I think there must be something on this sweater," Sunny said, carefully rising to her feet. "Maybe I'd better be going."

"But you understand this is a terrible accident? That Festus wouldn't normally do anything like this?" Poor Leah Towle looked as confused and upset as her dog.

"I'll try to explain things the way you explained them to me," Sunny promised gently.

She felt sorry for the Towles and their dog.

But . . .

Like Festus, both Chuck and Leah were large and strong—and their feelings obviously ran high.

Either could have sent a little woman like Ada Spruance flying down the stairs . . . with one hand tied behind his or her back.

10

Shadow blinked awake in his hiding place under Sunny's bed. He'd decided to get out of the way when she came and found the other female in the room. Among cats or two-legs, Shadow had noticed that when two females and one male were too close together, fighting often started.

The other female had left quickly, while Sunny had gone upstairs. That definitely hadn't pleased the Old One. Shadow had seen that as another reason to make himself scarce. From what he'd seen, two-leg males tended to take out their temper on furniture—and cats.

The space under Sunny's bed was dark but comfortable—no drafts because fabric hung down to the floor. It was clean, too, not like the space under the Dead One's bed. That was so dusty that even the daintiest steps raised a sneeze-inducing cloud. Best of all, there was a faint trace of Sunny in the air. Shadow liked that. He'd hunkered down, sphinxlike, closed his eyes, and dozed.

When he awoke, it was some time later. There was much less light. Shadow crouched, suddenly alert, when he realized what had roused him—footsteps, and they weren't Sunny's. He had to listen for a moment before he finally recognized them. The gait was different—quieter—but that was the Old One.

Shadow waited until the feet were almost back out the door before he stuck his head out from under the bedspread. He saw the Old One's back as the human stepped out into the hallway. But why was the two-leg moving with such exaggerated caution? Had he hurt himself? It didn't seem likely, since he kept moving around, sticking his head into each room. Shadow followed behind him, investigating each room after the Old One left it. Nothing seemed out of the ordinary since the time Shadow had last explored them.

He trailed behind as the Old One went down the stairs, placing his feet carefully to keep the treads from creaking as they usually did. Moving on the tips of his toes, the Old One went into the room with the picture box—but he didn't turn it on. Instead, he peered around to the corner where Shadow's bed lay.

When he saw that, Shadow made a quick move for the dining room, climbing onto the seat on one of the chairs. From there, he could look out between the wooden spindles on the back of the chair without much danger of being spotted—the stripes in his gray fur blended into the shadows beneath the tabletop.

As Shadow watched, the Old One came past, still moving in that weird attempt to step soundlessly; at least soundlessly for a two-leg's hearing. It almost seemed like a very clumsy attempt—

Shadow slipped down to the floor, fascinated. Could it be? Was the Old One trying to stalk like a cat? Shadow trailed along as the Old One headed toward the kitchen. Of all the two-leggity types he'd lived with, Shadow had never seen any of them play this game.

But what was the human stalking? Had a mouse or squirrel raised his stupid head?

The Old One reached the kitchen and peered in the dusk at the litter box and the food bowls.

Shadow blinked in amazement. *He's stalking* me*!*

Almost unbidden, a meow came from his throat.

The Old One jumped and spun around, one hand on his chest. Shadow streaked away. Although he was always careful to stay out of kicking range, sometimes the two-legs threw things. Shadow considered that extremely unfair.

Before the Old One could get close again, Shadow darted into the living room and squeezed under the couch. It was a tight fit, but Shadow was reasonably sure a human like the Old One wouldn't be in the mood to creep around on the floor looking for him.

He was right. Springs above him compressed as the Old One sat down, mumbling annoyed sounds. Then the picture box went on.

Not long afterward, Sunny returned. Shadow heard her steps coming from the door and felt a little surprised, not having caught the sound of her car coming up.

Before he even thought about it, he found himself popping out of his hiding place and padding toward her. Shadow forced himself to slow down. After all, this was just a quick check for interesting scents—and maybe a little marking to let the neighborhood cats know that Sunny was taken.

Then he stopped cold, his snout wrinkling. The stink she'd brought in the night before was bad enough. But now she reeked of Biscuit Eater. Shadow knew that for some unknown reason, many of the two-legs tolerated the mangy creatures—the large fawning ones or the little ones that scurried around yapping—all of them eager to slobber down their stupid biscuits. Not like a self-respecting cat.

One more sniff confirmed his initial suspicion; he smelled the Biscuit Eater who had killed Patachou on Sunny. Shadow had always thought that teasing a creature with fangs large enough to crush the biggest cat's skull was just looking for trouble. Patachou's death showed exactly how dangerous a game it could be.

But what could Sunny have to do with such a killer?

He stalked away, offended, and refused to be tempted back, even when a can of tuna was opened.

While the two-legs ate, Shadow sulked in the kitchen. From the sound of it, he was just as glad to be out of the way. The Old One's voice was low and grumbling, while Sunny's voice was high and quick. It sounded like an argument—something else the two-legs spent so much time on. For Shadow, a show of claws and a sharp hiss was often much quicker and easier.

Besides, arguments like this often led to Shadow losing his place to live. So he tried not to get too attached. That was why it was better to keep his distance from Sunny—especially since the Old One obviously didn't want him around.

Shadow made his way to the top of the box that kept food cold. That was another weird thing about the two-legs. They'd take food from a box that made it cold and put it in a box to make things hot. Shadow didn't even try to figure that out. The cold box was good, though. It offered a good high spot where he could look down on the room and the hallway beyond. And sometimes there was a hum deep within the box—interesting and pleasant to feel.

For a while, Shadow drowsed. He heard Sunny go up the stairs, and the Old One turned on the box of pictures. Sometimes the pictures were of interesting things, but the only smell the box ever gave off was of something burning, and it sent out an odd sensation that made his whiskers tingle.

Still, he thought he might as well take a look.

The picture showed a man and woman sitting behind a desk, talking. One of the more boring things that turned up on the box.

As he turned away, though, Shadow caught the scent of tuna. He raised his head, taking a deeper breath. Yes, definitely tuna, floating on a wave of cool air. It must be coming from the open window. Usually when it got dark the glass was down. Shadow found glass fascinating, like hard air you could see through but rest a paw against. He'd never found tuna out there before. This was definitely worth investigating.

The easiest way to get to the windowsill was from the couch.

Shadow looked up at the Old One, who sat slumped,

his eyes closed, his breathing regular. Three good bounds took him to the bottom of the sofa, then a careful leap to land as lightly as he could. The Old One was likely to shove if he was awakened.

Padding softly to the arm of the couch, Shadow climbed up to the back of the seat. The scent of tuna was stronger, coming in on a cold breeze. Shadow crouched low. A piece of wood rested on the couch back, creating a bridge to the windowsill. And outside the open window in the darkness, yes, he could smell tuna.

Shadow stepped onto the wood, placing his feet carefully, then with more confidence. He advanced on the tuna, licking his chops. But as soon as he was beyond the window, the wood beneath his feet suddenly shot forward. The cat found himself falling, barely twisting in time to land on all fours.

A noise above him caught his attention—the window going down.

This male Old One is different from the female Old One, he thought. *Full of tricks!*

The cold air began to make itself felt. Shadow shivered, rippling his fur. Then he began casting around for the morsel of tuna that had gotten him into this situation. It might be a while before he had an easy meal again.

Once he'd found it and finished eating, Shadow set off on the next most important thing—watering the plants the Old One set such store by.

After that, he searched for a place to sleep. Shadow had been outside on far colder nights than this. He needed a place that would be sheltered from the wind and hard for larger creatures like the Biscuit Eaters to get into.

The low deck behind the garage offered a perfect space. Shadow had to crouch to get underneath the wooden slats. Some leaves had blown in, and he gathered them together, walked in a circle to trample them down, and then lay with his legs tight to his body and his tail curled around his feet.

He was comfortable enough and not hungry. So he slept.

In the dream, the world was dark, but Shadow was warm, pressed against a warm fur body, and there was milk, and the very good smell of belonging. It jarred him to wake up in a chilly den with the smell of decaying leaves.

Had he ever really known the happy time that he lived in that dream? Shadow wasn't sure—he certainly didn't remember it.

He strained his ears, probing for whatever strange noise had roused him. Then he heard the low, muttering sound of a car engine—a car that hadn't been here before—and the scrape of shoes on the driveway.

By the time Shadow came around the garage, he didn't see any people. But a huge vehicle still stood on the drive, its engine rumbling.

He took a few running steps and leaped for the top of the hood. No one sat behind the wheel.

Some cats in the streets crawled up in the open spaces under cars for warmth. But doing that while the car acted alive could be dangerous. The metal pieces were hard, and hungry for cat tails, or even legs.

Jumping to the ground, Shadow circled the car's great bulk. Then he froze in disbelief. He'd never seen a car with a tail. Approaching cautiously, he tried to figure out what this might be. It looked like a made thing—some humans he'd lived with had one that squirted water, and looked like an enormous snake. But Shadow didn't see any water.

During his wanderings through more rural areas, Shadow had come across snakes and found them pretty good eating. The ones he'd hunted smelled like the flowers or plants they lived among. Sometimes, when they got upset or frightened, they let off an odd, musky sort of odor. The problem was, this thing didn't smell like any snake he'd ever encountered. All he got was the scent of dust and a trace of mold.

Shadow hesitated. Was it food or not? Maybe it was a sick snake. The stupid thing had somehow stuck its head into the part of the car where bad smells came from. That couldn't be good.

A low cough came from inside the big machine, and the snake-thing quivered. The movement made Shadow's mind up for him. This was possible food.

Shadow immediately leaped to the attack. He went for a grip on the neck, putting as much power as he could into his jaws. Sometimes that was enough to take a snake's head right off. This time, though, something was wrong. The snake's body gave under his teeth, and it tasted wrong. The body felt flabby as he savaged it with his rear claws. And then he was spitting and sneezing, enveloped in smoke!

Coughing, Shadow rolled out from under the vehicle, his tail rigid with disgust. There was nothing here to eat. The snake was empty, a made thing filled with choking smells.

That Old One, he sure has lots of tricks, Shadow thought darkly as he stalked back to his sleeping place.

The night had gotten colder, and he was starting to feel a little hungry again.

But there was one part of him that was full again. Shadow changed course to give those plants a little more attention.

11

An hour before her alarm clock was supposed to go off, Sunny jerked awake to hear her father bellowing, "What the hell is that truck doing in our driveway?"

She shrugged on a bathrobe and jammed her bare feet into a pair of running shoes, tucking in the laces because she didn't have time to tie them.

Even as she did that, she could hear her father's angry footsteps clomping down the stairs.

Since the heart attack, Dad hasn't even wanted to go driving because he's afraid of the stress involved, she thought ruefully. *But he's ready to go down and wage a war over somebody invading our sacred driveway?*

She got to the front door and opened it, expecting to hear Mike roaring to the neighborhood in general.

Instead she found him standing in silence, his hands jammed into his bathrobe pockets.

"Are you okay, Dad?" she asked.

His voice came out very low, almost in a stammer. "I—I was coming back from the bathroom, passed the window, and saw this thing down here. But now—"

Mike took a hand out of his pocket and pointed to the rear of the big, bright maroon Jeep Wrangler. "Do you see it?"

Sunny blinked her bleary eyes, trying to make sense of what she saw. The end of a black garden hose—their garden hose—lay under the SUV's exhaust pipe, a tangle of duct tape wrapped around it. The hose stretched from the driveway to the house, to one of the cellar windows where a pane of glass had been broken and the other end of the hose poked through, jammed in place with a bunch of rags.

Car—hose—everything sealed . . . carbon monoxide!

Enough brain cells finally woke up, and she let rip with a fairly naughty word, adding, "Somebody tried to kill us in our sleep!"

"But did you see who stopped it?" Mike bent over the taped end of the hose. Sunny joined him, now making out the tooth and claw marks in the plastic.

"Shadow?" she whispered in disbelief.

"The cat saved us," Mike said. "He saved us, in spite of what I did to him."

"What do you mean? What did you do to him? Why was he outside in the first place?"

Her tone of voice must have penetrated Mike's thoughts, because he quickly straightened up. "We'll talk about that later," he said. "Right now I think we'd better call the police."

*

Sunny had enough time to get dressed before a police cruiser arrived. A stocky guy in the uniform of a town constable got out and came up the walk. Sunny opened the door before he rang. "We left everything exactly the way we found it," she told him.

As he tried to come up with a reply, she saw the ID tag on his chest: B. Semple.

So this is the guy who should have shown up when I found Ada, she thought. *The one who's good at giving out traffic tickets.*

"Dispatch said this wasn't exactly a police emergency," Constable Semple said in some confusion.

"It might have been a medical emergency, if it had worked out the way it was supposed to," Sunny told him. "Or a job for the coroner."

She pointed to the end of the Jeep. "Go take a look."

Semple took a long minute looking over the nasty little setup. Then he hustled back to his patrol car and got on the radio.

Probably asking for instructions, Sunny thought.

But a moment later, the constable put down his mike and took out a cell phone.

That's probably Nesbit, Sunny realized. *Whatever he's got to say, he doesn't want it going out over the public airwaves.*

Semple finished his conversation and headed back up

the walk, doing his best to keep a poker face. "This vehicle doesn't belong to you?"

By now, Mike had come down to join them. "It's not ours. I never saw that Wrangler in the neighborhood before."

"Okay. When did you first notice it?"

That sent Mike off to the races, giving the whole story, chapter and verse, excluding the fact that the cat had saved them.

Semple went back out to examine the hose again. When he returned, he looked more harassed than poker-faced.

"So, you found this car parked outside shortly after dawn. Did anything wake you up? Did you notice any odd noises?"

"I was sleeping," Mike said.

"So was I," Sunny added.

The constable took them through their routine of the night before. "I went upstairs fairly early," Sunny told him. "I'm working on a story for the *Harbor Crier*, and I was transcribing notes and working on the lead."

"I watched some television until the late news," Mike said. "Then I went to bed."

"So you didn't actually see one another for a good part of the evening?"

Mike shrugged. "Not till I popped my head in to say good night. Sunny was working on her computer."

Semple nodded. "You didn't hear anything? Anyone coming or going?" He directed the question to Mike. "Since you were on the ground floor."

Sunny could feel warmth flooding her face. *And since*

Nesbit apparently wants to dismiss this as another public-ity stunt. Angry words came to her lips, but she stifled them somehow, even though the effort of clenching her jaws made her teeth hurt.

Mike apparently didn't catch the constable's drift. "No-body went in or out." Then he paused and muttered, a little shamefaced, "Except for the cat."

Semple's police-issue poker face took another hit with that response. "The cat?" he repeated in bewilderment.

"We've had a kind of annoying cat staying with us—always turning up where he wasn't wanted," Mike ex-plained, getting a bit red in the face himself. "Last night I sort of . . . tricked him . . . out the window."

Sunny shot him a "we are definitely discussing this later" look.

At least Semple had the grace to look apologetic when he came to his next question. "Please understand that I have to ask this. Carbon monoxide poisoning usually hap-pens as the result of an accident—"

"That setup outside looked pretty much on purpose to me." Sunny didn't even bother to keep the anger out of her voice.

"—or suicide," Semple went on, bracing himself for the reaction he expected.

He might have gotten that and more, except the doorbell rang. When Sunny answered it, she found Will Price stand-ing outside. "I was still up after my shift and caught the call on my scanner."

And apparently rushed right over after a hearty break-fast, Sunny grumpily thought.

As if reading her mind, Will went on, "I was a little

delayed because of another crime report. Sal DiGillio said a 2007 Jeep Wrangler was stolen out of his service station."

He turned to Mike. "Mr. Coolidge, you drive a maroon pickup, right?"

Sunny's dad nodded. "Yeah, a Dodge Ram. Guess it's about five or six years old now."

"And it's also at Sal's service station?"

"Sure, he towed it yesterday." Mike was getting a bit confused with this line of questioning, and his face showed it.

"Just one more question," Will promised. "What color would you call that SUV outside?"

Mike was definitely wondering if Will had been up too long. "I dunno. Kinda maroon?"

Will nodded. "So if I were to tell someone, 'Take the maroon truck from the service station and bring it to such-and-such an address,' it wouldn't be such a surprising mistake, would it?"

Semple decided to give up on the subtle approach. "The sheriff says—"

"Did the sheriff tell you that Sal reported the license number for that stolen Jeep?" Will interrupted. "It's the same as the one outside."

That shut Semple up, but Will went on, "And if our glorious leader is suggesting that someone here went out to get the car—what? They can't recognize the difference between their own pickup and an SUV? Not to mention, both of the two family cars are out of commission. Sal's place is on the interstate. I think somebody riding a bicycle would have stood out a little."

Will looked at the other officer. "Ben, I know you don't

like to get involved in politics. But in spite of what Nesbit says, I think we've got to treat this seriously."

"As serious as—" Sunny bit off what she was going to say because her father was standing next to her.

But her dad finished it for her. "As a heart attack," he said.

Sunny grinned, but that faded pretty quickly as she turned to Will. "If what you're saying is right, that means someone had to be watching the house in order to see Dad's truck being towed."

Will nodded. "Maybe several people. The meth business can quickly involve a lot of folks—someone to cook the stuff, someone to provide supplies, dealers—and security. This looks like a pretty good plan. The problem is the follow-through. After hitting the pipe, tweakers can be up for days at a time. They're called tweakers because they try to fill the time fiddling with things."

"Like maybe the gizmo that wound up in my car?" Sunny asked.

Will nodded. "Often, by the time a tweaker's finished tweaking with something, it's useless." He took in the look on her face. "Hey, look at it this way. If someone was after me, the best description I could hope for would be 'incompetent.'"

"I'd prefer 'gone' or at least 'arrested,'" Sunny told him.

"I can talk to the other guys," Semple said. "Explain the situation to them. Make sure we manage to swing by here and keep an eye on things." His lips curved in a faint smile. "We can always write more tickets next month."

"And to think, it was the cat that saved us." Mike shook his head, still not quite able to believe it.

"That cat you've got here saved you?" Will shot a sharp look at Sunny, who just shrugged. This was her father's story. She'd let him handle it.

Mike ushered Will out to check the evidence, determined to prove his theory. Sunny and Ben trailed behind.

When Will straightened up from looking at the teeth marks on the hose, he was trying hard not to laugh.

"What's so funny?" Sunny demanded.

"Of course, you don't know the reason why this thing was at Sal's in the first place." Will tried to keep a straight face. "The fuel gauge is screwed up. It reads full when the tank is almost empty. No matter what the cat did, the Jeep's engine would have conked out in minutes."

"So there wouldn't have been enough carbon monoxide to kill us?" Sunny said.

"Not based on what Sal told me," Will replied. "Of course, if the thief was a tweaker, he might not even have checked the gas gauge anyway."

"So maybe the cat saved us, maybe not." Mike stood over his winterized plants. "One thing I know for sure. That fur-coated little s.o.b. peed all over my roses!"

*

Sunny decided that carbon monoxide poisoning—even attempted carbon monoxide poisoning—offered a reasonable excuse for a mental health day. While the police prepared to tow off the maroon Wrangler (Will had successfully prodded the sheriff's department into action by suggesting that possible grand theft auto should justify dusting the SUV for fingerprints), she phoned Ollie and told him he'd have to arrange some coverage for the office. He growled and grumbled, but Sunny stood her ground until he gave in.

Then, as she was making breakfast for her dad and herself, Sunny got a call from Ken Howell at the *Crier*. "Heard there was some excitement up by your way this morning," he said.

"I'd like to say I'm getting used to it, but that wouldn't strictly be the truth," she told him.

"Not sure I like it when reporters end up in the middle of the news instead of just writing about it," the editor told her. "On the other hand, I'm thinking about running a sidebar—"

"That's the last thing I want," Sunny interrupted.

"I hope you're not having second thoughts about the story." His voice rose in an anxious tone. "We're supposed to be going to print tonight."

"I was going to do a quick phone interview with the Ellsworths," Sunny said. "But since I'm not going in to MAX today, I'll do it in person and work it into what I've already got. Don't worry, you'll have your story."

"Yeah, everybody's looking forward to it," Ken informed her dryly. "Veronica Yarborough was on the phone to me just yesterday, reminding me that the homeowners' association keeps lawyers on retainer."

"Lots of fun." Sunny sighed and shook her head as she and Ken ended the call. It would probably ruin his breakfast, but it looked as if she'd have to tell Mike more about the unwelcome present in her car.

"Dad," she began. "About the Mustang . . ."

"Useless when winter really sets in around here," Mike said. "Just as well that jackass fooled around with it and killed the steering."

Sunny stared at him for a second, openmouthed. "You knew about that?"

"I suspected something was fishy when you first told me, and Helena Martinson filled me in on the rest. We figured you didn't want to talk about it to keep me from getting upset."

They both involuntarily glanced toward the front of the house where the Wrangler had been left to kill them. "Looks like that worked out just fine," Sunny said wryly.

"Speaking of Helena, you may want to ask if you can borrow her car. It's a haul to get out to the Ellsworth place, especially if all you've got is a bicycle."

Sunny phoned their neighbor and barely got out her request before Mrs. Martinson said she'd bring the car right over. The woman was as good as her word, delivering the car and then quickly walking out with a minimum of conversation.

That's not like the Helena Martinson I know, Sunny thought. But then she remembered the last time they'd seen each other, and what Mrs. Martinson and her dad were probably doing. *Maybe she's a little too embarrassed to chat easily,* Sunny decided. *Which is fine by me, too.*

She settled herself behind the wheel of the car, a good, dependable Buick, for the trip to the Ellsworth farm. It was another clear morning, a nice day to enjoy a drive out to the country. On the other hand, there wasn't much country left nearby to enjoy anymore. The rising tide of development kept turning old family farms into spreads of half-acre homes.

Years ago, when Sunny was a kid, her parents would choose a good, crisp autumn Saturday and head off to Old Man Ellsworth's for an afternoon of apple picking. She could remember sitting in the backseat, watching miles of fields pass by. Now it was a lot of would-be stately homes until at last she saw the big white barn she remembered, with the familiar sign, WELCOME TO ELLSWORTH'S PICK 'EM YOURSELF. Back in second grade, they used to joke that the sign referred to noses.

Sunny pulled up in a gravel parking lot, empty today, and headed for the farmyard where she'd spotted a man—at least the bottom end of him. His head and arms were hidden by the innards of his tractor.

"Hello?" Sunny called.

The man uncoiled from the tractor to reveal himself as a tall, lanky guy in overalls and a flannel shirt, with a surprisingly boyish face.

Sunny suddenly recognized him as the tall, gangly boy who'd been a couple of grades ahead of her—the one with a perpetual cowlick. He never could hope to be one of the cool kids. In fact, he had been the butt of that nose-picking joke.

Well, he'd filled out a bit since grade school. Sunny couldn't tell about the cowlick. He was wearing a John Deere cap.

"Hope you weren't all fired up to go apple picking," the man said with a cheerful smile. "I'm afraid we're closed today. Open Tuesdays, Thursdays, Saturdays, and Sundays," he recited. "The rest of the week we spend keeping the place going."

When Sunny introduced herself and explained why she was there, the man wiped away some oil on an old rag and presented a hard, callused hand to shake. "Nate Ellsworth. So you want to talk about our trouble with Mrs. Spruance." He sighed. "I hoped it'd be over when that poor woman died. Hear the animal control people collected all her cats."

"It's pretty amazing that they would come all this way," Sunny said.

"To tell the truth, we thought so, too," Nate replied. "I guess we're the nearest working farm to town." He grimaced. "Town keeps coming closer and closer, these days." Gesturing to the fields around him, he said, "We've had four generations of Ellsworths farming this land. Thirty acres."

The orchard was pretty much as Sunny remembered it, neat rows of trees stretching off into the distance. A rounded hill rose in the middle of the land. To Sunny's younger self, it had looked as if a giant had been buried up to his eyebrows, the foliage on the rounded knoll being his hair.

"My granddad went over to the pick-it-yourself business," Nate went on. "Dad put in the cider press. We introduced lower trees—easier for the kids to get at the apples—and put in about fifteen acres of blueberry bushes. That way, people can come and pick something anywhere between July and November, if we're lucky. Got a few pumpkin vines, too, for jack-o'-lanterns and Thanksgiving."

As he spoke, a brown hen came wandering around the tractor, her head bent over in search of food. She halted in surprise to encounter Sunny's running shoes—a strange pair of feet—and scuttled off in a new direction.

"Oh, yeah," Nate said with a laugh, "and Isabel brought in some chickens. Why don't you come in and meet her?"

Nate led the way to the farmhouse porch and opened the door. "Isabel?" he called. "Company."

Isabel Ellsworth was a trim, bustling woman in comfortable jeans and a flannel shirt. With her strong features and deep tan, she looked like Hollywood's idea of a farm wife.

When Nate explained that Sunny was writing a story about the cats and the chickens, Isabel shook her head. "It's sort of traditional that farmyards should have a flock of chickens scratching around, and we decided they ought to be free-range. There's lots of room for them to wander in the orchards."

"And lots of bugs out there for them to eat," Nate put in. "Helps to control the insect pests."

"Then, too, the flock gives us a supply of eggs."

"Both for our kitchen and for Isabel's famous blueberry-cider doughnuts," Nate put in.

Isabel ducked her head at the compliment. "And every once in a while we'll dress a capon to sell at Judson's Market. This isn't some sort of factory farm, with thousands of birds in cages. It's just enough to feed us, and maybe bring in a few extra dollars."

"Like Isabel said, these are free-range. We don't fence the chickens in." Nate picked up the story. "The more adventurous ones will even go as far as the berry patches. They all come back at night to roost in the chicken coop at the side of the barn."

"When you let the chickens out like that, you've got to

expect to lose some," Isabel said. "There's foxes and half-wild dogs around here."

"And lately folks have even spotted coyotes," Nate added. "So it wasn't exactly a surprise when something started raiding the hen house. That's when we put in the cameras."

"And then we got the surprise," Isabel said. "Show her, hon."

Nate opened an old rolltop desk to reveal a laptop computer. A few taps and clicks, and a fuzzy, grayish image appeared on the screen.

"It's low-light stuff, so the picture looks a little weird," he said apologetically.

But it was clear enough to show a long, lean cat shape creeping into the chicken coop, grabbing a bird by the neck, and skedaddling.

Sunny asked to see it again. It was hard to make out details like stripes, but . . .

Is that Shadow? she wondered.

"Once we saw it was a cat, we checked around and found out about all the cats Mrs. Spruance kept," Isabel continued.

"And when we went over there, we found a whole bunch of bones in the backyard—chicken bones," Nate said. "Including a leg with one of our ankle tags on it."

Isabel's eyes narrowed, emphasizing the crow's-feet in her deep tan. "This was right after she made such a fuss about that dog going after one of her cats. But she didn't seem to mind her cats coming after our chickens."

Probably because she saw the cats as her friends, Sunny thought, *while the chickens were just . . . food.*

"Anyway, there was a lot of back-and-forth in your newspaper, people writing letters to the editor and such." Isabel rolled her eyes. "It seemed pretty simple to me. That woman said the dog should have been controlled. Well, shouldn't she control her cats? And frankly, she had so many she couldn't keep track of them in the first place."

"That was all annoying enough," Nate said. "But folks around here began taking it personally. Customers we've had for years suddenly weren't coming by. We even had a bunch of tour groups cancel. They just didn't want to get in the middle of anything."

"It sounds like a real mess," Sunny said sympathetically.

"We're trying to make a living here," Isabel said. "This whole debate definitely didn't help."

"So did you do anything to deal with any other possible predators?" Sunny asked.

Nate nodded. "Bought myself a varmint gun." He pointed toward the fireplace. The gun rack over the mantel was pretty old, but the rifle hanging there was obviously brand spanking new.

"Fellow at the store wanted to sell me a .22, but I wanted something with a little more oomph. That's a .308 caliber."

"Have you tried it out?"

"No," Isabel replied sharply. She clearly didn't like the idea of a gun in the house. "This isn't the country anymore. There are houses sprouting up all around here, and that means kids. So no shooting. We keep the bullets locked up separate from the gun."

From the look on Nate's face, this was an argument

they'd had more than once. Obviously, he didn't want to get into it right now.

Sunny closed her notebook. "Well, thank you for talking with me. I wanted to make sure I got your point of view."

They saw her to the door, and she set out for the parking lot and her car.

She couldn't see the Ellsworths killing Ada over a couple of chickens. But if she'd continued the controversy, splitting the community so that fewer people went down to the farm, that could have threatened Nate and Isabel's ability to keep their place.

So, that was motive. As for means . . . well, farm chores kept them pretty strong. Sunny remembered Nate's callused grip when they shook hands.

And finally, she thought as she got into Mrs. Martinson's Buick, *there's that .308 rifle that Nate is so proud of. It's not exactly rare, but Isabel said that none of the ammunition had been used. If Will wanted to look in that box of bullets, I hope Nate didn't sneak off for a little target practice behind his wife's back.*

Sunny started the car and got onto the driveway heading back to the road. She had to veer suddenly as a foraging hen scurried almost under the wheels of Mrs. Martinson's big Buick.

Stupid chickens, she thought.

12

Thursday morning, Sunny was back in the MAX office, stifling yawns. The good news was that she'd finished writing the article for Ken with time to spare. Sal DiGillio had brought back her dad's pickup with plenty of apologies. Best of all, nobody had tried to kill her in the night.

The bad news—Shadow was gone. After saving their lives and irrigating Mike's prized rosebushes, the cat had disappeared. When she'd completed her article and e-mailed it off to Ken, Sunny had taken a walk through the neighborhood but had had no luck spotting him. She'd even driven through town in the evening in search of the cat, but there was no sign of Shadow.

It looked as if he didn't want to be found.

At work, Sunny shook her head when she found herself

reading the same e-mail for the third time. *Come on. He's a cat,* she scolded herself, trying to break out of her funk, *not the man of your dreams.*

The door opened, and Ken Howell came in, carrying a stack of newspapers. It was the week's supply of the *Harbor Crier,* destined for the wire rack beside the potted plant in the office window. Usually Ken took the day off after spending the night printing his paper, delegating distribution to some of the local kids. But today he made it personal.

"Here it is, reasonably hot off the press," he said with a smile, holding up one of the folded copies so Sunny could read the above-the-fold headline: LOCAL WOMAN'S DEATH LEAVES UNANSWERED QUESTIONS.

Sunny sighed. "It's not as dramatic as 'Murderer Revealed!' I didn't exactly crack the case."

"Still, it's a very professional story." Considering his surly reaction when she'd first approached him about a job, Ken was being positively jovial.

And the story *was* professional, Sunny had to admit as she took the copy Ken held out and looked it over. She'd used an old journalism trick—if you don't have many facts, ask questions. So, using the death of a fairly controversial local figure as a springboard, she'd raised a lot of questions. With Ada Spruance no longer on the scene, what happened to all the conflicts she'd engaged in? Would poor Festus still be labeled a dangerous dog? Sunny made sure to present the Towles' case fairly, and she only mentioned the Ellsworths in passing—as Nate said, having the cats rounded up probably ended the threat of chicken stealing. But then, what would happen to all the cats collected from the Spruance house? For that matter, what would happen to the house itself?

Sunny did her best to shine a powerful spotlight of publicity on the homeowners' association. Maybe that would slow Veronica Yarborough down if she went ahead with her attempt to force Gordie out of his childhood home.

Finally, there were the mysterious aspects of Ada's death. Sheriff Nesbit had simply issued a curt "no comment" about the case. Mrs. Martinson, never one for publicity, had flat-out refused to be quoted in the story, so Sunny had had to use the weaker "local sources" attribution about Ada being afraid of her kitchen stairs. However, Sunny had her own personal observation to go on when she mentioned the steps in the cellar appearing unused and the fresh paint chips broken off when the long undisturbed doors to the kitchen had apparently been forced open.

And then there was the biggest mystery of all—that legendary lottery ticket. The clerks at Judson's Market confirmed that Ada had regularly bet on 13, 23, 40, 51, 59, and the Powerball of 14. And they confirmed that those were the winning numbers that had been chosen a year ago. But the countermen couldn't say for certain whether Ada had purchased a ticket on the given date.

The cutoff to apply for the prize was now barely a week away. If the day passed without a claim, that might be the biggest unfinished business of Ada's life.

Then Sunny caught the headline on the story below the fold: QUESTIONS CAN BE DANGEROUS. Ken had written the story himself, covering the booby trap in Sunny's car and the discovery of the stolen Jeep and the hose outside her house. He didn't step on Sheriff Nesbit's toes by calling the incidents attempted murder, instead framing the situations as attempts to intimidate a *Crier* reporter who'd merely been making inquiries for a story. But the facts in each case were there to let the readers draw their own conclusions.

"I thought we agreed not to go with that story," Sunny complained.

Ken just shrugged his skinny shoulders. "You may not like it, but it's news—the biggest news in these parts in quite a while."

He deposited the papers in their rack, yawned, and then turned back to Sunny.

"Funny thing happened this morning," Ken said. "I got a call from Ollie Barnstable."

Sunny set her shoulders, waiting for bad news. But Ken surprised her.

"He said if I valued my editorial independence so much, maybe I should buy him out of the paper. Named an amount that would half kill me to raise, but oddly enough, it's less than what he put in. So is your boss getting a bit forgetful, or is he having money problems?"

Ken's eyes might have been half closed, but his gaze was keen as he looked at her.

Sunny had to shrug. "We don't sit down every evening and count his money," she told the editor. "So how should I know? Maybe he decided to cut his losses—or to cut you a break."

Ken shook his head. "That doesn't sound like the Ollie I know," he said. "For him, a free press is never free. For him, it's always a question of dollars and cents."

He yawned again, said good-bye, and headed out.

From her desk, Sunny looked at the pile of papers and debated shifting them to someplace less conspicuous. But that wouldn't even put off the inevitable. There were dozens of places all over town where Ollie the Barnacle could pick up the *Crier*. And if he really was having cash problems, his uncertain temper would be even worse than usual.

It was midafternoon before her boss finally called. "I hope Howell cut you a nice check for the story you wrote for him," Barnstable growled over the phone. "Because you aren't getting paid for that sick day you took."

Sunny had had enough of tiptoeing around her boss. "Ollie, did you even read the paper? There's no mention of mad murderers roaming the streets of Kittery Harbor, just a local story about local questions. Ada Spruance spent her whole life in this town. I think she deserves better than to have 'accident' stamped on her forehead before being dumped in the nearest grave. There are questions that had to be raised."

She took a deep breath, wondering how she could get through to him. "I mean, my parents knew her. I bet yours did, too."

Ollie was, after all, a hometown boy who'd gone off to the big city and then come back, flush with cash.

He cleared his throat, actually sounding a little embarrassed. "Yeah, Mom and Dad knew her before she became"—the word "crazy" hung unspoken in the air—"the way she was."

After that, the subject got dropped, and Ollie toned down the sarcasm while they discussed a couple of business matters. But even so, Sunny had the uncomfortable feeling that if interns could handle the website, she'd be out of a job.

She sat feeling gloomy after Ollie hung up, trying to get work done and only creating more for herself.

Then Will Price walked in, going directly to the newspaper rack and picking up a copy of the *Crier*, holding it at arm's length to admire the front page. "So there it is," he said. "A lot of questions—but you missed the million-dollar one."

"You mean the six-to-eight-million-dollar one," she told him.

"I mean the big question: why did Gordie Spruance murder his mom?"

His casual attitude toward the whole affair ticked Sunny off. "Well, if you're so sure that you have a line on the killer, it's a shame you didn't outline your case for the story." She paused to glare at him. "Oh, that's right. You were staying on deep background for political reasons. So I got to make a target of myself stirring the pot while you watch to see what comes to the top."

He fiddled with the paper uncomfortably before finally saying, "I wouldn't quite put it that way."

"So what have you turned up that makes Gordie a stronger suspect than the Towles—or the Ellsworths, for that matter?"

"Well, I might start with that six to eight million you mentioned," Will offered. "A big-money motive is a strong motive."

"So is love—and the Towles really love their dog, Festus. Ada wanted him destroyed." Sunny also pointed out how the local dog-cat-chicken controversy had hurt the Ellsworths' business. "They love their land—the family's been farming there for four generations."

"We can rule the Ellsworths out on opportunity," Will told her confidently. "Saturday is a big day for their self-picking operation. Nate was there all morning, running hayrides full of tourists to and from the apple orchards. And Isabel was behind the counter, selling doughnuts and cider."

Sunny nodded. "And do the others have alibis?"

"Chuck and Leah Towles took Festus for a walk in Windward Point Park," Will reported. "It was morning, but not too early. A jogger spotted them around the same time you discovered Ada's body."

"That doesn't let them off the hook," Sunny objected. "All we know is that Ada died sometime before I found her. You didn't take her liver temperature or anything, did you?"

Will rolled his eyes. "People watch a couple of *CSI* shows, and then they expect miracles."

"I'll take that as a no, then," Sunny said. "If your jogger is the first time somebody spotted the Towles, either of them could have gotten up earlier."

Will doggedly continued down the list. "Veronica Yarborough sleeps late on Saturdays."

"And probably every other day, too," Sunny muttered.

"On weekdays, though, she has staff coming in," Will went on, ignoring her comment. "Not so much on the weekends, unless she's having a party. The Saturday in question was not a party weekend. That means the first corroboration on her movements was a luncheon date well after the presumed time of death."

"That leaves her in the picture, too," Sunny argued.

"Although I expect she'd prefer having one of the servants throw Ada down the stairs," Will said with a wry smile. "After all, that's the sort of job that could soil her lily-white hands."

"So what about Gordie?" Sunny pressed on.

"We can't trace his movements from the night before until almost eleven in the morning, when one of our officers apparently woke him up to give him the news about what happened to his mom," Will reported. "The last time he was seen before that—by anyone who'll admit to it, at least—was one a.m., the last call for drinks at O'Dowd's."

"Is that place still around?" Sunny asked in shock. "When I was home from college, my friends and I used to sneak over there because they'd serve us even though we were underage." She shook her head. "It was pretty down and dirty."

"Well, it's only gone further down and gotten dirtier," Will told her. "And I don't say that just because Gordie Spruance hangs out there. It's, like, lowlife central for Kittery Harbor."

He ticked off the points on his fingers. "So, we've got a strong motive, we've got at least possible opportunity, and as for means . . ."

Sunny remembered Gordie heaving around that big bag of cat food. "Yeah," she reluctantly agreed, "he's strong enough to have done it."

"What hit me last night, the clincher as far as I'm concerned, is what's happened to you in the last few days." He frowned, trying to organize his case. "That bullet in your car, the hose outside your house—"

"I can't imagine Gordie coming up with those slick criminal plans," Sunny told him.

"But could you see him as the guy who screwed both of them up?" Will asked.

That stopped her for a second, but she shook her head, remembering the lost, scared look in Gordie's eyes when he talked about his mother. "I just don't buy it. He was really upset about Ada's death."

"Sure, he was upset," Will argued. "It's called regret. Remember, Sunny, he's a tweaker. No impulse control. He could freak out and kill someone, then still feel really bad about it afterward. As for those half-assed booby traps and stuff—hell, they just stink of tweaker."

"So that's your case? Stinks, and what-ifs, and conjectures?" Sunny said. "If you had anything solid, you wouldn't be here talking to me."

Will grimaced. "True. If I had even a scrap of real evidence, I'd risk going over Nesbit's head straight to the district attorney. We did everything but put both cars under a microscope, hoping to find Gordie's fingerprints, but all we got were smudges. He may be a tweaker, but he was smart enough to wear gloves."

"So what are you going to do?" Sunny asked.

"Well, you said it—he's upset. After stewing about it for a few days, he might be ready to talk."

"You're going to question him?" Sunny stared in disbelief. "How are you going to do that? On what pretext? You can't just haul him down to the station. What are you going to charge him with—drugs?"

Will shook his head. "I don't think Nesbit would go for

it—even if it were a simple drug bust. We've got to go at this a different way."

"We?" Sunny said.

"I'm a cop. He's just going to shut up the minute he sees me," Will told her. "But you—you grew up with Gordie. I could see it when you guys were talking. He responded to you."

"So you think he'd confess a murder to me?"

"I think he might mention something to you that we could use," Will said. "Gordie is in O'Dowd's most nights. If you happened to come in for a drink, it would be the most natural thing in the world for you to have a little chat with him."

He saw the look on her face. "Hey, I'd be right outside the window for backup. If I see anything weird, I'll be right in there." Will shrugged, spreading his arms. "Just talk to the guy, that's all. I get an hour for meal break. So if you came in there, say ten thirty, eleven o'clock . . ."

*

How did I let him talk me into this? Sunny wondered as she pulled her dad's pickup into a space in front of O'Dowd's. It was a long, low wooden building in need of a coat of paint. The place didn't even have a proper sign, just a neon beer advertisement in one of the small windows.

Sunny opened the door and slid down to the pavement. She shook her head in amusement when she recognized the tan truck parked next to hers. Gordie Spruance's.

Well, at least I know he's in there.

She looked around until she spotted Will's patrol car parked across the street.

Okay. No more putting it off.

Finding her hands suddenly damp, she wiped them on the sides of her jeans. From what she remembered of the decor in O'Dowd's, she'd chosen essentially the same outfit she'd worn to clean Ada's house, with the addition of an old leather jacket.

Her dad thought she was going out searching for Shadow again.

Maybe I'd be smarter if I were doing that, Sunny thought ruefully. Instead, she straightened her back and headed for the gin mill's door.

The unpainted wooden panel had swollen over the years, sticking in its frame. Sunny had to pull hard to open it.

She stepped into a cloud of cigarette smoke. *Guess I shouldn't be surprised. A place that serves underage drinkers wouldn't care much about a nonsmoking law. Or maybe the regulars consider this their private club.*

In a way, the smoke served a useful purpose. It cut the stink of stale beer and less pleasant substances that had soaked into the raw wood walls and floors over the years.

The jukebox was playing loud country music with an amped-up bass thumping away, battling with the high-decibel babble of voices all trying to make themselves heard over the din.

A loud—and familiar—laugh cut across the noise. Sunny was shocked to discover that she recognized the woman behind the bar. Back when she last went to O'Dowd's, her male college friends all hoped that Jasmine the barmaid would fall out of the skimpy outfits she wore.

Nowadays, I think folks might be afraid of that happening, Sunny thought.

As Jasmine threw back her head for another laugh, doughy flesh jiggled wherever her tiny tank top didn't reach. And the unnaturally black hair that Sunny remembered now had an inch and a half of gray roots showing on either side of the center part.

No, Jasmine was not the barroom femme fatale anymore, explaining why a couple of guys at the bar were checking Sunny out as she stood by the door. She studiously avoided their gazes and then spotted Gordie sitting alone at one of the tables scattered around the room, a beer in front of him.

Sunny dug out a bill and headed to the bar. "Can I get a glass of red wine?" she asked Jasmine.

She'd already noticed that beer only seemed to come by the bottle or pint, she didn't want to be drinking hard liquor under the circumstances, and soda would have made her motives for being there, alone, seem even more questionable than they already were.

The barmaid scooped up a stemmed wineglass from a shelf behind her—Sunny noticed it was dusty—and the wine itself came from a box.

Not a big seller, apparently, she thought. *I just hope it hasn't turned to vinegar.*

She left a tip, strolled over to Gordie's table, and sat across from him.

He looked up from the half-empty beer he'd been contemplating and stared as if she were Dracula's daughter, inflamed zits showing up even more clearly on his pale face. "What are you doing here?"

"I was in the mood to go out for a quick drink. Been a while since I was in here, though."

But as Sunny put down her drink, she found some things never changed. Ever since she could remember, the tables at O'Dowd's had been cheap rounds of plywood on top of heavy steel pillars. The bases never sat straight, and the tops could give you splinters at a moment's notice. They still could. The table wobbled, causing her wine to slop around in its glass.

"Heard you wrote a piece about Mom in the paper." Gordie looked down at his beer. "Sorry, I haven't read it yet."

"It was more about the unfinished business she left behind," Sunny told him.

"If you mean the ticket, I haven't found it yet." She had to strain to hear Gordie over the rowdy background noise. "Maybe she never actually bought the damned thing. Mom was getting a little older. She'd started losing track of stuff sometimes."

"I know you're depending on that money to fix up the house and get things on an even keel," Sunny said. "Not getting it would be a real killer."

She'd decided to approach this talk the same way she did search engine optimization for her website—throwing out keywords and checking the response.

The word "killer" didn't seem to have any effect on Gordie. She decided to try another.

"Poor Ada changed a lot from the way I remember her as a kid. But I guess we all have." She smiled, gesturing to Gordie. "Look at you, how you've slimmed down. I hope you didn't do it the dangerous way—with amphetamines or something."

Gordie flinched and took a quick look around the nearby tables. A bit of an overreaction, since they were all empty. Okay. She could mark down a definite hit at the mention of amphetamines.

"I hope you don't mind that I wrote that article," she went on. "Maybe I should have mentioned it the last time we talked."

"Why?" Gordie asked. "Did you say something bad about me—or Mom?"

"No, but ever since I visited with you, somebody's been playing tricks on me."

Except for a little interest, Gordie wasn't really showing a reaction.

"Yeah, somebody got into my car, somebody was making trouble outside my house—"

Again, nothing appeared to register with Gordie. He blinked at her, a little puzzled, and said, "That's messed up."

All right, Sunny thought, *looks as if I'll have to up the ante.*

"It made me wonder if someone was afraid of that story I was doing." She gave him a hard look. "Afraid that something might turn up to suggest that what happened to your mother wasn't an accident."

She had all of his attention now. "What do you mean?"

"When's the last time your mom used those cellar stairs?" Sunny asked.

For a long moment, Gordie's eyes refused to meet hers. "I dunno," he mumbled. "But then, I haven't lived there in a while." He looked as if he were trying to push something away.

"But you were there when your father was still alive. I hear that's when she stopped using those stairs."

This turn in the conversation had him definitely uneasy. He tried to take a sip of his beer, but stopped when he saw how his hand was shaking.

"Ada at least tried to clean up the places where she usually went," Sunny told him. "But there was thick dust on those stairs. Years of it."

"Just what are you saying?" Gordie demanded, his fists clenched on the table.

Impulse control issues, Sunny thought, remembering Will's list of tweaker tip-offs. *Let's see if I get a reaction if I start circling around Ron Shays.*

"I'm saying it could be dangerous for an old woman to have something worth a lot of money, when there's criminal stuff going on around her. What do you think?" Sunny stared Gordie right in the eye. He looked as if she'd morphed from Dracula's daughter to the Prince of Darkness himself.

But before he said anything, angry voices rose over the crowd noise and the music. Sunny turned to see a big, beefy guy in a hooded sweatshirt with a mullet and a healthy beer gut shove a skinny guy whose beard didn't hide the acne scars on his face. Screaming like a banshee, Skinny launched a roundhouse right. Fatso ducked the wild swing, then slammed the other guy into the bar. Skinny came back with a bottle in his hand, smashing it against a bar stool.

Somebody ran past their table as people started to intervene.

Sunny turned back to Gordie to find a changed man.

Staring pale faced at the fighters, he muttered, "I know those guys, and they're bad news." Still staring, he bolted up from his seat. His hip jostled the unsteady table, and Sunny's wineglass fell over.

Before she could grab it—or him—Gordie was out the door. Sunny had never seen him move so fast.

A second later, Will Price entered, his expression hard, his right hand hovering beside the pistol at his hip. He came right over to where Sunny was still sitting. "I saw Gordie run out and heard sounds of a fight when the door opened. Everything okay?"

Behind him, except for the thumping country music, the place had gone dead silent. When Sunny looked over at the bar, the crowd had gotten a bit smaller, as if several people had preferred not to be seen by a representative of the local law.

So much for my undercover career, Sunny thought.

"I'm fine," she said, wiping at her lap as red wine began to dribble onto her jeans. "Nothing a wash won't fix."

She tilted the rickety table so the wine went the other way. Of course, that sent the glass rolling, too. Sunny grabbed it, then stared. "What the—?"

A lumpy mass sat in the bottom of the glass, stained the same color as the wine. At first she thought it might be past-due sediment, or maybe a drowned creature. Yuck.

But as she brought it closer, she saw that the lump was made up of a bunch of smaller globs, some kind of melting capsules . . .

Capsules that were supposed to have dissolved in her drink.

13

Will's eyes went wide as he took in the gooey mass of pills in the glass. He whipped out a handkerchief, wrapped the glass up, then pulled Sunny to her feet. "We've got to get you to the hospital. Who knows what this stuff is."

Sunny resisted. "I didn't drink any of it. There are two guys you'll want to talk to. They were fighting—"

She stopped, looking around at the crowd. Somehow, Fatso and Skinny had disappeared.

"Gordie got spooked when he saw them, but they're all gone now."

Will turned to the crowd. "Anybody know the guys who were fighting?"

"What guys?" Jasmine the barmaid tried to give Will a sexy smile, but the effect was a bit ruined by her missing front tooth. None of the other patrons said a word.

Claire Donally

Will's face got stony as he scanned the boozy wall of silence lined up in front of the bar. "And I suppose you have no idea how that broken glass happened to wind up on the floor over there?"

Jasmine peered over the cheap plywood bar, her cleavage dangerously straining her little tank top. "Somebody musta got careless and dropped a bottle." She bustled out with a broom and pan. "Thanks for pointing that out, Constable."

As the barmaid straightened up with her load, Will approached her, looking at the shards of glass in the pan. "Where's the top of the bottle?"

If he got hold of that, he might get some fingerprints, Sunny realized.

But Jasmine looked around, making a big show of puzzlement. "I dunno."

Sunny's shoulders fell. Skinny probably took it with him.

Will looked mad enough to spit. Instead, he reached into his pocket and pulled out a buck, which he dropped on top of the mess in the pan. "For the lady's glass," he told Jasmine, gesturing with the handkerchief-wrapped wineglass in his other hand. He came back to Sunny. "Let's get out of here."

She followed him back to his patrol car, where he carefully stowed the glass. "I have to go in and get that analyzed." He looked at her with worried eyes. "You're sure you didn't drink any of it?"

Sunny gave him a crooked smile. "It wasn't exactly the most appetizing vintage."

Will relaxed a little. "That's good." Then he switched

to superserious mode. "What'd you ask Gordie that made him decide to spike your drink?"

"I don't see how he could've," she objected. "The glass was sitting right between us while we talked."

She stopped for a second. "Of course, I turned away for a couple of seconds when the fight broke out."

"What were you talking about when that happened?" Will asked.

"The conversation was just beginning to get interesting," Sunny said. "I raised the possibility that his mom's death wasn't an accident, and he really got bent out of shape."

"And you wonder why he tried to poison you?" Will demanded.

"Not *that* kind of bent out of shape," she tried to explain. "More like he was dealing with an idea he didn't want to think about. And he seemed seriously scared when he saw the two guys go at it." She went back over the series of events. "Besides," she continued, "he knocked my drink over. I can't see how that would help him much if he really wanted to poison me."

"I think we might be able to file that under 'Henchmen, Fumbling,'" Will told her. "It sounds as if the fight was staged to distract you while the pills got into your drink."

"But nobody knew I was going to be there," Sunny protested.

From the look on his face, Will didn't want to think about that right now. "Can you describe the two guys?"

She tried to replay the fight again. "One was fat—big beer gut, but he was wide, too. Brown hair in a mullet, unshaven. Dark eyes, I guess. He was wearing jeans and a T-shirt with some kind of beer logo on the chest—I didn't really see—and a hoodie over that. The other one was smaller—skinnier—with lighter hair that really needed to be cut. He had a full beard that was darker than his hair, and he had acne scars." She paused. "Most of the time he had his back to me. He had jeans and a tight T-shirt, and I think he may have had a tattoo on his arm—his right arm. That's the hand he used to wave the bottle around."

Will jotted down the descriptions. "Okay. Why don't you go get into your car, and I'll see you home."

"I don't—" Sunny began in annoyance, but then her voice faded as the significance of what Will was saying sank in. "You think someone's been following me?"

Will scowled. "Let's call it a possibility." His words came out very grudgingly. He tore off a piece of paper and scribbled on it. "This is my cell number. I'll try to rustle up one from Semple, too. Whenever you have to go some-where, give us a call."

"And if I go potty, whom should I announce that to?" she asked sweetly, her frown now matching his.

For a second his eyes snapped, but when he spoke his voice was quiet, almost mild. "I just think it's a good idea that the good guys know where you're going to be," he said.

Sunny shivered, positive she was thinking the same thing he was.

Because, apparently, the bad guys will.

*

Shadow lay very still, trying to ignore the waves of pain coming from his side. He'd been hurt before—worse than this, even. Usually the thing to do was to find a good hiding place where he could heal up.

This time was very different.

He closed his eyes, but found himself reliving the events that had brought him here.

He'd been out foraging, roaming the part of town where the two-legs weren't so careful about wrapping up their trash. They often tossed out food, and on the street any chance to eat was a good one.

Shadow found some salty things that he licked, but he kept on, looking for meat. If he didn't find it in the trash, well, perhaps a nice fat mouse would come looking for a meal, too . . . and end up becoming one instead.

He was crossing a street when he stopped, sniffing the air. It wasn't food. Just for a second, he thought he caught a trace of Sunny.

Sunny was gone. The Old One had tossed him out just like the trash lining these streets. Shadow had his pride—he knew where he wasn't wanted. Best not even to think of it—

A door on one of the buildings flew open, releasing a wail of noise into the street. Shadow flinched. The two-legs could be so loud sometimes!

A whole array of smells billowed around him as the release of warm air dissipated. Then his whole snout wrinkled as he detected a particular odor. Was that the Stinky One?

The Stinky One moved very quickly across the street. Shadow followed, curious. The scent grew stronger, and then he heard the familiar rumble of the Stinky One's car.

Shadow watched in satisfaction as the despised human

hurriedly left. He took a victory lap around the space the car had vacated.

Too bad I didn't have a chance to let my claws hurry him along.

That little moment of triumph was a mistake. When you wandered the streets, you always had to be wary, on guard against attack. But he was concentrating so much on the Stinky One, he ignored the second blast of noise, the pair of two-legs running into the street.

They were arguing, he could tell that from their voices.

But Shadow didn't realize how close they were until the Fat One made loud, angry noises.

He never saw the kick the Skinny One sent into his side.

But he felt it as it sent him rolling into the gutter. He wanted to squall his fury, but even taking the breath hurt all over.

Shadow lay there for a while until the first pain faded a little. Then he slowly, awkwardly got to his feet. Standing around hurt on the streets was an invitation to get attacked. He had to find somewhere to hide, somewhere safe—

He inhaled deeply, trying not to mewl as the pain flared again. Was that another trace of Sunny?

It seemed to be connected with the truck he lay under. Shadow went to the tires. They had new smells from things they'd rolled through. But beneath that, they smelled of Sunny's Place—the place of the boxes!

Painfully, he cast around the big vehicle. It was taller than her car. The doors and windows were high above him. And besides, they were closed.

But this thing had the big flat part in the back. Shadow had visited it while exploring the place of boxes. Of course, it was much easier to get in there when there were piles of boxes to climb.

Here he saw his only chance was to get onto the trunk of the car parked next to the truck. Shadow circled around the car, trying to ignore the new hurts his exertion brought to life. He spotted a couple of boxes leaned against a light pole nearby. One box was open, filled with rotting food. The other was closed. He could only hope it would take his weight—

Shadow jumped, landed, and jumped again. For an instant, he thought he was going to fall back, his back claws scrabbling against the metal until he managed to pull himself forward.

He made his way across the expanse of the car's trunk. It sloped down to the right, his uninjured side. That was a good thing. Ahead of him rose the side of the truck, which still rose up higher than his vantage point. He still couldn't see where he'd end up landing.

Would he be able to make it? Shadow knew he'd only have one chance. Already he felt dizzy and sick.

He backed up until his rear paws almost went off the trunk. Then Shadow ran forward, ignoring the pain screaming from his side. At the last moment, he launched himself, trying not to think of the hard concrete flying by beneath him.

Shadow barely cleared the truck's side wall. But he was coming down into a place of safety—or so he hoped.

He didn't land well, stumbling instead of catching himself on all four feet.

Red pain flashed all over him.

Then everything turned black.

*

Nothing exciting happened when Sunny crossed back over the street to her dad's pickup. No sniper fire, no garbage truck careening down the street to run her over.

She started the engine and pulled out, feeling a little numb.

All the way home, she keep looking in the rearview mirrors, trying to spot a tail.

Of course, she had one. Will's police cruiser rolled along behind her.

I hope he's looking behind him, she found herself thinking, then shook her head at such foolishness. If someone had been following her, seeing a police car on her trail would probably discourage them.

The lights were still on when she arrived home. Her father was probably still up, watching the late news.

Sunny pulled up in the driveway and got out to wave to Will.

That was when she heard it—a low, mewling moan.

The noise seemed to be coming from the truck bed.

Instead of heading for the door around the front of the pickup, Sunny went to the rear and peeked in.

A furry shape lay sprawled on the metal bed.

"Shadow!" she cried.

She had to climb halfway into the truck to get at the cat.

Usually Shadow was totally aloof, a real "don't touch me" cat. He darted away if Sunny so much as extended a hand to pet him.

But now he just lay limply, blinking up at her in misery as she gently gathered him up in her arms.

Will came hustling over to see what was going on.

"You remember Shadow?" she said.

He nodded. "From the scene of the crime."

Sunny probed the cat with careful fingers. Shadow gave another low moan when she touched his ribs.

"He's hurt!" she said, and then she turned to Will in real horror. "You don't think that *they*—"

"Can't say." He looked down at the huddled gray form in Sunny's arms. "But this is really one of those times that I wish cats could talk."

14

Sunny burst into her house, Shadow in her arms, Will
Price at her heels.

Her dad jumped up from the couch at the commotion.
"Constable! What's going on? Is everything all right?"
Then he saw the cat. "Did she have you out looking for
this mange-ball?"

"Shadow's hurt," Sunny said. "We have to get him some
help!"

She turned on her heel, heading for the kitchen, then
turned back. "Do we still have a yellow pages?"

"In the cabinet," Mike said, following after. "You're
not just going to put him on the table, are you?"

"You're right." Sunny glanced over her shoulder at Will.
"Bring a pillow from the couch."

Once Shadow had been arranged as comfortably as possible, Sunny attacked the directory. "Pet hospitals," she muttered, flipping through pages.

Tucking the receiver from the wall phone between her ear and her shoulder while holding a finger on the number she wanted, she punched on the keypad.

On the other end, the phone rang four times. Then came a click, a moment of dead air, and a whirring sound with an obviously canned voice saying, "Thank you for calling the Kittery Harbor Pet Hospital. Our hours of operation are from eight thirty a.m. to four thirty p.m. Monday, Wednesday, Friday, and Saturday, and from ten a.m. to seven p.m. Tuesday and Thursday. Dr. Rigsdale and our staff offer a wide range of affordable patient care for small animals, large animals, and exotics—"

Sunny hung up. "I'm getting their machine. Where are the white pages?"

Silently Mike dug out the other phone book. "I know that look from her mother," he muttered to Will. "That's the 'don't argue with me' look."

"Rigsdale—good. There's only one in the book." Sunny copied the address, picked up Shadow on his pillow, and headed back down the hall.

"Aren't you going to call?" Mike called after her.

"And give this Rigsdale character warning that I'm coming?" Sunny almost snarled. "He's not going to hide behind an answering machine this time."

Will could only shrug and follow her.

When Sunny went to place the pillow on the passenger side of the pickup, Shadow mewled piteously at her. "It's okay, it's okay, we're going to get some help for you, just take it easy." She clipped on her seat belt, then carefully set Shadow and his pillow on her lap.

It was close to midnight by the time they got to the address. Will got out of his patrol car and came to her driver's-side window, doing a double take at the sight of the cat in her lap.

"Sunny, the place is dark," he said, pointing out the obvious.

"And this is an emergency," she snapped. "I'll carry the cat; you ring the bell."

Will muttered something about improper use of authority, but did what she said.

"Lean on it," Sunny said after Will rang the bell twice without getting any answer. "And if that doesn't work, we'll try your siren—wake up the whole neighborhood if we have to."

He leaned on the bell. A light came on in one of the upstairs windows, and then a head appeared, silhouetted against the light.

"What the hell is it?" a woman's sleep-fuzzed voice called down.

"We've got a veterinary emergency down here," Sunny said. "Don't we, Constable Price?"

"Constable Price?" The woman upstairs leaned out farther. "Will?"

Will's jaw dropped as he peered upward. "Jane?"

A moment later, the woman was downstairs. Even in a bathrobe with bed hair, she was a blond knockout.

Now it was Sunny's turn to stare. "Jane Leister?"

Jane had been the golden girl of her high school class:

valedictorian, most pretty, most popular. While Sunny and most of the girls were killing themselves to get pimply-faced juniors to notice them, Jane was going out with a college guy.

"I didn't even know you were back in town," Will said. From the look on his face, he and Jane had History with a capital *H*.

"Yeah, well, I didn't know you were, either," Jane said. "And my name is Rigsdale now. My husband—ex-husband—we were partners in the practice. I got the hospital in the divorce, and I kept the married name since I'm known professionally as Dr. Rigsdale."

She glanced over at Sunny with a half-puzzled. "Don't I know you?" kind of look.

Sunny sighed and introduced herself. Jane nodded. "Oh, of course, we went to school together. You were on the yearbook, right?"

No, and I wasn't part of your fan club, either, that uncharitable part of Sunny's mind silently answered.

Just as well, because the vet made another connection. "You wrote the article in today's *Crier*," Jane said. "I'd like to talk to you a bit about what happened to Ada Spruance, and what they intend to do about her cats. But first, we've got business."

She turned to the cat in Sunny's arms. "So this is the emergency patient? I warn you, I'll do this once because you're a friend of Will's—"

Jane broke off in surprise. "Hey, Shadow," she said in a gentle voice. "Whatcha doin' here?"

Shadow stirred and meowed at her.

"I thought you and all of Ada's cats were with Animal

Control." Jane gently scratched the cat between the ears, talking to Shadow as if it were the most natural thing in the world.

Sunny couldn't help noticing that Shadow didn't shy away from Jane's fingers.

Great—she's also the most popular with cats, Sunny fumed.

The vet turned to Sunny. "I gave all my medical files on Ada's cats to the folks at the shelter to try and help get some adoptions set up. She probably spent more time and money taking care of her strays than she did for herself." Jane smiled. "Guess I'll have to get Shadow's back." She pointed over her shoulder. "Bring him into the kitchen. I'll examine him there."

Following Jane's instructions, Sunny deposited Shadow on a kitchen island that probably cost as much as her year's salary at MAX.

"It's his side," she said as the vet helped Shadow to sit up. He was obviously favoring one side.

Jane nodded. "Cats usually don't show much when they're hurting. Out in the big, bad world, a small animal that acts lame or starts crying is just asking to be attacked by something else. It's simple survival to be stoic."

Sunny blinked. "But Shadow cried out. He was in the back of our truck when I passed by, and I didn't know it until I heard him."

Jane looked surprised. "I don't think he ever talked to Ada. Guess he must like you." She continued her careful investigation. "He's definitely hurt—probably a kick. His breathing seems all right . . ."

She stepped around to pull a stethoscope from a drawer.

"Don't hear anything wrong with his heart or lungs. The little guy may have some bruised ribs, but I don't think anything is broken. You can bring him in for X-rays tomorrow"—she looked at the clock—"make that later this morning. Or you can keep an eye on him for a day. If you see breathing problems or if he suddenly doesn't want to eat, then I'd be worried."

Jane gently petted Shadow. "Don't give him any pain medicines. It's not just a question of dosage; cats' systems—or dogs', for that matter—don't handle them the same ways ours do. The best thing right now is just to let him rest."

Will kept glancing anxiously at the kitchen clock. "Look, I've got to go back on patrol."

"I'm just going home," Sunny told him. Will said his good-byes hurriedly and rushed out the door as Sunny turned to Jane. "I'm sorry for barging in like this. Maybe I overreacted."

But the vet shook her head. "That kind of trauma can mess up a cat's lungs, even his heart. You did the right thing." She saw Sunny to the door. "Besides, it was interesting to see Will again—and you, too, Shadow," she added, running a finger under his chin.

She glanced over at Sunny. "You don't seem too familiar with cats, if you don't mind my saying so. What'd he do, adopt you?"

"I—I guess so," Sunny admitted.

"As I said, I can retrieve his medical records if you're going to keep him. He can be a handful, but he's healthy. If you're still making up your mind, I have to warn you— he's starting to bond with you."

Sunny looked down into Shadow's oddly flecked eyes. "Yeah," she said softly. "I think I am, too."

＊

Her dad was in bed by the time Sunny got home. His light was off, and Sunny suspected he had the covers over his head, hoping to avoid her righteous indignation over the results of his attempt to evict Shadow.

"Too bad, Dad," she muttered. "I think your fiendish plan to toss Shadow out completely backfired on you."

How was Mike going to get rid of the kitty that had saved Sunny and him from being gassed, especially when the feline hero came home injured?

Sunny transferred Shadow to the pet bed, which had remained in the corner of the living room. Then she carried him, bed and all, up the stairs to her room and put him down in front of her bookcase. "G'night, Shadow," she said, getting a drowsy "Mrrrrow" in response.

Smiling, she went off to her own bed.

＊

Sunny's alarm rang all too early the next morning. She staggered downstairs to find Mike already making breakfast—his idea of a peace offering.

She decided not to beat him over the head. Instead she just repeated Jane Rigsdale's advice about listening to Shadow's breathing and letting him rest.

"Let him rest?" Mike muttered incredulously. "How is that different from what he usually does?"

Shadow came into the kitchen. He was still moving carefully, but already he seemed a bit better. After a brief detour to snag some dry food, he came over and nudged Sunny's ankle with his head. She reached down and scratched him behind the ears, smiling when he didn't shy away this time.

Mike watched and gave a helpless shrug. "So that's the way it is now?"

Sunny didn't even answer, gulping down her coffee and heading for the pickup truck. She made it to the office on time and spent most of the morning trying not to fall asleep on her desk.

Guess it's just as well I'm not doing anything critical today, she told herself.

She tried to look bright and chipper as the office door opened—although the effect was spoiled a little when her mouth dropped open in surprise. Jane Rigsdale walked in. "Several of my patients mentioned you this morning," the vet said.

"Parrots?" The snarky question came out before Sunny could think to stop it.

Jane grimaced. "I guess the ladies who talked to me consider themselves my patients' mothers. So you were down in New York being a journalist? Now that I think about it, it wasn't yearbook, was it? You were on the school paper back in the day."

Yeah, while you were student government president and prom queen and—Sunny broke off that line of thought. Her high school annoyance at Perfect Miss Jane was almost fifteen years in the past. Why was she getting so riled up about it now?

She tried to keep that ancient irritation from her voice as she answered. "Yeah, that's what I was doing until my dad got sick and I came up here to take care of him." She shrugged, giving Jane a crooked smile. "I took a leave of absence, and then I got laid off. The newspaper business isn't as healthy as it used to be."

Once again, Sunny had to hand it to the gossip establishment over the local media. Here Jane had her whole backstory, not to mention clearly pinpointing where she worked now, all thanks to a couple of conversations with people bringing their sick pets in for treatment.

If Ollie could figure out how to tack advertising onto that, he'd be a megagazillionaire, Sunny thought. Out loud, she said, "So what brings you back to the old hometown?"

"Business," Jane said shortly, drawing herself up. Then her shoulders slumped. "Martin—my ex-husband—had a practice outside of Boston. That's how I met him, actually. In the vet trade, you essentially start off as an apprentice to an experienced practitioner when you come out of school." She sighed. "Martin was a very good vet. As a husband, though, not so much. There were problems, financial and personal. I thought we could make a fresh start up here, but—" Jane made a helpless gesture. "Long story short, it didn't work out. Martin moved on, and I stayed here with the pet hospital."

After a moment's silence, Jane pulled herself together, becoming a businesslike veterinarian again. "I had an early lunch, so I thought I'd stop by and see how your patient was doing." She colored slightly. "The furry one, not your father."

"I guess both patients could be better," she told Jane. "Shadow is walking around a little lopsided, and my dad is bent out of shape because there's a cat in the house."

Jane laughed. "I've seen that syndrome before." Then she got serious. "On the other hand, there are some studies that show having a pet around can help a sick person's recovery."

"Let's hope so," Sunny said, "because up to now all Shadow has done is raise Dad's blood pressure." She shook her head. "That's not altogether true. Dad did promise to keep an eye on Shadow while I'm at work. Although he did ask what the difference was between Shadow resting and the cat's normal day."

"Recovering cats rest by night as well as by day. So if your father has to get up at some ungodly hour to go to the bathroom, he *won't* bump into Shadow wandering around on midnight patrol." Jane smiled. "Shadow's a healthy, resilient little guy. If he's walking around, even a little lopsided as you say, that's a good sign. I expect he should recover quickly. But it's good to have someone keeping an eye on him, just in case."

She paused for a moment, then said a little too casually, "It was great seeing Will Price last night. Has he been helping you with the investigative story?"

Several possible answers flitted through Sunny's mind. *No, he's actually my helpless love slave* sounded a little too silly (not to mention untrue), while *Yes, and we're also playing detectives in our spare time* was perhaps too much information.

She decided on the literal but uninformative truth. "He was the one who first responded to my 911 call when I found Ada dead, so he has an interest in the case."

"Ah." Jane raised a hand to brush her blond hair behind her shoulder. "You don't know if he's . . . seeing anyone, do you?"

Sunny put on her best helpful expression. "He hasn't mentioned anything like that."

Jane nodded. "Just wondering. Well, keep me posted on how Shadow is doing. I called this morning to get his records back. It was good seeing you guys last night. We returnees ought to stick together."

Right, Sunny thought as she watched Jane walk out of the office. *Maybe we can get together and form the Busted Lives Club.*

She threw herself back into work, trying to squelch that dismal thought.

Will Price's call a little while later didn't help much on the cheering front, either.

"I had a friend in the Portsmouth crime lab take a look at the gunk in the bottom of your wineglass." He sounded even grimmer than his usual cop voice.

"Oh," Sunny said. With all the other excitement later in the night, she'd almost forgotten about their abortive undercover operation. "What were they? Some kind of knockout drugs?" She made a face. "That date rape stuff?"

"Not unless Gordie was into necrophilia," Will told her. "It was a mixed bag of sleeping pills. Addicts often carry them to come down from a long meth jag. That many pills, though, would have put you to sleep permanently. Gordie must have had a handful of them, and his sweaty palms glued them all together. It's beginning to look like a Wile E. Coyote adventure," he said wryly.

"Who?" Sunny asked in confusion.

"You know, the coyote from the *Road Runner* cartoons? The one who's always coming up with a clever plan, which then falls apart, usually biting him on the butt." He gave a dry chuckle, but Sunny just rolled her eyes.

"It didn't have to be Gordie," she said, running back over the sequence of events again. "Somebody came up behind me when the fight got serious. At the time, I thought they were running to help separate the two guys."

"They?" Will repeated. "Not he or she?"

"Come on, there was a bar fight going on, which kind of distracted my attention. I never really got a look at the person behind me," Sunny confessed. "But whoever it was, they were close enough to drop something in my drink."

"Be that as it may, I'm very eager to have a chat with Gordie Spruance," Will said. "He lives out in the country— outside the town's jurisdiction. I can't get Nesbit's people to help on this, but Ben Semple and the guys in the department are stopping by to check around Ada's house and keep an eye out for Gordie and his pickup."

"And what are you going to do if you get him?" Lurid images of blackjacks and waterboarding flashed through Sunny's mind.

"I'm going to show him the glob of pills in your glass and the other stuff that was used to try to get at you," Will replied. "If he is involved, I ought to get some kind of twitch out of him. If he's not involved, as you seem to believe—well, maybe all that stuff will shock him into talking about his criminal associates."

"And then maybe you'll have something to take to the district attorney?"

"Yeah." Will sounded as tired as she felt. "Maybe, maybe, maybe."

After Will said good-bye, Sunny tried to occupy herself with the lowest kind of grunt work—the stuff she usually put off because it was so tedious. Unfortunately, that left her mind free to keep jumping around in very unsettling ways.

She almost welcomed the interruption when the phone rang again.

It was Ollie Barnstable at his most charming. "Sunny, I need you to go into my files," he said. "Get the folder marked 'Investment Opportunities' and bring it to the Captain's Table. I'm having a business lunch."

And apparently you want to impress whoever is eating with you by having a flunky appear, she thought.

"So get to it." With that encouragement, he hung up. Sighing, Sunny opened the cash box for a special set of keys. The back wall of the office held a row of file cabinets with Ollie's personal files. They were supposed to be kept locked and never opened unless he asked for something.

Sunny suspected that half the cabinets were empty or held old tax papers. Some of the drawers had pretty cryptic inscriptions.

One of these days, preferably while Ollie is away on vacation, I'll have a look into some of those, she promised herself. For now, though, she went to the first of the alphabetized cabinets, unlocked it, and searched under the Is.

There it was—Investment Opportunities. Sunny slipped the file into a large envelope and headed for the front door, stopping to lock it on her way out.

*

The Captain's Table offered the best dining in Kittery Harbor—not to mention the best views. The owners of the restaurant had renovated a warehouse in the old waterfront district, with outdoor dining on the old pier. Between the quaint buildings surrounding them and the vista of the cove that had served as an anchorage, the Captain's Table would have drawn crowds of diners even if the food hadn't been fantastic—which it was.

"Just the place to go to impress some rich out-of-towner," Sunny muttered as she set off down the sidewalk. Any trip downtown was like a journey into the past, especially the past of narrow streets. She could reach the waterfront district faster on foot than taking her dad's truck.

Main Street lost a couple of lanes at the Redbrick Tavern, another high-end restaurant and one of the few historic buildings not constructed of hemlock and spruce. Just as she reached the corner across from the landmark, Sunny stopped and stared as Gordie Spruance came out the front door of the tavern, rubbing the back of his hand against his mouth. He was wearing ripped jeans and a paint-stained gray hoodie, clothes more suited to O'Dowd's than a nice place like the Redbrick. And, she noticed, he had the hood up—as if that could hide his beaky nose and the flaming acne across his cheeks.

"Gordie!" Sunny yelled. "Hey! Gordie!"

He took one look at her and ran around the corner. Sunny dashed after him, digging out her cell phone, wishing she'd put Will on speed dial.

Behind her, she heard the roar of an engine, then wild horn-honking.

Sunny turned to see a huge blue SUV barreling through traffic—coming straight at her. The fight-or-flight response kicked in. If Sunny had been running before, she almost flew now, reaching the far sidewalk. But the big vehicle kept coming, climbing the curb.

Oh my God! Sunny thought, hurling herself to the left. The envelope she was carrying slipped from under her arm, and her phone flew from her hand as she skidded along the sidewalk. The truck flashed by, going way too fast . . . then hit the brick wall of the tavern.

They built things pretty solid back in the day. The wall may have shaken a little, but the front fender of the SUV crumpled. Sunny heard the *bang!* of an airbag going off, and a sort of rattling roar that built up to a huge crashing noise.

She pushed herself up onto her knees as the door of the truck opened. The driver wobbled out, but he had no interest in Sunny. His hair flew wildly around his head, and he held a hand over his nose and lower face. Bright red blood dribbled between his fingers.

A nondescript Toyota pulled up in the street. "Come on!" a voice yelled to the injured driver, who stumbled into the car as it fishtailed away. By the time Sunny got into the street, it was too far away for her to make out the license.

Sunny lurched back to the sidewalk, managing to retrieve her phone and her envelope as people poured out of the tavern, staring at the abandoned SUV.

Then a scream came from around the corner. Sunny forced her shaky legs into another run, skirting the rear of the SUV and swinging around.

Bad idea.

A young woman rammed into her, running blindly, still screaming at the top of her lungs. Sunny tried to step back, but the crowd from the tavern had surged after her, blocking any hope of retreat.

Now Sunny knew what had made that rattle-crash sound right after the truck had hit. Like many buildings from the old days, the Redbrick Tavern had a slate roof. The shock of the crash had dislodged a bunch of the thin slabs of rock and they had cascaded down onto a passing pedestrian.

Somebody in a paint-stained gray hoodie that was rapidly turning red.

15

The screaming woman finally quieted down just as
screaming sirens announced the arrival of the Kittery Harbor Police. The first responding officer was Constable Ben
Semple. He looked a lot more authoritative today as he
ordered the crowd back, called for backup and an ambulance, and then asked if anyone had witnessed what happened.

Sunny raised her hand, and he turned to her, his eyes
going wide in recognition. "Ms. Coolidge!"

She mustn't have looked her best, because the next thing
Semple said was, "Are you all right?"

"You've got to call Will Price," Sunny said, trying to
keep her voice low and steady. She'd tried to get him herself, but her fingers were shaking so much, she kept hitting

the wrong buttons on her cell phone. "I don't know if you recognized him, but that's Gordie Spruance under there."

More officers arrived, helping to herd the onlookers out of the way while Semple made a phone call and then knelt for a real examination of the bloody form on the sidewalk. The constable glanced at Sunny, giving her a brief, negative headshake. Rising back to his feet, he craned his neck to look at the roof.

"Was Spruance trying to avoid the SUV when it crashed?" he asked her.

She shook her head. "Gordie was trying to avoid *me*. *I* was trying to avoid the SUV."

As she told her story, the constable began to get that glazed look she'd seen on his face before. "I don't know what the sheriff's going to make of this."

"That makes two of us," Sunny muttered.

Will arrived, using his badge to get past the police line. He looked bleary-eyed, as if Semple's call had hauled him from a deep sleep.

He's on the swing shift, Sunny thought. *That's exactly what that call did.*

He also appeared to be a bit grouchy at being woken up. "Weren't you supposed to call about wherever you were going?" Will demanded.

"I had to deliver—" Sunny broke off, looking at the envelope she'd been carrying. "Oh, God. I've got to get this to the Captain's Table. Ollie Barnstable's been chewing me out ever since I agreed to do that story for Ken Howell. This will give him an excuse to fire me."

"Well, I'm sorry, but you can't go," Semple said. "You're

a witness to"—he gestured at the scene all around them—"whatever this is."

"Looks to me like someone leaving the scene of a fatal accident—at the very least." Will took the envelope from Sunny. "I'll head over to the Captain's Table and get this into Barnstable's hands."

"Also, tell him to call someone in to cover the office," Sunny called after him. She turned to Semple. "Something tells me I'm not leaving here anytime soon, am I?"

*

Sunny's suspicion turned out to be all too correct.

After canvassing the crowd, Constable Semple wound up taking her and a couple other witnesses to the police station, where they were divided up into separate rooms and asked to give statements.

By the time she finished with that, Will had reappeared. "Barnstable was wining and dining some foreign guy," he reported. "And you were right, he was not happy when I told him what had happened. He seemed to think you tried to get yourself killed just to inconvenience him."

"I'd say it was a bigger inconvenience for poor Gordie." Sunny shook her head. "How could this stuff be going on? This is Kittery Harbor, where nothing happens."

Will's initial grin faded into a serious frown. "So would you mind going over the sequence of events again for my benefit?"

She explained about getting the call from Ollie, bringing the package, seeing Gordie . . . and what had happened as a result.

As she did, Will kept looking at some papers in his hand. "The getaway car—you said it was a Toyota?"

She slowly nodded. "I saw the logo on the trunk. But I was still getting up. I never got a decent look at the license plate. I can't even say if it was from Maine or New Hampshire."

"And the car's color?"

"It was one of those new bland metallic colors." She shrugged her shoulders. "I don't know what you'd call it. Cream? Sand?"

"Well, that falls in between the person who called it silver and the one that called it tan." Will sighed.

"And the one that almost hit me was blue," Sunny suddenly said.

"Yeah." Will drew out the word a little. "Easy to check on, since it's still stuck against the wall at the Redbrick. If you want to be precise, I believe it's sport blue clearcoat metallic."

"A Ford Explorer."

Will gave her a bemused look. "That's right. You must really fixate on logos if you noticed that bearing down on you while busily jumping out of the way."

Sunny shook her head. "I saw it before. That day you gave me a lift, that—that monster truck was following me on my bike." She began to shake again. "It would have been really easy to wait till we got out on an empty road and—"

Will grabbed her hands. "They didn't then, and they didn't now," he broke in forcefully.

"But you can't put this down to a Wile E. Coyote

foul-up." Sunny paused for a second, struck by a thought. "Or can you? Was Gordie there to lure me into position for that truck? Or was he just really unlucky—in the wrong place at the wrong time?"

She gave an impatient headshake. "That doesn't work out. Even if it was a two- or three-man operation, Gordie, the guy in the explorer, and the guy in the getaway car, how would they know I was going in that direction? So they had to be following me."

"I'd like to worry a little less about the theoretical implications of the attack and concentrate more on cold, hard facts—especially while they're still fresh in your mind," Will said. "What can you tell me about the driver from the Ford?"

Sunny shrugged. "I only saw him for a few seconds, and not from a good angle. I was on my hands and knees at the time, climbing up from the sidewalk."

She frowned, shutting her eyes, trying to call up a picture of the guy she'd seen stumbling from the wrecked SUV. "He had a bloody nose, that's what really leaps out. The blood was trickling down between his fingers." She opened her eyes and shook her head. "That bloody hand was covering everything from his nose to his chin. I just saw bright red—didn't even notice the color of his eyes."

After a second she said, "He had a lot of hair. Long. Maybe it had been pulled back in a ponytail and got loose, because it was all over the place."

"Long hair," Will repeated. "His hand couldn't have blocked all of his face. Try to remember. Was he clean shaven, or did he—" He broke off with a frown. "That could be leading."

"What could be leading?" Sunny asked. Then the light went on over her head. "You think it might be that Ron Shays guy?"

Again, Sunny tried to visualize the man making his way out of the blue Explorer, struggling to bring the edge of his masking hand into focus. Could there have been a beard under there? Or was this what Will was afraid of? Had he planted the idea in her head?

"Sorry," she said unhappily. "I just can't say."

"It would have been nice." Will straightened up the papers in his hands. "Because if you hadn't realized it yet, I just lost my prime suspect in Ada's murder."

"There's still Veronica Yarborough and the Towles," Sunny suggested. "Neither of them have alibis for all of Saturday morning. And do we know where anyone was on Friday night?"

Will nodded, but it was clear he wasn't rating the neighbors as hot suspects. Sunny wasn't so sure. For all her airs and graces, Veronica Yarborough didn't strike her as a good person to cross. As for Chuck and Leah . . . Sunny remembered how she'd felt when she found Shadow crying in the back of the pickup. *If I found the person who hurt him—*

Protecting a pet suddenly seemed like a much stronger motive now.

*

When Sheriff Nesbit arrived, he wasn't happy to find Will with Sunny.

This time, though, he can't shove what happened under the rug—there are too many witnesses, she thought. *And he's got to see there's no way I could have singlehandedly arranged an attempted hit-and-run against myself.*

But the sheriff's mood certainly didn't improve when Will started telling him some of the things they'd discovered about Gordie Spruance.

Nesbit smoothed down his silver mustache while his face turned dull red. Before Will got a full sentence out, the sheriff barked, "The two of you have been conducting your own little investigation, and now you've decided to let me in on what you've found out? How considerate of you!"

"It didn't start as an investigation," Sunny responded. "I just talked to the guy as part of the article about his mom's death—"

"A death that you insinuated might be murder," the sheriff interrupted. "And you weren't happy until you spread your theory all over town, were you? Look where it's gotten you."

"A death where the dead woman's son and heir was a tweaker," Will stepped in. "You don't have to take my word on that. I'm sure an autopsy will prove it."

"Maybe you're right, Will," Nesbit said grudgingly. "I don't want to speak ill of the dead, but you know there are weak-willed people out there who'll use drugs no matter how clean we keep things around here."

"Except Gordie was hanging around with a dealer who specialized in making places dirty," Sunny burst out. "Tell him, Will."

Will started explaining about Ron Shays and his business model of opening meth labs in virgin areas, but Nesbit cut him short. "You went to Portsmouth PD and didn't share this information with me?"

"What would you have done if I had?" Will challenged.

"It's irrelevant," the sheriff blustered. "Doesn't apply here."

"What doesn't apply?" Will wanted to know. "We have a guy who likes to open meth labs in quiet places, and we have the tweaker son of a lottery winner who could put up the money."

"Except nobody seems to know where this famous missing ticket ended up," Nesbit objected, "or even if it exists. To tell you the truth, I wish to God I'd never heard about it!"

You and me both, Sunny thought. *It may have gotten Ada Spruance and her son both killed. And I might be next.*

A knock on the interrogation room door interrupted them. The door opened, and one of Nesbit's deputies came in with Ken Howell.

"Sheriff—," the nervous deputy began.

"I don't have a comment to make right now," Nesbit barked. He turned furious eyes on Howell. "Especially not for your miserable rag."

"My 'miserable rag,' as you put it, is the least of your worries," the *Crier* editor told him. "The phone's been ringing off the hook in my office. Reporters from the Portsmouth paper, all the TV news types, even stations from Boston, they all want to pick up on the double tragedy connected to this lottery ticket."

He scowled. "Hell, I would, too. Just my luck this happens the day *after* the latest issue came out." Then he grinned at the sheriff, having kept the best for last. "It's a slow news day, Frank. You're gonna have yourself a media circus coming to town—and all the clowns will want to talk with the reporter who actually interviewed Gordie Spruance *and* witnessed his death."

"Oh, God," Sunny blurted out.

"Oh, *damn*," Frank Nesbit muttered.

*

Sunny quickly called her dad and filled him in. This was something she did *not* want him discovering on the TV news. Then, all too soon, Sunny found herself standing beside the sheriff in the local press room, a utilitarian space with cream-colored walls and a low dais where Nesbit positioned himself behind a simple lectern, facing an array of microphones and cameras. It wasn't just the regular media contingent that she saw on TV. She also spotted a lot of people she'd encountered while beating the bushes for a journalism job in the area—would-be newspaper stringers and unemployed reporters who called themselves freelancers.

I think anybody with a press card within a hundred miles has turned up, she thought. *Oh, Lord, I hope I don't look like a deer in the headlights.*

Nesbit stepped up and gave a carefully edited summary of the facts in the case. "A sport utility vehicle climbed the sidewalk in downtown Kittery Harbor, narrowly missing one pedestrian and causing the death of another. We cannot speculate at this time as to how or why this happened. The driver of the SUV fled the scene. Our mechanics are examining the vehicle to determine whether there was any sort of mechanical malfunction."

Period.

He handled the storm of questions that followed like the political professional he was. Yes, it appeared the car had been stolen several days ago in Portsmouth. No, his department had no idea as to the identity of the driver yet. Yes, the deceased was the son of the supposed lottery winner, who herself had died less than a week ago. No, the lottery ticket had not yet been found.

Nesbit wrapped it up pretty quickly, then turned to Sunny. "Ms. Sonata Coolidge is the person who survived this traffic incident. She also works as a reporter for our local newspaper, the *Harbor Crier*."

Out in the wolf pack, Ken Howell grinned broadly.

"Ms. Coolidge recently wrote a story on the death of Ada Spruance, in the course of which she interviewed Gordon Spruance, the young man who died in this occurrence. She is assisting us in our inquiries."

Thanks to her experience from the other side of interviews, Sunny handled herself pretty well. There were a couple of ticklish moments, like the question from one reporter who'd done her homework.

"You suggested that there were mysterious circumstances in the death of Ada Spruance." The skinny young TV journalist curved her bloodred lips in a predatory smile aimed at Sunny. "Do you think these circumstances might also apply to this woman's son?"

"I outlined apparent discrepancies regarding Mrs. Spruance's death that I was able to substantiate," Sunny carefully replied. "There were other rumors that could not be substantiated."

Translation: *If I couldn't use the information I'd dug up for my own story, why would I air it for yours, honey?*

"But are the two deaths connected?" the female reporter persisted.

"That's for the police to determine," Sunny honestly answered. "All I can say is that buying that lottery ticket seemed to use up all the luck the Spruance family had. If the ticket actually exists, it hasn't done them much good."

After a few more questions, Sheriff Nesbit stepped in to wrap things up. But just as he was doing that, a deputy came hotfooting it into the room. "Sir, urgent call from the fire chief over in Sturgeon Springs. We transferred it in here." He pointed to a phone off to the side of the podium.

Nesbit impatiently snatched up the telephone handset. "What is it, Joe?" he barked. But as he listened, his face went white.

"Huh," Ken Howell said from the middle of the crowding journalists. "Good thing I left my cell on vibrate. It's a source on the Sturgeon Springs Fire Department."

He listened for a moment, and his smile only got broader. "Well, what do you know? Gordie Spruance's place has exploded in flames, and they're having a hell of a time putting it out. My guy says it looks exactly like a training film they just watched—about dealing with fires in meth labs."

16

For the briefest of moments after Ken Howell spoke up, the crowd of media people stood silent.

Then they all burst out in a frenzy of shouted questions to the sheriff.

Sunny certainly had no reason to like Frank Nesbit. But watching him standing at bay with the phone in his hand, she couldn't help but feel some sympathy for him.

He's been on with the fire chief for maybe a minute, Sunny thought. *What in-depth information do they think he could suddenly tell them?*

Turning to the collection of news gatherers slavering for the merest sound bite, she had to wonder, *More to the point, why would he* want *to tell them anything?*

After a moment of pandemonium, Sheriff Nesbit showed his years of experience in news management. Gesturing for silence, he said, "There's a preliminary report of a suspicious fire at the site. I'm heading over there immediately for a personal inspection. After I've ascertained the facts—"

Translation: When he comes up with a good spin on all this, the snarky voice in Sunny's head suggested.

"—I'll be glad to share them with you." Nesbit told the fire chief he'd be there as soon as possible and escaped from the room, followed by a ravening horde of newspeople.

Sunny watched them go, feeling a little embarrassed for her chosen profession.

"I'd say that went well enough." Will Price appeared beside her, now wearing his uniform. "At least no one got trampled in the mad stampede."

"Are you going out to the fire?" Sunny asked.

Will shook his head, wearing his most expressionless cop face. "I have another important assignment—seeing you home."

"Are you sure you've got the okay to do that?"

"Hey, it came from the sheriff himself," Will told her with a lopsided grin. "Local law enforcement wouldn't look too good if we allowed something to happen to you after that awfully public near hit-and-run. And it doesn't hurt that it'll keep me out of Nesbit's hair. Not only did he show concern for your safety, he actually expressed worry over my own health."

Sunny gave him a doubtful look. "He did? Really?"

"Oh, yeah. He said, and I quote, 'No more of this extracurricular fooling around.' At least it was something like 'fooling'—had the same first letter. 'You were up to something last night, and you were in here worrying about that girl when you should have been sleeping. I don't need some blinking zombie patrolling on the swing shift.' " Will grinned. "Trust me, that's pretty much verbatim, with some of the more colorful language toned down a little."

"So, you were worried about me?" Sunny asked, feeling her face get a little warm.

Will's expression got more serious. "Worried as hell," he admitted. "That's another reason why I don't mind making sure you get home in one piece."

Remembering Gordie's fate put a chill on whatever warmth Sunny had been feeling. "Guess we'd better get started, then," she said.

Will gave her a lift in his patrol car back to the New Stores, since she'd walked downtown. He got out himself and ran a quick check on Mike's pickup truck.

"No nasty surprises," he reported. "Did you see what I did?"

"It was pretty hard to miss when you dropped to the sidewalk," Sunny told him.

"I was looking to see if anything had been left under your truck," Will replied, deadly serious. "It wouldn't be the worst idea if you did the same thing before you climbed aboard in the future."

Sunny couldn't come up with a snappy answer to that. So she walked in silence over to the pickup, got in, inserted the key, and started the engine.

The journey to Wild Goose Drive was pretty tame. No attack helicopters swooped down, no wild SUVs came barreling out of nowhere at her.

Will beckoned Sunny over after she pulled up in her driveway.

As she walked to his car, he rolled down his window. "I know you probably think it's overreaction," he said in a quiet voice, "but a little prevention and forethought results in nice, boring trips like these." He smiled, lightening the mood. "I'll try to give you some sort of report on the excitement we missed at the fire scene. Later, okay?"

Sunny nodded. When she turned in the doorway to wave good-bye, she noticed that he stayed in place until he was sure she was safely inside.

"Hey, Dad," she called as she came into the living room, "did the people on TV completely blow things out of proportion?" She'd done her best to minimize things in her phone call to him, but God only knew how the newspeople had decided to spin the story.

"They say some idiots nearly killed you—again," Mike replied. "How close does that sound?"

He was trying to put a good face on it, but he sounded worried. "I don't like this, Sunny," he finally admitted.

"Neither do I," she said. "At least the sheriff's finally started to take things seriously."

"If he took things seriously, he'd resign and let someone who actually knows about crime prevention take over."

Mike might had continued in his tirade, but the phone rang. Sunny picked up the receiver.

"Ollie Barnstable," the voice on the other end announced, as if Sunny would have trouble identifying those accusing tones. "The office was closed for hours today because you were off talking to the police and getting yourself on television."

"I didn't have much of a choice," Sunny protested. "It was a murder case, and they needed a statement."

"Well here's a choice for you," Ollie snarled. "Make up the four hours you owe me tomorrow, or have them docked from your pay."

What a public-spirited prince you are, Ollie, Sunny thought. But aloud she said, "Okay. I'll come in for the morning."

When she told her father what the call was about, Mike had some choice comments to make about Ollie the Barnacle. Then he broke off, looking over to the doorway. "I must have woken up your friend. He spent most of the day sleeping in that expensive bed you bought him—and shedding hair on my good coat lining."

Sunny watched Shadow come into the living room. Even on less than a day's rest, he seemed to be moving with a lot more of his usual grace.

"How's his breathing?" she asked.

"Well, he didn't snore."

Sunny shot a look at Mike. "Did he eat?"

"Not when I was around," Mike told her. "But whenever I look in the kitchen, his bowl is always miraculously empty."

Shadow wound himself around her ankles with more interest than usual.

Well, Sunny thought, *even if I wasn't in a cell, I was in the jail. Guess I must have picked up some interesting smells while I was there.*

She dropped to one knee and went to scratch Shadow behind the ears, half expecting him to pull away now that he was obviously feeling better. Instead, he pushed his head against her fingers. Sunny gently ran her hands along his furry sides. Shadow was fine with that, except for a little squeak when she passed his left ribs.

Claire Donally

"I'd be afraid to lose a couple of fingers doing that," Mike told her.

"After what you pulled on him, I wouldn't be surprised," Sunny responded with a shake of her head. "Tipping him out a window into the cold like that." She was still annoyed about her dad's little trick, but the words came out in a sort of crooning tone as she petted Shadow.

"He seems to be okay," she said, looking up from the cat. "No swelling, and not that much pain, as far as I can tell. Looks as if he's getting back to his normal self."

"Great," Mike grunted. "Should I start nailing the lamps to the tables?"

Sunny ignored him, finally rising to her feet. "I'll start making supper."

"Wash your hands first," Mike called after her as she headed for the kitchen.

*

Shadow felt much better. He had appreciated the safe, warm place to rest, but now that Sunny was home, he couldn't keep himself away from her as she worked in the kitchen. As the room filled with the smell of cooking, he twined around her legs, even though she'd been thoroughly marked.

She talked to him and even put a bit more food in his bowl. He ate a little, just to be polite, and then kept following her.

When she and the Old One sat down to eat, Shadow positioned himself under the table, butting against her shins every once in a while. He stayed away from the Old One, even though he'd been careful and kind today. From harsh experience, Shadow knew that two-legged males might well kick when they thought no one was watching.

When the meal finished, Shadow accompanied Sunny back and forth to the kitchen as she cleared the table. The Old One took up his usual place, looking at the picture box.

Sunny came out and sat down, and Shadow sat at her feet. After a little while, though, she got up and went back to the kitchen. But she didn't go for food. For a moment or two she rummaged in a drawer. Then she came out with a ball of string.

Shadow ran circles around her as she returned to the other room, but then she sat on the floor instead of back in her chair. Were they going to play with the string? He remembered chasing and rolling with the stuff, but he hadn't played those games since he was a kitten! Trailing the end of the string along the rug, Sunny brought it to the corner of the chair. Just before it passed out of his sight, Shadow pounced on it.

Sunny flicked out the end of the string, and again began pulling it out of sight. Again Shadow pounced just before it would have escaped.

Shadow crouched low to the carpet, hoping she'd flick out the string again. She did.

They played the string game for a while, and Shadow managed to get a claw into the string itself. He pulled the ball to him and lay back, playing with it. The ball got smaller and smaller as loops of string piled up around him.

Sunny made happy noises, and even the Old One joined in, showing his teeth in that peculiar way the two-legs had.

At last there was no ball left. Sunny stayed on the floor,

rolling it up again. Shadow lay beside her, resting against the side of her leg.

He was almost surprised at the contented sound suddenly welling up from within him.

*

Sunny gently petted the warm, furry body beside her.

"Are you purring?" she asked Shadow.

Mike used the remote to push up the volume on the show.

Then the phone rang.

"Who can that be at this time of night?" Mike grumped. He picked up the receiver and a moment later held it out to Sunny. "It's Will."

"I'm on meal break," he said when she got on the phone. "If you don't mind the occasional sound of me eating pizza as I talk, I'll bring you up to date on what I heard happened out at Gordie's place."

"Okay," Sunny said. "So what's the story?"

"They finally got the fire put out and started investigating the cause. More or less as we, or at least I, suspected, it looks like Gordie was apparently trying to synthesize crystal meth."

Sunny passed that information along to Mike.

"How do they do that, anyhow?" he asked.

Will must have heard him over the phone. "To put it very simply, you add certain kinds of cold medication to a solvent to strip away some of the active ingredients you want," he said. "Gordie had a pretty bare-bones setup. For a solvent, he'd managed to get his hands on some ether. For the rest, he had a bunch of different cold pills. Either he was buying them in different stores or taking them with a five-finger discount. More likely the second, since he had no money."

"Maybe that explains why he went into the meth production business in the first place," Sunny suggested. "He might have been desperate to raise money. Think about it. If he told Shays that there'd be cash to fund a serious meth operation and then there wasn't, Gordie would have found himself in a real bind."

"That does make sense," Will said. "Anyway, it looks as if Gordie had laid everything out for a trial run before he went into town. But he didn't close up the ether container tightly enough. The stuff must have begun to leak out. Since it's heavier than air, the ether just filled the house out there on the edge of town until finally it reached the pilot light on the stove and—kaboom."

Sunny relayed Will's explanation to Mike, who nodded.

"That's how some of our demolition guys used to take out tunnel complexes back in 'Nam. All they needed for the job was a can of ether and a candle."

"Well, it certainly blew the hell out of that old farmhouse—and did a pretty good job on Frank Nesbit's PR, too." Will reported. "Those camera crews followed him out to the fire. His whole 'Keep Elmet Safe' campaign sounded a little hollow when a meth lab turned up under his nose. He's been trying to spin it, saying that this was the work of evil outsiders, but Gordie was a local boy."

Mike cackled when Sunny told him that.

"Another interesting point," Will went on. "Gordie was paying week to week to stay at this old farmhouse—a distressed property picked up by none other than your beloved boss, Oliver Barnstable." He paused. "With luck Ollie will be lying low for a while."

"Now, that would be good news," Sunny said.

"There's one more thing." Will sounded more tentative now. "I'll be switching to the day shift come Monday, which means I'll actually have both days of this weekend off."

Sunny had stopped passing along Will's conversation to her dad, sensing this was going to be more personal.

It was.

"Look, um, would you like to have dinner on Saturday to discuss the case—or whatever?"

"Sure," Sunny said aloud.

Especially whatever, she added with a silent smile.

17

Saturday started off dull, which perfectly matched the way Sunny felt as she sat in the MAX office, trying to get her keyboard into focus. Well, if Ollie Barnstable came by to check on her today, he'd find her working very early, if not so bright.

I've just got to make it to noon, she thought sleepily. Her first visitor of the day appeared even less well rested than Sunny felt. Ken Howell walked in with a thin pile of papers, looking heavy-eyed and moving like a much older man.

"Got a collector's edition here," he announced, his voice raspy. "First time the *Crier*'s put out an extra—God, since Will Price's father went off the road."

He held up the top paper so Sunny could see the head-line: HIT, RUN, AND FIRE.

"I tapped some people as soon as Nesbit left that press conference, and we worked all night." He stifled a yawn. "I'm getting too old for this nonsense. Anyway, it's four sheets—figured if you wanted, you could wrap it around the edition that just came out."

He paused for a second. "Hope you don't mind losing the front page."

Sunny shook her head. "Really, Ken, it's all right with me."

"Good, good." Ken left the pile of papers on her desk. "If you want to do it, fine. I really am done. Instead of sleeping yesterday, I pulled myself out of bed for Nesbit's media circus. That plus an all-nighter—" A mighty yawn escaped, and he looked embarrassed. "Pardon me. Just do me a favor, Sunny. If you're going to get involved in something else exciting, could you hold off until, say, Tuesday?"

With a rueful smile, Sunny promised she'd do her best as Ken shuffled out of the office, looking dead on his feet.

She picked up one of the extra editions and read through it. Stories recounted the events at the Redbrick Tavern, the press briefing, and the fire out at the farmhouse in Sturgeon Springs where Gordie Spruance had been staying. Pictures showed the crashed SUV and what looked like a mug shot of Gordie. Ken had also gotten somebody out to the scene of the fire to take some action shots there. Sidebars explained the use of dangerous solvents to create crystal meth and the fire dangers, including the possible explosive results of using ether.

Sunny noticed that she was quoted in the hit-and-run story—snippets from the press conference.

Thank God he didn't go for an exclusive interview, she

thought. *That would've probably been enough to get me fired.* She sighed. *Much as I hate to admit it, Ollie does have a point. I'm supposed to be boosting local tourism. I can't imagine this is going to do the industry much good.*

She wondered when Hurricane Ollie would come roaring into the office. *On the other hand, he's got the fire—and the meth lab—on his property to occupy his mind.* She sighed. *Here's hoping.*

Finishing the articles, Sunny had to hand it to Ken Howell. Not only was the extra edition a very competent piece of news gathering, but he hadn't editorialized on the situation. Just a bald recounting of the facts made Sheriff Nesbit look bad enough.

Sunny's second visitor of the day looked about as groggy and sleep deprived as Ken had.

"Will!" Sunny said, taking in his rumpled uniform. "Are you still working?"

"I'm going home to get some rest right now," he promised. "Your dad told me you were here, so I thought I'd stop by on my way and tell you how things shook out from last night's happy hoopla."

He dropped into a chair. "First, Sheriff Nesbit finally got in touch with the Portsmouth drug squad to ask about Ron Shays."

"Did they get hold of him?" Sunny asked.

Will shook his head. "Nobody's seen hide nor hair of him for a few days now."

"That could be good," she said cautiously. "If he saw that his deal was going down the toilet, maybe he just got out of the area."

"Leaving his henchmen behind to clean up any loose

ends?" Will added. "As it turns out, that's the line Nesbit's taking. His theory is that the hit-and-run was actually aimed at Gordie, not you, as revenge for screwing up the deal. Not only does this theory blame outsiders for all the trouble, but it ties up the case in a neat knot. Justice triumphs in the end—the bad guys have fled town."

The two seconds of relief that Sunny had felt quickly passed away. "It's neat, but there are questions that theory doesn't answer—like why Gordie was producing meth in the first place. If he was getting a lab up and running, wouldn't that mean he was trying to make good on the deal? Why then would Shays or his henchmen try to kill him?"

Will closed his tired eyes. "Gordie was obviously cooking the stuff on a shoestring budget. Maybe he got bounced from the deal and decided to try on his own. If so, Shays might've considered him competition in his new territory."

He opened his eyes, a troubled expression on his face. "This might be just the beginning of more trouble."

"A lot of this seems to depend on Shays," Sunny said. "Do the Portsmouth cops have any idea where he might have gone?"

"I talked to some guys outside of regular channels," Will admitted. "As far as they can tell, Shays just picked up and left. There's no reason other than the glitch in his supposed deal here. Things are quiet between the dealers."

He shrugged. "Well, as quiet as you can expect between a bunch of drug-addled, paranoid businessmen. It's always possible that some competitor thought this was a nice, peaceful opportunity to take out Shays, and he's actually floating somewhere in the Piscataqua heading out to sea."

"So what you think we have here are several bumbling henchmen trying to carry out plans their late boss came up with while trying to get some sort of business going on their own?"

Will gave her a lopsided grin. "And not doing a great job of any of it. With that scenario, it's possible that Gordie was actually working with them. They not only accidentally knock him off, they let their meth lab blow up."

"I like that one," Sunny said. "Not only is it entertaining, but it means that around about now the bad guys should be getting discouraged enough to head out of town."

She breathed a long, drawn-out sigh. "The problem is, the real situation could be any of these, or something we haven't even thought of. Don't start," she said, raising her hands at Will's thoughtful expression. "You're overtired as it is. Coming up with more off-the-wall theories isn't going to help you sleep."

"Okay." He dragged himself to his feet. "Home. Sleep." His expression brightened. "And dinner later tonight?"

"Dinner tonight," Sunny agreed. "Do you know where you'd like to go?"

"Not the Captain's Table or the Redbrick—I think that might be a little too soon for you. And for them, actually. What do you think of someplace out of town? I've got a place in mind," Will said, "but I'll have to see if I can get a table on short notice."

"Well, call me during the day if you're successful," Sunny told him. "If not, Lord knows I've got a list with lots of places." Sometimes it seemed as if half her job at MAX involved recommending restaurants for visitors. "Some of them even give me coupons."

*

As the morning slowly passed, Sunny really began to worry about how badly all the negative news coverage might have hit Kittery Harbor's tourism. E-mail traffic was way down, and the phone didn't ring at all.

At this rate, Ollie the Barnacle will have a whole new— and justifiable—reason to fire me, she worried.

As she sat at her desk, laboring through the tedious task of updating the website's software, Sunny could look out the plate-glass window and see Kittery Harbor PD cruisers passing by at irregular intervals. Ben Semple she knew already, and repetition made the other officers on the day shift become familiar, at least by sight.

Sunny decided to stay barricaded behind her desk rather than going out for a snack, unable to decide whether to be comforted or annoyed by so much police attention.

Just as the noon hour approached, she got a visit from the week's biggest tourism spender—Raj Richer.

"I wasn't sure the office would be open," he said. "But then I noticed you in here as I walked by."

"Just putting in a few extra hours. How's your genealogy research going?" Sunny asked, only to get a shrug.

"There are some possibilities," Raj said, "but I would have to get more of our family records before I could pursue them."

"Ah," she said, trying to keep disappointment out of her voice. "I guess you'll be leaving soon."

"Not for a few more days," he replied. "In fact, I'm here to make another payment."

More big bills came out of his wallet. Sunny made out a receipt and put the money in the cash box. "So you're enjoying your stay?"

"It's restful," Raj said. "It's been nice for a while to escape from business—which reminds me—"

He opened a leather portfolio and removed several sheets. Sunny saw Oliver Barnstable's letterhead on top, then in large letters, "Investment Opportunities."

So Raj was the rich out-of-towner that Will had seen lunching with Ollie.

"I wanted to return these." Raj put them on Sunny's desk. "Please forgive me for leaving them with you instead of delivering them to Mr. Barnstable in person. He is a very persuasive man, with an interesting vision for this town. However, after the unpleasantness yesterday, I'm reluctant to make an investment."

Raj leaned over to pick up a copy of the newly published issue of the *Crier*. "I saw this when I went out for breakfast this morning. It quite shocked me to read that the building that burned down—the one the drug people were using— had belonged to Mr. Barnstable." He shook his head in distaste. "Really, I don't think this is an appropriate situation for an investment at this time."

"Do me a favor," Sunny told him. "Don't mention that to Mr. Barnstable."

Raj glanced over at her. "I also read the issue with your article. Very interesting, I thought. The whole state of affairs must be very difficult for the family—Spruance, is it?"

"I don't know if there's much of the family left to be upset," Sunny told him. "The father died some years ago, and Gordie—Gordon—was an only child."

"Somehow that makes it even sadder." Raj paused for a second as if searching for words. "There was another article, insinuating that there have been attempts to intimidate you?"

"A couple of . . . things happened," Sunny said, trying to keep from getting too specific. "Upsetting, maybe, but I try not to get too excited about it."

As she spoke, one of the town's dark blue patrol cars came by. Constable Semple was behind the wheel and actually waved at her. When Sunny nodded back, Raj turned to see what she was looking at, a smile tugging at his lips. "Well, it seems the local police take a more serious position on these matters."

He said good-bye, and the hands of the clock at last reached noon. Sunny hesitated for a moment. She had promised to call Will so that he could escort her home before she set off. But he'd looked so tired, maybe she should give him a little more time . . .

As she dithered, Sunny watched the minute hand pass beyond noon, and realized something that made her smack herself in the forehead. She'd forgotten about all that cash Raj had given her—and with Saturday hours, the bank was now closed!

Guess I'll have to take the cash box home again, she thought, dialing Will's number.

Will sounded reasonably coherent when she finally rang him up. "Be there in a few minutes," he promised.

Soon enough, she spotted his black pickup on the street outside. Will flipped up his sunglasses and gave her a smile. Sunny already had everything on her desk turned off. She tucked the cash box away in a bag, came out, locked the door, and headed for her dad's truck.

The loud honk of a horn sounded as she reached for the door handle. Sunny turned around to catch Will pointing at the ground under her truck and shaking his head emphatically.

Sighing, she dropped to the pavement as he'd shown her to look for bombs.

"You okay, ma'am?" a young voice said from above her. Sunny looked up to see a twelve-year-old in a Boy Scout uniform hovering anxiously over her. "Are you feeling ill? Do you need help getting up?"

Even when she told him she was fine, he still offered a hand. "I thought I dropped something and went down to look for it," Sunny lied to make him go away. When she glanced over at Will, he was cracking up behind the wheel.

Sunny did her best to ignore him as she climbed into the truck.

The ride home was uneventful. They talked for a few minutes about plans for the evening when Sunny pulled up in front of her house. Once again, Will waved good-bye when Sunny was inside the door.

She said hello to her dad and Shadow, went to the kitchen, dug out a block of low fat, low-sodium cheddar, and used the toaster oven to make grilled cheese.

It wasn't an outstanding lunch, and neither was the table talk. Sunny apologized for having such a dull morning. Mike was interested when she gave him the new edition of the *Crier*, though, saying, *"Extra! Extra!"*

Sunny collected the plates and washed them. Then she joined Mike in the living room, sitting on the floor to play with Shadow. The cat had devised a new game.

*

Shadow backed up almost to the box that held cold things. Then he crouched low and sprang into a run, through the kitchen doorway and down the long hallway that led to the front door. The kitchen floor was shiny and a little slippery under the pads of his feet, but he got better traction on the wool runner in the hall. His legs ate up the distance until he was almost to the archway that led to the room with the couch and picture box. Then he launched himself into the air, ignoring the twinge in his side as he twisted in mid leap, extending his forepaws to catch the side of the arch about six inches off the ground. At the same time, he brought his rear legs down on the plaster and pushed, caroming off the entranceway and sailing in to make a perfect landing in Sunny's lap. He didn't even need claws to grab on to her jeans. He scrambled to his feet, looking up at her laughing face above him, and then climbed over her leg, dashing down to the kitchen to start the wild race all over again.

After about a dozen repetitions, Shadow had burned off his burst of energy and lay down beside Sunny. He arranged himself on the rug so that his furry shoulder and flank leaned against Sunny's denim-clad thigh. Nice. Warm. Comfortable. Just the way he liked it.

Then Sunny's hand descended to pet him. Perfect.

*

Sunny glanced up at her father as she ran her fingers through Shadow's gray fur. "Looks as if he's healing pretty quickly," she said.

Mike put down the *Crier*. "Talked with Sal DiGillio today," he reported. "He went down to the impound lot and had a look at the cars."

"Cars?" Sunny echoed.

"Yours and that Jeep Wrangler that wound up in front of the house," her dad explained. "He says the Mustang is shot."

"Tell me about it." Sunny sighed.

"No, he says that between the steering column and the windshield, it's not worth trying to fix the car." Mike spread his hands. "You know Sal's honest, and he tries to keep from gouging people. When you racked up the door, he kept it cheap for you."

And loud, Sunny silently added.

"But this is going to be parts and labor. You may even have to go to an auto glass place to get the new windshield put in."

Sunny winced, imagining a stream of dollar bills flying out the window. Shadow leaned up and put a paw on her arm.

"You can drive my truck, of course," Mike said quickly. "But you should consider getting a car for yourself."

Sunny nodded, wondering, *With what money?* She'd made a decent salary in New York, but it had been an expensive town. And even though she'd lived frugally since coming home, shipping all her stuff up here had put a serious dent in her finances—a dent that her pay from Ollie Barnstable did little to fill.

"Sal also told me a bit about that Wrangler," Mike went on. "Says it's a good machine, but it hasn't been taken care of for months." His voice dropped. "Used to belong to the Winslow boy."

Sunny glanced up. Stevie Winslow had been a local high school kid, looking forward to a great senior year, when a boating accident tragically ended his life. It had happened this past summer, and Sunny had followed the sad story along with everyone else.

"The Winslows sent the Jeep to Sal to fix it up and sell it." Mike's voice took on a coaxing quality. "I could talk to him—"

"You think it's a good idea to buy a car that almost killed us?" Sunny interrupted, staring at her father. "Doesn't that seem like bad karma or something?"

Mike shrugged again. "If we could get it cheap," he said, sounding like the quintessential Yankee trader. "Better suited for the area than what you had."

When Sunny declined to talk any more about it, her dad returned to reading the *Crier*, rattling the pages. Apparently he had something else on his mind. He finally put the paper down and made a noncommittal noise.

"So, you're going out with Will tonight."

"If there's something you'd especially like to have to eat while I'm gone, we'd better go shopping for it." She paused, still looking up at him. "It's just dinner, Dad."

Mike harrumphed. "Well, your mother and I just had dinner once upon a time—back in the Stone Age—and look what happened."

He looked as if he were going to add something else, when he got cut off by a howl of sirens in the distance.

"Oh, God, what's happened now?" Mike said, sitting very straight on the couch.

As if in answer, the phone rang. He fumbled the receiver off the cradle with nervous hands. "Hello! What? Oh, Will. Yeah, I understand. I'll tell her. So long."

Mike hung up, then turned to Sunny. "Will said he's sorry to be so brief, but he's dashing out the door because of a call on the police band radio. He figured we'd hear the sirens and wanted to let us know what's going on. Seems somebody got spotted trying to break into Ada Spruance's house."

18

Sunny shot to her feet, startling Shadow into jumping away. "We've got to go over there and check it out," she said.

Mike glared at her. "You don't *have* to do anything of the sort!"

She stared at him wordlessly, finally realizing how tightly wound this whole situation had him.

When he spoke again, his voice was a bit calmer. "The only reason someone would go into the Spruance place is to look for that damned lottery ticket—the one you think got two people killed already."

He raised a hand, cutting Sunny off before she could speak. "The people involved in that also tried to kill you four times—and me once. You don't want to be out on the street when guys like that are around."

This isn't my job anymore, Sunny told herself as her dad's words sank in. *I'm not going to break the big story.*

She forced herself to sit down, and they flipped through the channels on the TV, searching for some sort of local coverage. But it was much too soon, and they couldn't find any mention of an attempted trespass, a police chase, or anything even remotely criminal sounding.

Sunny sat down on the couch beside her dad, taking his hand.

"Gonna fight me for the remote?" he asked.

"Nope—just glad we have one sensible person in this house," she said.

That got a smile out of him.

They watched the countywide news channel, but again, no luck.

Then the doorbell rang.

Mike's hand tightened under hers, but Sunny got up.

"I'm dialing up 911," Mike called, making sure his voice was loud enough to carry outside. "Anything funny happens, the call goes right to them."

Sunny looked through the glass panel and saw a nervous-looking Ben Semple. "Don't have your dad call anything in," he begged. "I'm not supposed to be here."

"Hang up, Dad," she called over her shoulder. Then she opened the door for Ben. "Why—Sunny began, but he was talking already.

"Will asked me to stop by and tell you what happened. One of the other constables was driving by, keeping an eye on the Spruance place, and he saw someone sneaking up the driveway. Dispatch sent everyone screaming over there, and the noise spooked whoever was inside. Although our guy was covering the front, one person can't surround a house. The intruder took off through the backyards. We're searching, but I don't have much hope."

"And Will?" Sunny asked.

Semple shrugged. "He turned up, and the sheriff is keeping him on the scene. Since he's been in there before, maybe he'd notice if anything has been disturbed. The perp didn't have much time inside, so we don't think he found anything. But if we knew where he'd been, it would be easier to look for evidence."

"Other than not catching him, though, nothing bad happened?" Sunny felt a little silly, but she wanted it spelled out.

"Everything is fine," Semple assured her. His lapel radio squawked. "I gotta get back to my car."

He dashed down the walk. Sunny went to close the door.

"All clear," she called. "No more excitement."

Then she saw another visitor approaching—Helena Martinson.

Sunny reopened the door. "Hi," she said, "coming to see my father?"

"No, dear," Mrs. Martinson said in a determined voice. "I'm taking you for a haircut. I've already made you the appointment. It's long overdue, especially since I understand you have a date tonight."

Sunny shot a look at her father, who pretended to be absorbed in the weather report. She tried to decline Mrs. Martinson's overeager gesture gracefully, but the neighbor lady put her foot down. "This is the first time you've gone out since you came up here. And, frankly, my dear, you have to do something about your hair."

Sunny raised her hands in mock surrender. "All right," she said meekly. "I know. Thank you, I guess."

Looking relieved that warfare had been averted, Mike shut off the TV and got up from the couch. "While you're gone, I'm gonna take a page out of the cat's book and have a nap."

The salon was in an upscale enclave outside of town—and from the outside it looked pretty busy. Sunny wondered how much social extortion Mrs. Martinson had used to shoehorn Sunny into the schedule. Did the stylist know what she was in for?

As she opened the door, who should come out but Veronica Yarborough, a triumph of the beautician's art. She stared down her nose at Sunny, who bit her tongue to keep from saying something snarky.

Instead, she gave the head of the homeowners' association a pleasant smile. "Wow, looks like you got the whole spa experience, Mrs. Y," Sunny let her smile get wider. "Must have had you up a little early for your usual Saturday." As she spoke, Sunny remembered that Veronica still had no alibi for the morning when Ada Spruance had died.

Veronica's eyes got big and she made low gobbling noises as she stomped off.

Grinning in triumph, Sunny went into the salon and put herself in the hands of the professionals.

She heard a lot of tsking from overhead as her shaggy mane got shampooed. Frankly, after all the chemicals and treatments Sunny had tried to make her hair straight or mildly wavy, it was a wonder she had any hair left at all. She'd finally found a Manhattan stylist who knew how to manage rebellious curls. But since she'd come home, Sunny had let her hair alone. If it frizzed till she looked like she'd stuck her toe in a light socket, fine. As long as she could pull it back out of her face, she was willing to make do.

Her heart sank as she moved from the sink, hair wrapped in a damp towel, to wait for her stylist. Of all people, sitting in the chair next to her was Jane Rigsdale, looking like a queen in her salon gown. Even without makeup, the planes and angles of her face spelled "knock-out."

What's the matter with me? Sunny asked herself. *I just faced down the neighborhood queen bee without a problem. Why does Jane rattle me so much?*

She couldn't worry about that now. Jane had already spotted her and smiled. "Talk about a coincidence! I didn't know you used this place. It's my best discovery since I came back here."

Like you really need beauty treatments, Sunny thought. Instead, she gave Jane a tight smile and took refuge in the truth. "It's my first time here."

"Oh." Jane's pale eyebrows rose as she glanced around, perhaps trying to figure out who'd gotten bumped from the crowded Saturday schedule to accommodate Sunny. "Helena Martinson," she muttered, then blushed when she realized she'd spoken aloud. Trying to change the subject, Jane asked, "So, is this for a special occasion?"

Sunny felt a little warmth flooding her own cheeks as

she said, "Not really." That might be the literal truth. Will *had* even mentioned business. But no way, no how was Sunny going to discuss a date with Will—not to his gorgeous former flame. "I guess Mrs. Martinson got tired of my Sasquatch hair. She's a . . . good friend of my dad's, you know."

Jane didn't know, but she didn't ask any more questions, either. They chatted a bit about fitting back into the swim of things in Kittery Harbor. Sunny got to hear a lot of news about classmates she hadn't thought of since graduation.

Finally Jane was called for her haircutting session. Sunny stared after her. *She was trying to be nice to me. So why do I get so witchy whenever I see her? I mean, I hated her Miss Perfect act back in high school, but I should be over that by now.*

Moments later, Sunny's stylist came and collected her. She was a very nice older woman. And very good. By the time she was done, Sunny's mane had been tamed into a very flattering cut.

Well, Jane was right about one thing, Sunny thought as she breezed out of the salon. *This may be the best discovery I've made since coming back to town, too.*

*

Shadow padded through the empty downstairs of the house, enjoying the silence. The past few days he had slept most of the time, even through the dark hours, trying to recover from his hurts. But now after napping when the Old One had gone upstairs, he'd awakened feeling refreshed and full of energy.

He had tried a few rounds of the race-and-jump game, but it just wasn't the same without Sunny to land on. So he had looked out the windows, sniffed around the doors, and finally come up the stairs. Shadow made his way slowly down the upstairs hallway, dim in this cloudy weather, stopping outside Sunny's door and inhaling deeply. He savored the sweet smells from the bottles and jars—and from Sunny herself. The door was slightly ajar, and for a moment he debated pushing against it and going in to explore those things on her table more closely. But he decided against it.

Regretfully, Shadow backed away—and then froze, hearing a shifting of bedsprings and a low groan. Then came footsteps and the faint creak of a door opening. This didn't come from Sunny's room, where Shadow had hidden by the partly opened door. No, this came from farther down the hallway. The Old One must be stirring!

Sure enough, the older human appeared in the hall. Shadow could see him clearly in the gray light, but, judging from the way the two-leg groped around, he could barely see his hand in the dimness, much less Shadow.

Keeping his own steps silent, Shadow crept forward as the Old One stepped into the room of shiny tiles and shut the door.

Sudden light from under the door made Shadow blink and shy back. Then he arranged himself just beyond the edge of the pool of light. He had played the jump-out-of-the-dark game with other old ones—females who screeched and jumped when he pounced on their feet.

The light went off, and Shadow braced himself for the

attack. But as the Old One came out, he gave a deep sigh, rubbing at his face. His footsteps seemed to shuffle, and his shoulders slumped in weariness.

Shadow had never pounced from the darkness on a sick, frail person. It didn't seem right, somehow; not fair.

He remembered that since Sunny had brought him home, hurt, the Old One had been kind to him in his gruff way. He made sure the bowls were full in the kitchen and had even extended his hand—slowly, carefully—for Shadow to sniff. Perhaps he was sorry for the tricks he'd played earlier.

No, Shadow decided as the Old One made his way back to his room. Another time, maybe, but not today.

*

Sunny returned from the salon to find her father up and watching college football.

Dad whistled his approval. "Lookin' good, kiddo."

Sunny couldn't help but smile. "Thanks, Dad." Then she glanced at her watch. "But we've got stuff to do."

Not only were there routine chores that had been neglected in a week of interviews and death attempts, stuff like laundry and housecleaning, but there were new tasks, like emptying Shadow's litter box. And then, as promised, Sunny took Mike out on a grocery run. Her dad wanted a prepared dinner that he could nuke, but all of them had either too much fat, too much salt, or both. In the end, Sunny suggested making an early supper with a snack later if he felt the need for it in the evening. "Just don't eat all the ice cream in the freezer," she said.

"If I'm hungry—" he began.

She rolled her eyes, not willing to get embroiled in this kind of argument.

In the end, they wound up collecting the makings for a beef stew. When they got home, Sunny got out her mom's old pressure cooker. Mike assisted in peeling carrots and potatoes while Shadow ran back and forth on the kitchen floor, excited by the activity. They sliced onions, which made the cat wrinkle his nose, and trimmed and split celery stalks. Then Sunny put a little olive oil in the cooker and seared the meat, tossing the onions in, too. The rich aroma had Shadow stretching up on the front of the stove, sniffing appreciatively.

After stirring the meat and onions around the bottom of the pot, Sunny piled on the other ingredients, adding some water, dill, garlic, and her mother's secret ingredient, half a cup of V8—the low-sodium variety. Finally she locked the cooker's top in place.

As the stew cooked, she and Mike cleaned up their mess from the prep.

"Your mom loved that thing," her dad said, pointing at the hissing cooker. "She used to say we could have a stew in fifteen minutes."

Sunny grinned. "That's true, if you just count the cooking time. Of course, we spent about forty minutes peeling, chopping, and so on."

By the time they'd finished with the cleanup, the stew was ready. Sunny ladled a serving onto a plate for her dad, her own mouth watering as she took in the savory smell. The rest of the stew went into sealed bowls to cool off and be refrigerated. They'd made enough for a couple of meals. And the longer the stew marinated in its own juices, the better it tasted.

"I bet you won't get anything as good as this when you go out," Mike announced, tucking in.

Sunny laughed. "You may be right."

"So where are you going?"

"Will suggested a place up in Saxon," she said, naming a wealthy township farther up the coast.

"Sounds fancy," Mike said.

Sunny shrugged. "He told me it's dressy casual."

She spent a while going through her wardrobe to create an outfit to match that dress code. In the end, she wound up with a soft wine-colored sweater over a pair of black cords that felt more like velvet. With her car-length leather coat and a pair of low boots, Sunny felt about as ready as she was going to be.

She was upstairs, making a last-minute inspection in the mirror, when the doorbell rang. She came downstairs to find Will chatting amiably with her father.

"Right on the dot," Mike said with approval.

Will took in her outfit and new hairdo. "You look great," he said.

She laughed as Shadow inserted himself into the group, twining around Sunny's legs and sniffing. "Apparently, I smell great, too." She gave Will an up-and-down look. "And you don't look so bad yourself."

Will wore a pair of polished boots, soft gray wool slacks, and a slightly darker V-neck sweater with a tweed hacking jacket that accentuated his solid shoulders. His face softened in a slightly shy smile, and Sunny thought she'd never seen him look so good.

Not only had Will polished up his boots, he'd polished up his truck. Saying good night to Mike, they went outside and climbed aboard. They rode up to Saxon, a town that nowadays seemed to go more for Beemers and Escalades, though Avezzani's, their destination, had a more rustic look, with plaster walls the color of parchment and exposed blackened beams.

A tall guy in an Armani suit and an apparent year-round tan greeted Will warmly at the door.

"Gene Avezzani was in my homeroom—now he runs this place," Will said, making introductions. "It's thanks to him that we got a table."

"You don't ask every day," Gene replied, making a courtly bow over Sunny's hand, "or bring such lovely ladies."

He personally took them to a table in the corner and presented them with a nice bottle of Barolo.

Will grinned at Sunny over his menu. "When I was in high school, we'd go to the deli Gene's folks ran next door for meatball heroes," he confided. "The deli's gone now—too downscale for the neighborhood—but the meatballs are the same."

Splitting an order of those meatballs as an appetizer, Sunny had to admit they were pretty darned good. So was the stuffed artichoke they also shared. The whole meal was a throwback to the glory days of Italian red-sauce cuisine. Along with a few glasses of wine, it made for a mellow mood. Sunny enjoyed Will's combination of ironic humor and self-deprecation.

"You went to school up here instead of in Levett?" Sunny said. "Why would you—oh, of course. Saxon Academy."

Will rolled his eyes. "Yeah, the snob school of Elmet County. I managed to get in on a scholarship—regardless, it was a pretty good four years."

He sipped his wine. "Of course, most of the kids who graduated tried for Ivy League schools. Some of the teachers were disappointed that I went for a school with a major in law enforcement." Will put his glass down. "So was my dad. Sometimes I think I've spent an awful lot of my life annoying the sheriff of Elmet County, no matter who it might be. See, my dad wanted me to be a lawyer—that was his idea of stepping up in the world."

"And you?" Sunny asked.

"I was interested in the law," Will admitted. "But mainly in enforcing it. Still, after college I entered law school, just to please the old man—until everything went to hell. When Dad died, I gave up on law school and signed up with the state troopers. Took a posting with Troop F, way on the other end of the state by the Canadian border. After a few years up there, I knocked around the state on different assignments. Then I decided to take a shot at city policing. Maybe Portsmouth wasn't the smartest idea for that. A lot of people on this side of the river were getting tired of Frank Nesbit and imported me as a thorn in his side." He sighed. "I want to be a cop, not a politician."

Sunny swallowed her bite of tender gnocchi in pesto sauce. "What about your mom?"

"She and Dad got divorced when I was still in grammar school. I didn't see much of her after she moved down to

New York and remarried. Never liked a city that big." He coughed and pushed his wineglass away. "Sorry. I know you lived there for a while."

"It was going to be my big move." Sunny let a little mockery into her own voice. "The *Standard* was expanding from the suburbs into the big city, and the chain that owned the paper recruited the best and brightest from their other rags to join the spearhead. I figured if I could establish myself in the big town, maybe I'd have a chance at the *Times*. Of course, the problem was that the paper business was all set to contract. While I was up here taking care of my dad, the *Standard* got rid of its city bureau—and my job. Even worse, I had been going out with the guy who ended up canning me."

She gave him an embarrassed smile. "Is that enough true confession for the evening? Or do I act like a pushy reporter and ask about Jane Rigsdale?"

"Ouch!" Will picked up his glass again. "My reaction when she called my name didn't hide much, did it?"

"Well, you obviously knew one another in a former lifetime," Sunny told him. "Hey, I went to school with Jane, although we weren't what you would call friends. Still, I remember hearing the rumors that she was going out with a college guy. And when I saw the way the two of you acted, well, duh."

Will took a sip of his wine. "Let's just say it was a bad breakup—on both sides."

Maybe it wasn't a good idea to bring up Jane, Sunny suddenly thought. *I get all defensive when I even think about her. It's not high school anymore. I don't have anything to envy her for.* Sunny almost dropped her fork when she realized that wasn't true. *I am jealous of her. Jane came back to Kittery Harbor on her own terms, she's got her own business . . . and she fits in. She even asked about Will before I even thought about dating him.* Sunny looked down at her plate. *I guess I'll have to be nicer to her the next time we speak.*

"Let's talk about something else," Sunny said, abruptly. "Did you find anything interesting at the Spruance place?"

"I learned that when a tweaker tries to search for something, he's not exactly methodical." Will sounded exasperated. "I spent some time over there this afternoon. Get this—the sheriff has actually encouraged me to poke around a little." He looked up, struck by a thought. "Would you like to come along tomorrow? What the place needs is a horde of CSI types, but of course Nesbit isn't gonna bust the budget or ask the state for help. So it comes down to me, and I'd be happy for an extra pair of eyes. Besides, you've been there before. You might spot something that I'd miss."

"Oh, you baited that hook very well," Sunny told him. But she did agree to meet him the next morning. After that, their conversation turned to more mundane but pleasant topics, and they somehow made their dinner last for hours.

By the time Will took Sunny home, it was a bit late. She saw that her dad had left a light on in the living room, just as he used to back in her high school days; she could see the glow in the window as Will walked her to the house. Reaching the door, they hesitated for a moment, facing one another in the dimness.

"Well, this shows how out of practice I've gotten with the whole social thing." Will sounded a little annoyed with himself. "I've gotten more used to handcuffing people than wishing them a proper good night." He hesitated for a second. "You would like a proper good-night kiss, right?"

"Some clue spotter you are," she told him, raising her face to his. Their lips met in a very satisfactory kiss. Sunny tasted the Barolo wine they'd both shared—and a touch of garlic.

Will stepped back, grinning like a schoolboy. "Tomorrow, then?"

"Tomorrow," she promised and went inside.

Given the hour, and maybe a sense of tact, Mike wasn't downstairs. Shadow was up, though, and he gave Sunny a warm welcome.

*

Shadow had been dozing on the couch that the Old One had abandoned when the noise of a key in the lock roused him. He went to the archway to see Sunny close the door and then hop around comically, trying to remove her boots silently. Maybe she did, as far as a two-leg might hear.

He made a beeline for her ankles, twining around them and sniffing appreciatively. He caught the scents of delicious food and strange spices. No wonder Sunny was in a good mood. She had eaten well. When she knelt to pet him, though, he also caught the sweet-sour smell of weird drink. Sometimes it made humans happy; sometimes it made them want to fight. Shadow had seen it go either way. One of the two-legs he'd lived with had even poured him some. He hadn't liked it.

Luckily, the stuff had made Sunny cheerful. She spoke to him softly as she petted him in all the most comforting places. He lay bonelessly at her knees as she spoke to him softly and chuckled. He purred back at her.

*

Smiling, Sunny gave Shadow a tummy rub, not minding the cat hair she'd undoubtedly get all over her cords. It had been a good night indeed, getting to know more of Will Price. For the first time since she'd come back to Kittery Harbor, Sunny didn't feel so . . . lonely. With a little surprise, she realized that she hadn't even admitted that feeling to herself before.

Shadow gently butted his head against her hand, demanding a little between-the-ears scratching. Sunny obliged, softly saying, "Y'know, cat, besides you and that glitzy salon, I think I've discovered another great thing since I came home."

After Shadow had gotten the full treatment, Sunny collected her boots, doused the lamp, and tiptoed up to her room. She put away her clothes and slipped into a comfortable pair of pajamas. Making sure not to disturb her father, she quietly walked to the bathroom, removed her makeup, and brushed her teeth. Then, returning to her room, she went off to sleep with happy thoughts swirling in her brain.

But it seemed that Sunny had barely closed her eyes when she heard her father's voice calling. She sat up, blinking, and looked at the clock. The display said it was after three in the morning.

Padding down the hall, she tried to clear away the fog in her head. But when she saw Mike half reclining on his bed in the pool of light from his nightstand lamp, she jolted awake. His face was pale, his eyes were wide and scared, and his hand clutched his chest. "I've got pain," he said hoarsely.

"It's probably angina." Sunny tried to sound matter-of-fact. "You've had it before."

But Mike hadn't had those kinds of chest pains in months. *Please let it be that,* she silently prayed as she opened the drawer in the nightstand to pull out the bottle of nitroglycerin tablets.

Trying not to rush and scare Mike even more, she went to the bathroom to get a glass of water and suddenly discovered she had a furry companion in the hall. But Shadow didn't try to get into Mike's room.

Sunny helped her father sit upright in bed, arranging the pillows behind him. She let him take a sip of water to rinse his mouth, then he spat it back into the glass. Finally, she slipped one of the little pills under his tongue. She sat on the edge of the bed, holding his hand and timing five minutes on his clock.

"All gone?" she asked.

He opened his mouth and showed that the pill had dissolved.

Sunny didn't have to ask if he was feeling better. Mike's hand remained pressed to his chest. Another five minutes went by, and she gave her dad another tablet. Though she did her best not to show it, Sunny felt a little nervous. The nurse who had arranged Mike's departure from the hospital had been very clear about what she called the "three strikes" policy. In case of chest pain, Mike got one nitro tablet. Five minutes after that one dissolved, if the pain didn't let up, he got another. And if the condition didn't abate, he got a third. If that didn't work, Sunny would call 911 and take her dad in to the emergency room.

Long minutes passed. At last Mike leaned back, letting out a sigh. "It's going."

Sunny rearranged his bed so he could lie down again. Mike wished her a good night and turned off his light. By the time she got to the door, Sunny could hear regular breathing on the edge of sleep. She left Mike's door open— her own, too.

I want to make sure I hear anything, she thought.

As she lay in the darkness, though, she couldn't hold back a grin that mixed exasperation and humor. Dad has a heart episode, takes two pills, and drifts right off to sleep. Sunny the caretaker, however, can't seem to close her eyes.

Maybe I'm *the one who needs a couple of pills,* she thought.

Her door pushed open slightly, the hinges making the faintest of noise. Sunny heard a couple of light footfalls, then she made out the slightly darker form of Shadow walking along her bed. He came up to her shoulder, butting his head against it gently, and rested a forepaw there.

Shaking her head, Sunny reached up to pet him. "Yeah," she whispered. "More excitement than we needed."

He stayed with her, a warm, comforting presence, until she finally drifted off to sleep.

19

Sunny felt brightness against her closed eyelids, opened one eye to a slit, and quickly closed it against the glare. Had she left her blinds open? If sunlight got from the edge of the blinds to her pillow, that meant it was pretty . . .

Late!

She remembered what had happened the night before and sat bolt upright in bed. A glance at her clock showed that it was, indeed, late. Almost flying out of bed, Sunny went down the hallway to check on her dad.

Mike lay on his side, his breathing deep and regular as he slept. Watching him, Sunny wondered, just for a moment, if the whole angina attack thing had been some sort of nightmare. Then she spotted the bottle of nitroglycerin tablets on his bedside table.

Sunny reached over and touched his shoulder gently. "Dad? How are you doing?"

Mike opened his eyes and peered at her for a second. "Huh," he said. "Kinda late to be sleeping." He stretched. "Feels good, though."

Then he woke up enough to remember the previous night's attack. Reflexively, he put a hand to his chest and then dropped it. "No, really, I feel okay."

"Good enough for breakfast?" Sunny asked, and he nodded.

She made a brief detour to her room and her cell phone, calling Will Price's number. When she explained what had happened overnight, he readily agreed to push back the time they were supposed to meet by an hour.

By that time, Sunny had showered herself awake, fed her father, Shadow, and herself, and put on clothes appropriate for traipsing through a dusty, dirty house.

Mike had established himself on the living room couch with the Sunday paper, assuring her he was fine. "You know how these things go," he said. "They always happen at night. I take the little pills, go to sleep, and I'm right as rain in the morning."

He made shooing motions at her. "Go and do what you have to do. You're only gonna be a couple of blocks away, not a couple of towns. And you've got your cell phone."

Even as he spoke, she was checking the charge on the battery.

"Okay," Sunny said, still feeling a little nervous about the situation.

Will must have picked up on it when he came to the

door. He made a point of coming inside and saying hello to Mike.

When they finally left, Shadow darted out the door before Sunny could get it closed. He managed a neat trick—evading Sunny's attempts to pick him up while staying close to her heels. She looked up at Will, who was trying not to laugh. "Do you mind if he comes along? Maybe he knows where we're going."

When they had settled themselves in the pickup, Will said, "By the way, your dad looks okay. You're who I'd have picked as the one who was up all night with chest pains."

"Just with worry," Sunny replied, blinking in the sunlight. Damn! She'd forgotten her sunglasses. "He hasn't had one of these episodes in months. That leaves me wondering. Dad's tried to put a good face on it, but I think this whole situation, especially the nonsense aimed at us, or rather, at me, is stressing him out."

"Then let's hope we find something to crack this case," Will said.

That sentiment seemed overly hopeful when they arrived at the Spruance place. Sunny could see that Gordie had moved a lot of stuff around, but he hadn't gotten rid of anything. Black trash bags lay everywhere.

Probably afraid that if he threw anything out, the lottery ticket would be hidden in it somewhere, she thought. She flexed her hands, trying to get used to the feel of the heavy rubber gloves Will had insisted they wear . . . along with face masks.

They stood in the living room, a glare of sunlight coming in through the window that had lost its drapes.

"This has to be where our man outside saw the flashlight," Will said. "So we know the intruder was in here somewhere."

"Well, we know this is one of the rooms she used," Sunny pointed out. "It would seem reasonable to search in places she frequented. Ada said she'd lost the ticket. She didn't say she'd hidden it and forgotten where the damn thing was." The possibilities involved in that theory made her shudder. "Imagine checking under the liner in the litter box."

Shadow circled around the room, making little grumbling noises. Sunny watched him, fascinated. Was he looking for the other cats who used to live here? Was he just responding to the way Gordie had rearranged things in this once-familiar room? Or had Shadow forgotten about Ada's death—was he looking for his former mistress amid the mess?

The cat kept sniffing around Ada's chair and acting generally unhappy.

Will watched him for a moment, then said, "You know, people who spend a lot of time in meth labs hang around some pretty unpleasant-smelling chemicals. Could our furry friend be reacting to that?"

"How do we know it's not just Gordie's smell, since he was setting up the lab himself?"

"We don't," Will admitted. "But I'm betting Shadow's responding to the freshest scent."

He got down on one knee. "The chair's been moved," he announced. "You can see the indentations the legs left in the rug." He looked at the slightly shaggy upholstery and shook his head. "Nothing here that would take a print."

Examining the table next to the chair, though, he got a

little more hopeful. "The dust is disturbed where someone might have picked the table up or shifted it." He pointed, keeping his finger carefully above the surface. "Whether there are prints, smudges—or if the guy wore gloves like us—I'll leave that up to the lab people."

"It makes sense," Sunny said, peering around the pieces of furniture. "Ada spent a lot of time here. Do you think we should have a look?" She pointed at the chair cushion.

"I don't think it would hurt. As I said, there are no prints here." Will pulled the cushion loose to reveal a comb, several hard candy wrappers, an emery board, and a catnip mouse that had all gotten tucked down the seams. No lottery ticket, though.

"I'll take a look for any marks in the kitchen," Will said. "That's the only other place the intruder could have gotten to in the amount of time he was here."

Standing alone in the dusty living room, Sunny tried to imagine what it would be like to live here, with her life bounded by the few little areas that Ada had struggled to keep clean. The living room chair and the TV. The kitchen. She'd use the stairs in the back to get to the cellar if she needed anything from there. The kitchen door, for bringing in food supplies. Maybe the pantry area could do with a search.

Sunny glanced over toward the front door. Would Ada ever come and go that way? She walked over to the foyer and the little odds-and-ends table that stood beside the door. It was just the place to pick up a purse or car keys before going out—or perhaps to rest a bag when coming back from shopping.

A thick layer of dust covered the surface of the table,

however, so it was clear that nothing had rested there for a while. A row of three small, impractical drawers stretched under the tabletop—pretty, but you couldn't fit much in them. Two held buttons, spare keys, change—the sort of stuff that gets emptied out of pockets. The middle one, though . . . Sunny's heart almost stopped when she saw the lottery logo printed on the back of the paper. Fingers trembling, she turned it over . . .

And snorted at herself. Oh, it was a lottery ticket, all right. But it was dated about a week before Ada died.

"Did you find something?" Will was back in the room, looking eagerly at the ticket Sunny held.

"Not unless lightning struck twice," she told him, pointing out the date. "Bad enough to be searching for a winning ticket when there might be a year's worth of losers lying around the house, too."

She bent down to pat Shadow, who stood beside the table, looking up at her.

*

Shadow watched as Sunny waved the piece of paper in front of the Big Male. Were they going to play with it? If they let it go and it floated down, there might be some pouncing games they could play.

The male—Will, he seemed to be called—shifted his feet, and Shadow sidled away. He was very aware of feet after what he'd smelled around the chair, and even though his side felt much better, remembered soreness seemed to stiffen his gait.

There was no mistaking it—the memory of this particular scent had been reinforced with severe pain. The one who had kicked him so badly had been here. That was a bad two-legs, and smells like that always seemed to be connected to bad things. Shadow shifted uncomfortably as he watched Sunny and Will talk.

Even though he'd lived here, and the other smells were familiar, he wanted to leave this place. It made him nervous.

*

They went upstairs to check Ada's bedroom. Gordie had apparently put in his most serious search efforts here. The closet stood empty and so did the dresser, the clothes bundled into those ubiquitous garbage bags and piled on the unmade bed.

"I wonder if he checked the pockets," Will said, poking at the emptied contents of one bag.

A small jewelry box stood on the dresser. Sunny picked up the top to find the interior almost empty, although slots for rings showed impressions of use.

"I didn't look very closely when I found Ada," Sunny admitted. "Was she wearing jewelry when she died?"

Will shook his head, looking into the box. "Probably either she or Gordie was pawning stuff."

He pointed at several faded family photographs with brighter edges scattered across the bleached wood top. "Those were probably in silver frames. Pawned, too, I bet."

Sunny turned away, not wanting to look at these relics of a miserable, lonely life. "Let's go downstairs."

They ended in the kitchen, following Sunny's notion of walking in Ada's footsteps. The cans that had filled the cabinets were still on the counter. The shelves themselves were empty, lined with adhesive plastic sheets—still sticking on, but faded.

"My mom told me that they used to have special shelf paper that was supposed to get switched out once a year," Sunny said. "Her mom used to slip a dollar under the paper as a reward for whoever changed it." She tapped the faded floral pattern. "Nothing like that here."

One drawer revealed knives, forks, spoons, and a can opener. The other held a tape measure, a handwritten phone book, and a lot of nondescript junk. Sunny peered at the cabinets under the sink. One held cleaning products. The other was full of pots and pans. "You think a ticket could have fallen down here?"

"I'm beginning to wonder if one of the cats ate it," Will told her.

"The only other place I could imagine her going was the pantry." Sunny started for the narrow, shelf-lined hall that led to the cellar door.

Shadow suddenly appeared underfoot, meowing at her.

"What?" Sunny took a step. Shadow butted his head against her shin. Taken aback—literally—she retreated a step, and Shadow butted the other shin.

"People talk about herding cats when they want to describe a hopeless job," Will said with a laugh. "But here we've got a cat herding you."

*

Shadow glared up at Sunny, her face disappearing as memory put another set of features on them—the Old One–Dead One–Gone One, in her familiar housecoat, her mouth open in shock, her eyes wide with fear.

He'd been sleeping in the pantry, caught unawares as she was flung past him, the screech of the door as it tore open drowning out her weak cry as she went down, down, down.

Shadow leaped from stair to stair after her, though he knew he was too small to be of help. The door above banged shut behind him, cutting off the light from the kitchen. That didn't matter to a cat's eyes, though. He could see clearly enough that the Old One was no more.

Then that Other One came running down the stairs, the noxious stench on him like the stink that rose from the Old One's son, only a hundred times more poisonous . . .

No! He would not let it happen again!

Seeing Sunny by that deadly door, and the male behind her, Shadow couldn't help himself. Even though they didn't smell the same, dread overcame him.

He would force her back, pushing, crying out warnings, using his claws if he had to.

She would not die here!

*

"This is silly," Sunny muttered, feeling her cheeks getting warm. She retraced her steps into the pantry, but couldn't concentrate on checking the shelves with all the noise Shadow was making. "What is your problem, cat?"

Shadow walked back and forth in front of her as if he were on sentry duty, his tail lashing around, unhappy sounds coming from deep in his throat.

"Maybe he doesn't like being trapped in that little space," Will suggested.

"He's not trapped," Sunny said impatiently. "He wormed

his way in ahead of me." She advanced on Shadow, trying to shoo him aside. He stretched up to press the pads of his forepaws above her knee, pushing her back.

"Shadow!" Sunny said sharply and regretted it a second later as the cat jumped away from her.

Then he did something really weird. Turning in midair, Shadow launched himself at the cellar door. It sprang open with an unearthly screech, but Shadow didn't go tumbling down. Somehow, he used the door's resistance to bounce himself back, landing almost at Sunny's feet. He looked up at her, making a low, unhappy, moaning noise.

Sunny stopped in her tracks. "All the time he's lived here, that door has been painted shut."

Will stood beside her, making Shadow crouch and lash his tail, his noises becoming bloodcurdling. Frowning, he said, "So the cat couldn't have known it would open—unless . . ."

Sunny looked from Shadow to Will, her throat getting a little tight. "You know, ever since he came to us, he's been obsessed with pushing things."

Taking her arm, Will pulled Sunny back from the spitting cat.

Shadow calmed down and followed them to the living room, where Sunny knelt down and stroked him.

Will joined her. "Wow, little guy," he said, offering a hand to be sniffed. "It's really a shame you don't talk. Because I think you were an eyewitness to a murder."

20

"Shadow, come on now." Sunny tried to sound stern, but even she noticed the desperate note creeping into her voice. "We've got to go."

"Dumb cat," Will muttered. "This is the way we came in, and he was fine."

That was the problem. They'd entered the house through the open cellar doors and up the stairs into the pantry. That was their only route out, but Shadow pitched a fit every time Sunny tried to go through the door leading down to the basement.

"How are we going to do this?" she asked, watching the cat get more and more upset.

Will frowned, studying the situation. "I think we'll have to be ungentlemanly," he finally said.

"What do you mean?"

He grinned. "Ladies last."

When Will headed down the narrow pantry, Shadow didn't have a problem at all.

"Apparently, it's only seeing you come down here first that sets him off." Will gave one good shove, and the door stiffly swung open, the accompanying shriek piercing Sunny's eardrums.

He went down a couple of steps, then turned back. "C'mon, Shadow."

Shadow trotted to the open door and climbed down into the cellar. Will turned to block the stairway while still holding the door open, and Sunny hurried through.

Holding tightly onto the banister—she didn't want to follow Ada's unfortunate example—Sunny quickly made her way downstairs, then up and out the cellar doors.

"We don't have much to show for an afternoon," she said as she joined Will out in the backyard.

"Potential fingerprints on that living room table," he pointed out.

"And piles of clothes with pockets to go through," she added with a laugh.

"I don't know if Nesbit would authorize overtime to do that," Will deadpanned. "We may have to shoehorn the job into our copious spare time."

"There's not much of that—time in general, I mean." Sunny frowned. "The eligibility cutoff for that ticket is just a couple of days away."

"And what?" Will said, "you don't want to lose your chance of winning millions?"

"I think it may screw up our chances of finding the people who killed Gordie," Sunny told him. "As for Ada, I'm not so sure. It might not even be the same killer. We still have folks who had fights with Ada. You eliminated the Ellsworths, but not the Towles." Although she liked them, she had to admit they had a motive. "Or Veronica Yarborough," she added.

Will looked at her. "So you're suggesting two different murderers, with completely different motives? That's kind of messy."

"Sort of like life," Sunny replied. "Sometimes it doesn't tie up in a nice, neat way." She frowned. "The problem is, we've been playing defense since everything started happening around me, watching out for crazy drug dealers. The other suspects have sort of faded into the background. That's the other thing about the ticket. It messes up all the motives."

"So when it expires, that will go away," Will said.

"And so will the drug dealers," Sunny said gloomily. "The hope of cashing that in is the only thing that's keeping them around."

They were both silent, lost in their own unpleasant thoughts, all the way home. At the last minute, Sunny offered Will a lunch of leftover stew, only to be politely declined. He dropped her and Shadow off—Shadow following Sunny out of the pickup without any fuss—and drove away.

"Hey, Dad," Sunny called as she came inside, Shadow charging ahead. "What do you think of leftovers for lunch?"

She stopped at the entrance to the living room, afraid that Mike was in cardiac distress again. Then she realized her father was pale with anger, not illness, as he sat clutching a piece of paper. "Call that jackass Barnstable—he should still be at the office."

"What's the problem, Dad?"

"He accused you of stealing!" Mike burst out. "The idiot wanted your cell number—apparently he couldn't find it. I told him to go to hell!"

Sunny began to get worried. Ollie the Barnacle had not been happy with some of the stuff she'd done in the last week. Frankly, her job didn't look all that secure right now, and Mike's lack of diplomacy wasn't helping Sunny's cause.

She dialed the office number. Ollie picked up on the second ring. "Who is this?"

Before Sunny even got her whole name out, he growled, "Where's the goddamn cash box?"

Sunny blinked. This was his big problem? "I took it home for the weekend. Mr. Richer gave me a large cash deposit—you can check with him. I didn't think it was safe—"

"I don't care what you think!" her boss interrupted. "You bring that box back here right now! And if there's anything missing, even a penny, you'll be looking for a new job."

He slammed the phone down. Sunny was tempted to do the same.

Well, he'll look pretty stupid when he finds out we're several hundred bucks to the good, she thought. Had Ollie been drinking? God knew he didn't always wear his wealth gracefully. He could act like a spoiled child if he didn't get his way. She frowned, remembering the conversation with Will about the possibility of Ollie being a suspect in Ada's murder. *For someone who's supposed to be rich, he sure sounded awfully worried about the cash box.*

Sunny bit her lip. If he'd learned that Richer wasn't going to invest in any of his schemes, that disappointment, coupled with the embarrassment of discovering that one of his properties housed a meth lab and burned to the ground, might make his temper even more uncertain than usual. *And I get to be the one he takes it out on,* Sunny silently complained.

"It's just a misunderstanding, Dad," she told Mike. "But I've got to go into the office and straighten things out. Be back as soon as I can."

Sunny went upstairs, got the cash box, and climbed into her dad's truck. She'd gone about half a mile before she remembered her promise to call Will if she was going out alone.

Just as she reached for her cell phone, an SUV came roaring up behind her. Sunny pulled aside to let the maniac driver pass. But as the SUV came abreast of her, the passengerside window rolled down. A guy leaned out, his mullet streaming in the breeze.

Sunny immediately recognized Fatso from the brawl at O'Dowd's. The shotgun in his hands needed no introduction.

Oh, my God! A quick tromp on the gas pedal, and Sunny's pickup shot ahead before Fatso could get a shot off.

She heard confused shouting behind her, quickly

drowned out by engine noise as the SUV accelerated after her. It grew larger and larger in Sunny's rearview mirror as she zigzagged from lane to lane, trying to keep them from pulling beside her again.

The SUV got right behind her and rammed her rear bumper, sending her fishtailing along the road. Sunny had to grip the wheel with both hands, her phone dropping into the well beneath her feet.

Wonderful, she thought. *I can't outrun them, and I can't call for help.*

All she could do was hang on and hope she could control the speeding truck. If those guys made her spin out, that would be the end. She'd seen the look in Fatso's eyes. He fully intended to use that shotgun on her.

A second smack on her bumper jarred her, but she was prepared now. Sunny's hopes rose as the SUV shrank in her mirror briefly, but then it came at her again—the driver had just pulled back for a little more running room.

Then, up ahead, she saw her only chance: an old shortcut. Sunny hadn't taken that rutted, disused road since she was in high school. It wasn't even much of a shortcut, but bouncing along between the ruts was about the closest thing local teenagers had had to an amusement park ride.

The shortcut angled off from the road, and Sunny hit it at full throttle. Despite the fact that her dad had always dinned into her the importance of using her turn signals, for once Sunny was willing to be a bad driver if it didn't give those goons behind her any warning about what she planned. The pickup bounded into the air and landed with a shock strong enough to shake her fillings loose.

If I make it through this, I guess I'm going to owe Dad for a new wheel alignment, she thought.

The truck jounced over the ruts, flinging her against her seat belt until she was sure she'd have bruises. Sunny braked, forced to lose speed if she wanted to keep control. She grimaced as the front wheel dropped suddenly with a head-rattling bang. *Maybe I'll have to throw in new shocks, too.*

Her mirror had been knocked askew, so she didn't get a full view of the pursuing SUV. But she saw it take that same punishing dip that she'd just gone through.

Besides the rattling bang of protesting car parts clashing together, she also heard a lower, sharper *boom!* ring through the air.

Behind her, she saw the SUV slew erratically back and forth, finally jouncing to a stop. Sunny continued on her wild ride, content to see her attackers diminishing in the mirror.

She finally hooked up with a county road about a half mile away, well out of Fatso's shooting range, and brought her truck to a stop. Her whole body shook as she groped around under the seat for her phone.

Sunny finally got her fingers around it, got it open, and called Will. As soon as he answered, she spewed out, all in a rush: "I had to go in to the office—urgent call—and two guys came up and tried to shoot me—"

"Sunny!" he interrupted. "Where are you?"

"I'm at the southern end of the old shortcut." It used to have a name—what was it? "Ridge Road—that's what we used to call it. Do you remember it?" she said into her phone. "Look, I really have to get to the office. Barnstable is going to fire me if I don't turn up. The SUV that chased me looks to be stuck out there. They had a shotgun, and I think it went off—"

"Sunny, are you okay? You sound—"

"No, I'm not okay," she answered, cutting him off. "Somebody tried to shoot me with a shotgun." Sunny wasn't sure she could deal with that right now. What she could deal with was reaching the office and saving her job.

"You can't just drive off, Sunny." Will sounded every inch a cop now. "And you've got to call 911."

"No, I've got to get in to work. *You* call 911." Getting angry did one thing—it steadied Sunny's nerves and hands. She started up the truck and drove down into town and the MAX office.

*

She arrived to find Oliver Barnstable sitting behind her desk like a judge ready to pass sentence. "About time," he said, ostentatiously looking at his watch.

Sunny put the box in front of him and handed him the key.

Ollie the Barnacle unlocked and flipped open the lid, then gawked. Bouncing around in the cab of the truck had left bills, change, and receipts scattered all over the box. But he could still see the sheaf of hundreds at the top of the pile.

"Er—ah," he said.

"Maybe I lived in New York too long, but the bank had closed, and that seemed like too much money to leave in an office that's this open to the street. That's what I did with the last big cash infusion." Sunny tried hard to keep her voice calm. "I keep a running tally of income and outgo, so it should be easy enough to check."

"Um." Ollie's round, florid face was even redder than usual. "I can see that's probably not necessary. It's just—finding it gone after a rather difficult week—"

Excuses, but not an apology, she thought. *You really are a prince among men, Ollie.*

The opening door interrupted Barnstable's self-serving speech. "We're closed," he called, without even looking at the visitor.

Sunny turned around to recognize one of the constables she'd seen driving past the office in the last few days.

"Ms. Coolidge, I have to take you to headquarters," the cop said.

That got Ollie's attention. He goggled when he saw the uniform. "Oh, now what the hell is this?"

The constable ignored Barnstable, concentrating on Sunny as he spoke. "We have a report that you left the scene of a crime. The sheriff would like to question you."

"What crime?" Ollie's question almost came out as a moan.

"Attempted murder," Sunny told him.

The constable spoke at the same time, but his answer was shorter.

"Murder."

21

"**Murder?**" **Sunny echoed** weakly. Then her voice got louder. "What are you talking about? I'm fine."

The constable looked as if he'd just taken a big, healthy mouthful of spoiled milk.

He probably wasn't supposed to give that away, Sunny thought. But who got killed? Then she remembered the boom of the shotgun going off. She'd thought the SUV had gotten damaged. But what if it was the driver? That mental image made her queasy and weak in the knees.

The young man took her by the arm and tried to recover his authority. "You have to accompany me now, ma'am."

Sunny turned stricken eyes to Ollie Barnstable, who stared at her with something between amazement and fright. "Don't call my dad!" she begged. "This would just about kill him!"

Sunny clung to the hope that they'd quickly resolve this mess and she'd catch a little rest after the events of the early morning and the late afternoon. But that hope quickly died when she arrived at the police station. The place looked even busier than on her last visit, and it only got more so as people in state police uniforms appeared. Apparently a killing received a full-court press.

Then she got to sit down in an interrogation room with Sheriff Nesbit and a guy in a rumpled suit who turned out to be Lieutenant Wainwright, a state police homicide investigator.

For the next couple of hours, it wasn't so much good cop/bad cop as tough cop/furious cop.

"What the hell was the big idea of leaving the scene?" Nesbit demanded.

"I didn't think it was a good idea to stay around where their car stopped," Sunny replied with complete honesty. "Not when I saw one of them trying to aim a shotgun at me earlier."

"But why didn't you stay put after you'd gotten safely away and reported the crime?" Wainwright asked.

"I wasn't thinking straight," Sunny admitted. "My boss told me I had to get to the office for an urgent meeting or he'd fire me, so I was freaked out even before I saw the guy with the gun." She shrugged helplessly, looking at the men. "I need the job."

She glanced over at Nesbit. "Besides, I had no idea there had been a murder! When I made the other reports, it always just ended up in me wasting—uh, spending—a lot of time on them and then being told that whatever happened wasn't really a crime."

The sheriff swelled up so much, Sunny was afraid he was going to explode.

"What other reports?" Wainwright asked as Nesbit sputtered.

"I'll send for the files," the sheriff said shortly. He went to the door while Sunny happily outlined for Wainwright some of the things that had happened since she started looking into Ada Spruance's death.

The state police investigator listened, nodded, and then asked, "Do you own a gun, Ms. Coolidge? Have you ever handled one?"

Sunny stared at him. "No."

"Do we have your permission to search your car for any weapons?"

Sunny began to wonder if this was the time when she should start talking about a lawyer. But she gave her permission.

"She could have tossed it anywhere between the short-cut and reaching town," Nesbit growled.

Sunny stared back and forth between the two lawmen. "What's going on?" she said. "The only gun I know about is the shotgun one of those guys was carrying. I thought I heard it go off when they hit a major bump—"

"It did," Wainwright told her. "Wrecked the SUV's transmission and did quite a job on the driver's right ankle. He was a small-time Portsmouth thug named Eddie Deever."

"He bled to death?" Sunny asked, horrified.

"The constable dispatched to the scene found two men dead, both with bullet holes in their heads," Nesbit said. "Probably nine millimeter."

"And you think I shot them?" Sunny's voice rose to an indignant squeak.

"They match the descriptions you gave of two men involved in an altercation while you were recently in a known criminal hangout," Nesbit said.

"I was in O'Dowd's trying to talk to Gordie Spruance— you remember, the guy who got killed the next day? I think those two staged a fight to distract me while somebody else dumped a handful of pills in my drink!" she replied heatedly.

Both of them glanced at Lieutenant Wainwright and shut up.

"It raises an interesting question," Wainwright said. "The kill shots were at very close range. Deever's usual partner in crime, Vernon Galt, was the other person in the car. As you reported, he had a shotgun."

He looked at Nesbit, gesturing to Sunny. "If they'd been chasing this young woman with the intent of killing her, I don't think they'd have let her come that close with a weapon."

The sheriff didn't have anything to say to that, so Wainwright went on. "The fact that Galt let the shooter get so close suggests that he considered that person to be a friend."

Wainwright turned back to Sunny. "This young woman already gave a description of the two to the police in another complaint—that doesn't make her look like a friend."

Nesbit looked like a kid who'd just seen all his Christmas gifts go up in flames. For one bright moment, he must have thought he could get a quick solution to a murder case and get rid of a political thorn in his side at the same time.

Instead, he obviously faced a lot more work. There was

no way for him to pass off these two most recent murders as "accidents," and there went Elmet County's so-called spotless crime record.

Wainwright assumed the lead in the interrogation, taking Sunny through the whole chain of events. Along the way, he asked Sunny a number of questions she couldn't answer—for instance, had she noticed the SUV following her before the attack?

"I don't know," Sunny had to admit. "I saw it in the rearview mirror, zooming up, about half a mile after I left home."

The state police investigator thanked and dismissed her, but she still had to wait for her statement to be typed up so she could sign it.

Finally she was free to go—and found a strained-looking Will Price waiting for her.

"Well, at least they're not locking you up," he offered.

She managed a wan smile. "There is that."

"I called your dad to let him know you'd be a little delayed," he went on. "I didn't tell him why."

Sunny nodded, wondering if tonight would be another anxious bout with her dad's angina. "Thanks," she said.

The streets around the police station were pretty quiet early on a Sunday evening as they made their way toward the New Stores. Will told her he'd parked near the MAX office, figuring that would be easier for escorting her home.

"And I am escorting you," he insisted, "even if they screwed up this attack." He shook his head. "Looks like the Wile E. Coyote curse continues. I mean, how many times do you hear about hit men launching an attack and killing their own car?"

Sunny relaxed a little as they strolled along. "Actually they may have gone two for two, if they're the ones who planted that bullet gizmo. First they killed my car—at least the steering—and then their own."

"Bumbling henchmen," Will joked.

But all of a sudden, Sunny shuddered. "It's a shame their boss doesn't seem to have a sense of humor."

Will nodded, his face grave again. "This time one of the henchmen got seriously wounded. The damage to Deever couldn't have been fixed with a couple of bandages and a little bed rest. He would have had to go to a hospital, and Galt must have said as much when he called for help."

"How do you know he called for help?"

"We found a cheap cell phone in Galt's pocket. According to the records, he used it to make a lot of calls to another cell phone that, remarkably, isn't answering anymore. Whoever got the call must have flown over there to beat the squad car."

"So you're saying they called their boss for help, and this was his answer," Sunny said faintly.

"Well, hospitals are bound to ask embarrassing questions and make annoying reports to the police," Will explained. "So Mr. Genius decided to terminate Deever. And since Galt was likely to disagree, and he had a shotgun, he got taken out first."

"Brrrr," Sunny said, "that's cold."

"One man's cold is another man's business model," Will replied.

"Ron Shays," Sunny burst out.

Will nodded. "We know he likes to set up businesses with locals and then get rid of them. So he sets himself up in Portsmouth and recruits some goons. But this time the cycle ran a bit faster than usual. He ended up getting rid of his local talent before he even made any money."

"Do you think he's still in Portsmouth pulling the strings?" Sunny asked.

"The Portsmouth cops lost track of him almost a week ago," Will pointed out. "But I bet he was in Kittery Harbor today, pulling the trigger. Problem is, now he could be in the wind anywhere."

"No," Sunny said, and she said it quite definitely. "It's like you said—Shays hasn't made any money. Would you imagine a druggie with poor impulse control giving up on six million dollars?"

Will looked at her for a second, speechless. "Put that way, you might have a point."

"The question is, how do we make him stick his neck out?" Sunny smiled as the glimmerings of a plan began to come together in her mind. "Do you mind taking a little time before seeing me home? I need to talk with Ken Howell."

22

Ollie Barnstable was gone from the office when they finally got there, but Sunny called his cell phone. It would not be business as usual tomorrow. She needed a free hand to conduct phone interviews and even have news crews come in if she was going to accomplish what she hoped to do. He wasn't happy when he heard that, but Sunny gave him a pretty stark choice. Do nothing and let the town endure a wave of bad publicity from a double murder, or let her undertake this project and give the local media an alternative story to cover.

"Which headline do you think would be better for tourism?" she asked. " 'Two Thugs Murdered in Kittery Harbor' or 'Search Continues for Lottery Millions'? No, I can't guarantee finding the ticket. But either way, the problem will be finished by tomorrow."

The next step was to convince Ken Howell to use his media contacts and get some publicity. "It's a straight news story," Sunny told him. "Tomorrow evening I'll make a last-ditch attempt to find Ada's ticket. Ada asked me to help before she died, and Gordie did, too."

That was all literally true, but Sunny was hoping that a paranoid mind might start wondering what else Ada and Gordie had told her.

Ken worked up a story, including quotes from Sunny, and promised to do what he could with it.

Then Will saw Sunny home. She and her dad had a rerun of the stew for dinner, and she went to bed early—tomorrow was going to be a long day.

*

Sunny sat in the kitchen listening to the local news radio over breakfast. She usually did that to catch the weather report. Today, though, she listened for the lead stories. Had terrorists done something awful overnight? Had a political scandal broken? Had some Hollywood starlet gotten herself arrested for some stupid crime? So far, the answer was no. It sounded like a fairly quiet news day.

The morning news team bantered a bit with the weatherman, and then got serious to report the pair of bodies discovered in Kittery Harbor. A moment later they lightened up again, talking up the missing lottery ticket.

"Sources close to the family say that they'll attempt a final search of the house this evening," the female anchor reported.

"That's cutting it pretty fine," her male counterpart said. "They only have until tomorrow to submit a winning ticket."

Sunny grinned. The seed had been planted.

She did try to get some work done at MAX during the day, and in spite of the crime stories, tourism interest seemed to be picking up again. But she also had to make time for interviews. The phone kept ringing, and Sunny found herself either answering questions or agreeing to visits from camera crews.

Then came a very different call.

"Oliver Barnstable, please," a male voice said from the telephone receiver.

"I'm sorry," Sunny replied, "but Mr. Barnstable isn't in the office."

"He goddamn well isn't answering his cell phone, either," the voice said, losing a whole lot of politeness in the process. "I'm tired of leaving messages, too. So here's something you can give to him person to person. If Ollie imagines that by ducking me he won't have to pay what he owes, he's got another think coming. I'll start legal action to put liens on the insurance money he's expecting from that fire in Sturgeon Springs. If he thought the meth lab thing was embarrassing, wait till it goes into the legal record that he's defaulting on payments. I'm sure you've got a direct line to the big man, so you just tell him that."

"But I don't—," Sunny began. That was as far as she got before the phone clicked off in her ear.

She hung it up and sat for a moment, staring as if the handset might suddenly jump up and smack her in the head. *I guess the signs were all there,* she thought. *He's gotten erratic with my pay and even offered to sell back his piece of the* Crier *at a loss. It looks like Ollie does have money troubles. And if so, where is that going to leave me?*

The answer was way too familiar for too many people these days—out of a job.

"I've got to find out," Sunny muttered, getting out the cash box where the key to Ollie's supposedly secret files was kept. It was like the awful compulsion to stick the tip of your tongue into the gaping hole after the dentist drills out a cavity and before he fills it. She hurried over to the bank of cabinets along the back wall, painfully aware that everything she was doing could be clearly seen from the street outside.

All I need is for Ollie to come strolling in on his way to lunch. Sunny hesitated with the key, then thrust it into the lock. *To hell with it.*

She found the file she was looking for just a couple of dividers ahead of the "Investment Opportunities" folder she'd collected to deliver to him a few days ago. This one was headed "Bills," and it was stuffed with pieces of paper. The latest ones all seemed to be in shades of red with some version of "past due" on them. Even the Land Rover that Ollie was so ridiculously proud about—the dealership hadn't gotten a lease payment for months.

If this keeps up, he's going to be asking if he can borrow my old mountain bike, Sunny thought as she slammed the drawer shut and locked the cabinet again.

She went back to her desk feeling curiously light-headed. When Gordie had bad-mouthed Ollie, she'd just taken it in a sort of business-as-usual way. She'd even laughed when Will had outlined a motive, opportunity, and means case against her boss.

But if Ollie was up against it financially, then he had a real motive to get money out of Ada somehow. What had

Claire Donally

Will said? Big money—big motive? If he were desperate enough to pressure Ada into selling her house—or even to go snooping around in there, trying to find that blasted ticket . . .

Yeah, he could have sent the birdlike little woman flying.

So—motive and means, Sunny thought. Then she realized she might have a perfect witness: Mrs. Martinson. Her dad's lady friend must have been up early, baking that damned coffee cake for him. Helena Martinson's house was on the same block as Ada's, just across the street and a bit farther down.

Sunny dug out the local directory and got the number. Luckily Mrs. Martinson was home, answering on the second ring. "Hello, dear, I've been hearing a lot about you on the radio. Are you really going over to Ada's tonight?"

"I am," Sunny told her. "But I just thought of something else. You were probably up the Saturday morning when Ada died."

The older woman sighed. "I'm up most mornings," she admitted, then paused. "You mean was I across the street when this terrible thing happened? I never even thought of it that way."

"We don't know when it happened," Sunny said quickly, not wanting to upset her neighbor any further. "I was just wondering if you might have seen anything out of the ordinary." Given Mrs. Martinson's weakness for gossip, Sunny was sure the woman would keep a close eye on her own block.

Probably has a periscope in her kitchen to maintain surveillance, she thought.

"If I saw anything suspicious, the police would have already heard about it," Mrs. Martinson said. "But there was nothing, not even a car."

Sunny suddenly realized how tight her shoulders had gotten. But just as she relaxed them, her neighbor went on. "Except for that Barnstable fellow, driving around the neighborhood in that ridiculous safari truck of his. He was always looking for houses with realty signs, or where an owner had passed away, or where the house was getting run-down because the elderly owner was a little overwhelmed."

She paused for a second. "Like Ada."

"Ollie made an offer on the house," Sunny admitted.

"Did he, now?" Helena Martinson said tonelessly.

Somehow, Sunny managed to thank Mrs. Martinson and hang up the phone before her neighbor put any more of that picture together. She found herself gnawing one of her knuckles—a bad habit she thought she'd gotten rid of years ago—as she mulled this new information over.

Ollie was at least near Ada's house the morning she died, and he'd never mentioned the fact. Though, of course, they didn't have an actual time of death. Ada could have gone down those stairs the night before.

The phone rang, and Sunny almost jumped out of her seat. Maybe it was Mrs. Martinson, calling back to say it was all a mistake . . .

Instead it was Sunny's dad, sounding reassuringly normal. "You were on the noon news," he said, "looking very pretty behind your desk." He made an annoyed sound over the phone. "I should have recorded it."

While Sunny appreciated his compliments, the important thing was that the story was building some momentum.

"Your feline friend and I just ate," Mike went on. "I hope you don't mind that I didn't invite him up to the table." He took a sip of something. "Iced tea. Very refreshing. Have you had lunch yet? Where are you going to eat?"

For a brief, yearning second, Sunny thought of the bench by the wharf. All of a sudden the walls of the office seemed to be pressing in on her.

But with my luck, I'll end up dodging a sniper, or the Loch Ness Monster will attack, she thought sourly.

"I brought a sandwich, and I'll probably end up eating it at my desk," she told her dad. "There still may be newspeople coming by."

"In that case, make sure you clean up the crumbs," Mike said.

But the next person to stop by the office didn't bring a camera—just a large chip on her shoulder. Jane Rigsdale had a stormy look on her face as she rattled the door that Sunny had been keeping locked.

Sighing, Sunny went to open up. *What now?* she wondered.

Jane's heels made an abrupt rat-a-tat noise as she stalked across the wooden floor. "You know, I asked about as nicely as I could whether Will was seeing anybody." Her voice came out a little loud and her face was pink. "So when Donna Stavely comes down from Saxon to have me look at her Pomeranian, think how surprised I was when she mentioned seeing Will having a romantic dinner up at Avezzani's on Saturday night with you."

Sunny blinked. "I don't even know . . . who the heck is Donna Stavely?"

"She used to be Donna Allnut—and she certainly recognized you and Will."

The worst gossip in high school, Sunny thought. *This whole county is really too small to live in.*

"So you don't deny it?" Jane pressed, really getting into Sunny's face.

Sunny forgot her resolution to be nicer to Jane the next time they met. "What is there to deny?" she snapped. "We went on a date. Big deal. When you did that whole cutesy-wootsy 'Oh, is he seeing anyone?' routine, I honestly didn't know. I still don't. Will could be dating someone else or have a harem on the side. I just met the guy. We've been working together, trying to dig up the truth about what happened to Ada Spruance. And lately, he's been trying to keep me from getting killed."

Well, at least that stopped the flow of high-school-level complaints. Jane stared as if Sunny had just gone out of her mind.

"If you read the *Crier*, you'd know that somebody messed around with my car and outside my house," Sunny said. "And that car accident where Gordie Spruance got killed? That was an attempted hit-and-run on me. And that double murder that's all over the news?" She explained that story's background, which Sheriff Nesbit was keeping quiet for the moment.

"So in the middle of all this, Will asked me out to dinner to talk over the case, and I said yes. As you've noticed, he's a nice guy, and I'm a big girl. So what now? If you want to kill me, you'll have to get in line."

Jane changed her tune a bit after that, not so much ac-

Claire Donally

cusing Sunny of stealing her once and future boyfriend as blaming Sunny for ruining what could have been a beautiful friendship.

Sunny might have asked how strong this newfound bond might be if one friend came to jump down the other's throat because she went out with the one presentable man both of them knew. But she was distracted, having spotted a big red toolbox that lay apparently unattended on the sidewalk.

"Are you even listening to me?" Jane complained.

"To tell you the truth, no," Sunny replied. "The guys who've been after me have tried gas, poison, bullets, and speeding SUVs. That leaves bombs, and there's a big box sitting right outside." She pointed, and Jane was left staring again.

Sunny was just about to suggest a quick exit through the bathroom window in the rear when a guy in a Verizon hard hat walked past the window and picked up the box.

Jane headed back to the door, her heels tapping even more quickly. "I don't know what Will sees in you," she said. "You seem to have real problems."

Sunny bit the inside of her cheek to keep from answering with something she'd later regret.

But as soon as Jane was gone, Sunny sat glumly at her desk. *So much for treating Jane better. How does she manage to get under my skin like that? Maybe I do have a problem.* To rouse herself out of the dumps, Sunny reviewed her suspect list. She wasn't sure this ticket stunt would bring out the Towles or Veronica Yarborough. On the other hand, if the winning ticket expired without being found, Ada's death would certainly get a lot less attention.

So it was possible that, rather than going for the prize, a hometown killer might try to preempt the ticket's discovery.

Criminals like drug dealers would definitely want the money. And speaking of wanting money . . . Sunny found herself back to obsessing over her boss as a possible killer. The recitation of murder attempts she'd made to Jane would seem to weaken the case against Ollie. It struck her as a bit far-fetched that he'd hire a bunch of drug-running lowlifes who just happened to know Gordie Spruance. That whole side of the case had to involve the abortive crystal meth deal.

And yet . . .

Gordie had seemed honestly surprised—even shocked—when Sunny had tried to connect his mom's death to his drug-dealing associates.

What if Ollie committed the murder for his own completely separate motives? Sunny found herself wondering. *Trying to get the house or the lottery ticket—or maybe Veronica Yarborough put him up to it, offering money or clout with the homeowners' association. So that takes Ada out of the picture, and Gordie needs to find the ticket to get Ron Shays off his back.* She sighed. *And then I stuck my nose in, and Shays and his drug people came after me because Ron Shays didn't want his meth lab deal revealed.*

A worse thought hit her. *What if, when Gordie couldn't provide the money for the lab, Ollie got involved somehow? He has money problems, so he's probably looking for some way to turn a quick buck. And if he's desperate enough, he might not be too picky about how he does it.*

Sunny sat at her desk, resting her head on her hands.

Maybe Will was right. Maybe she got too caught up in the theoretical aspects of the case.

She sat up straight. Well, with luck she'd untangle all the nonsense tonight. Doing, not thinking. A van with a television channel logo on the side pulled up on the street in front of the office, which reminded her that she had another camera crew due for an interview. Sunny shook out her hair and went to the door. More bait for her trap.

*

I could get him, that stupid bird, Shadow thought from his perch on the top of the couch. He'd chosen this vantage point to see when Sunny might come back. But now all his attention was on the idiot bird hopping through the grass on the front lawn.

Shadow had hunted birds when he was out on his own and found that they could provide good meals—but plenty of frustration. An hour's worth of careful stalking could go to waste when they'd flutter up right as he pounced, just evading his paws to escape into the sky.

But if I was coming down on him, say from here, while he was trying to go up . . .

Licking his chops, Shadow stretched from the couch to rest his paws on the windowsill, stretching his long body almost to its limits. He quickly pushed off with his rear legs to bring his back paws onto the sill in preparation for a mighty leap . . . and his nose hit glass.

Oh. Right. The window's closed, he thought, flinging his rear legs back to the couch and scrabbling for a hold. He'd been so intent on the hopping morsel outside that he'd forgotten all about the window.

Now he found himself barely clinging with his front and rear paws, his body overextended and vulnerable. And then, from behind, he heard the footsteps of the Old One entering the room.

Shadow tried to twist and keep an eye on that tricky human, but that made him lose his precarious hold. After a second of skittering in the air, he plummeted down behind the couch.

He couldn't see the Old One from behind the piece of furniture. But Shadow could hear him. The two-leg didn't speak in his usual gruff way. In fact, he was making happy noises and saying the phrase that Shadow had often heard in his wanderings.

"Crazy cat."

I wonder what that means, Shadow wondered as he swaggered back around the couch. *Maybe "excellent fall"?*

*

By the time Sunny got home, she found Mike flipping between channels. "They said they were going to do your story on Channel 6," he said excitedly. "Now I'm checking Channel 8. This time I'm going to get you recorded."

She appeared on both those channels—twice—and on the later broadcast from the local CBS affiliate. Shadow had come into the room during one of her interviews. He'd stared at her image on the screen, then turned to her, extending a paw as if to make sure she was real.

Okay, she thought as the interview ended. *Looks as if phase one of the plan worked just fine.*

They sat down for supper, but Sunny couldn't eat much. *The butterflies are taking up too much room.*

She ended up putting her plate into the refrigerator and then went upstairs to change into the clothes she'd used to search Ada's house the day before—no use getting another set dirty.

All prepared, she went back downstairs and spent some time stroking Shadow, hoping that would calm her down.

Sunny looked up at her dad, who was pretending to watch the national newscast, and patted his knee.

"I wish I could go with you," Mike said quietly. "But I'm not in any kind of shape to be useful."

It was dark out by the time Will came to pick her up. "You don't have to do this," he said for about the fifteenth time since Sunny had come up with this plan. "We could just sit tight and let the word get out that you didn't find anything."

Sunny shook her head. "We're doing this to see if we can smoke this guy out," she said. "We have to give it a shot."

"I still think I should go in there with you," Will insisted.

"That might spook him off." Sunny patiently went through the plan they'd agreed on. "You'll drop me off, go around the corner to make sure you're not followed, park, and then walk back. I already checked with Mrs. Martinson. She has her car parked right across from the Spruance place. And she gave me her spare keys, so here, take them and you can get in her car and keep an eye on things. As soon as you see anybody else going in, you'll come out and arrest them"

"I talked to Ben Semple," Will added. "He'll be in the area if we need backup."

"We won't." Sunny did her best to sound confident. "Piece of cake." She took a deep breath. "Let's get this show on the road."

But when she opened the front door, she heard Mike swear. Then, as she turned, a gray streak flashed past her legs.

"Shadow!" she called. "Shadow, what are you doing?"

She glanced at Will.

"It's your call," he said. "If you want to spend the time chasing the cat."

"No." She shook her head. "We'll find Shadow when we come back."

But as she climbed into Will's truck, she couldn't shake the feeling that this was a bad omen.

23

In the darkness, Shadow crouched by the bushes at the end of the driveway. He'd enjoyed having Sunny pet him, but hadn't liked the scents coming off her. She smelled of the old place where he'd lived, the place of death. And he caught a whiff of something else. It wasn't quite fear—he knew that stink all too well. There was worry in there, too. He felt that in her touch. But there was also an odd tickle, the sort of thing he sensed when a strange cat had decided to fight.

Sunny was very quiet, talking with the Old One, so she wasn't going to fight with him. Then the new male came in. Something was going on between them, though it didn't seem like a fight, either. But something kept warning him of danger.

When he saw they were going out, he escaped before they could stop him. He heard Sunny calling to him, but stayed hidden. When she went to the door on the big vehicle, he dashed across the sidewalk and launched into a jump for the open back. His bruised ribs complained at the exertion, but he landed successfully.

Even better, no one had noticed him.

They didn't go far. But even though he couldn't look over the sides of this large box, his nose told him where they were. He stretched to hook his forepaws over the top of the wall, scrabbled over, and landed in the street.

Why did they keep coming back to the Dead One's house? Didn't they know that this was a Bad Place?

*

Sunny released a deep breath as she walked up the driveway to the rear of the Spruance place. She didn't want to admit it, but the house definitely looked creepier in the dark.

Pulling out a pocket-sized LED flash, she lit her way down into the basement and up into the pantry. She flipped a switch, and the kitchen lights came on. Sunny breathed a sigh of relief. The power company hadn't pulled the plug yet.

She prowled around the kitchen and then glanced at her watch. Five minutes had passed. Will should be in place by now. How to kill time before Shays turned up?

Sunny repressed a shiver. Maybe "kill" wasn't a good word to use while waiting for a murderer. She decided that she might as well actually continue looking for the ticket to spend the time and drifted back to the pantry to finish the search that Shadow had interrupted earlier.

All she found was more canned goods, more dust, and an unidentifiable damp patch that was unpleasantly sticky. She washed her hands in the sink, then tackled the cabinets beneath.

No errant lottery ticket had fluttered down to land among the cleaning stuff. Sunny was on her knees, shifting the pots and pans, when the pantry door screeched open.

"Wow, that was quick. Did you get them already?" Sunny began, but she stopped when she saw who was standing there. "Raj? What are you—?"

Sunny stopped again when he brought up his right hand—the one with the pistol in it.

"Recognize it?" he asked, his voice more nasal and a lot less polished. "It's your boyfriend's."

"He's not—" Sunny broke off her denial, realizing it wouldn't do much good arguing about her relationship status when a murderous character was holding a gun on her. Then a more important thought crowded out that reaction. "What did you do to him?"

"He just went nighty-night when a lost traveler asked him for help with an address, and then slugged him with a tire iron." Raj thought that was really funny and gave her a smile; a real, openmouthed smile, one that revealed his distinctive, brown, mismatched teeth.

"Ron Shays," Sunny said. "Well, you clean up pretty well."

Shays made an airy gesture with his manicured hand—

the one not holding the gun. "I do, even if I say so myself. Headed down to Boston for a haircut and beard trim, not to mention an improved wardrobe. Then I booked myself into an expensive spa—tanning bed, mani-pedi, all kinds of skin goo." He gave her another snaggletoothed grin. "I came out a new man."

"With a new name," Sunny said.

He nodded. "A lot of people, when they got to change their identity, choose something with the same initials. You can almost pick 'em out. Me, I go by sounds. Lately, I was doing business as 'Rob O'Shea.' You hear that in a crowded room, and it almost sounds like 'Ron Shays.'"

"And so, in a slurred kind of way, does 'Raj Richer.'" Shays beamed.

Sunny felt stupid to admit it, but she could see his point.

"A bit more upper-class," he said, falling back into the vaguely European accent he'd been using in his latest identity. "The only problem was the teeth. No time to get them fixed. But that whole British tight-lipped thing really made it convincing."

"Yeah." Sunny grimaced at her gullibility. "What I don't understand is why you came after me at all."

Shays shrugged. "A customer from up this way tells me some local gossip about a down-on-her-luck newspaper reporter poking into the old woman's death. I needed a place to lie low, and I wanted a look at the person who was following the news story. Figured I'd take care of both jobs by going to your office. And as soon as I saw you at work, finding me a place, digging up that genealogy crap, I knew you'd have to be stopped. You'd have kept digging, going after Gordo, until you found out about my business. So I figured I'd keep an eye on you—with an eye to getting rid of you."

Sunny suddenly recalled how she'd always happened to bump into her new pal Raj right before bad stuff started happening. He identified her car before the bullet gizmo got placed in it. He spotted her on the bike when that SUV started following her. She'd told him about her dad's truck being towed. And it would have been easy to have his stooges waiting for her when Ollie the Barnacle sent for that file. The only one that didn't fit the pattern—

"Did you have somebody follow me to O'Dowd's?"

Shays shook his head. "Eddie went in there for a beer and spotted you with Gordo. He called me, and I set something up quick." His lips curled away from those ugly teeth again. "Only those nimrods screwed it up—like they did every time. Even when I dropped the pills in your glass, Gordo knocked it over before you drank the wine." His teeth showed in an angry snarl. "I spent a lot of money acting like a rich guy. Now I gotta get paid." He was still dressed like Raj Richer, but with his lips twisted and his eyes angry, he looked a hell of a lot more like crazy Ron Shays.

"It's like there was a curse on us, right from the beginning, when the old biddy woke up and found me looking for her frigging ticket. I had to shut her up, and nothing's gone right since."

"Well, you kept me fooled," Sunny hastily said, trying to calm him down. She glanced at a big, cast-iron frying pan just beside her knee. If she grabbed that, maybe threw it at his face—

Shays must have read something in her expression.

"Don't fool yourself, now. You're too far away. I could put a bullet in you before you even get off the floor."

For the first time, he seemed to notice the pots around her.

"You're still looking?" the drug dealer burst out. "When I heard about you on the news, I figured you must have had some inside information from the old woman or Gordo." His eyes skidded around the room, and Sunny could almost see the thoughts bouncing back and forth in his meth-fueled brain. Paranoia, low impulse control, and the coldhearted business acumen that had made him a successful criminal . . .

Sunny could read it in his eyes. He'd decided to cut his losses.

And that included her.

"Get up!" Shays said, his voice hard. "Get over here!"

Is this what happened to Ada? Sunny thought. *Did she find him in here searching for the ticket? Did he try to get the location out of her?*

As Sunny slowly rose to her feet, a bloodcurdling moaning noise came up from the basement.

"What the hell is that?" Shays snapped.

Sunny had no idea. Ada's ghost?

The noise came closer, modulating into a deep, guttural growl.

"Shut up!" Shays's eyes were wild now, and he waved the gun at the door.

It flew open with a wild screech, and a lean gray shape came rocketing into the room—seemingly aimed straight for Shays's nose.

The man tried to twist aside, then screamed as Shadow

caught him. Claws raked across Shays's face, his hand jerked, and his gun went off.

Somehow Shays managed to shake the cat loose. Shadow landed on one of the pantry shelves, sending a row of cans cascading down, and bounced back at the killer.

That was what Shays looked like now—a killer. His lips were twisted back in a frozen snarl, baring his discolored teeth. Blood dribbled down from a set of deep gouges just over his left eye.

The claws on Shadow's other paw must have caught Shays's left ear. The lobe was torn, and blood poured down the side of his neck, soaking into his expensive coat.

Hissing and growling, Shadow was all over the dealer, clawing at clothing and whatever flesh he could reach.

Sunny snatched up the frying pan and tried to join the fight, but Shays saw her and snapped off a shot with his pistol.

The bullet must have hit the skillet, because it was torn from her grasp, leaving her hand numb. Sunny dived to the floor as more shots rang out. Something crashed behind her, but she didn't bother trying to look.

The problem was, she had no place to go. Shays still stood in front of the only door out of this place.

Using both hands, Shays finally managed to push Shadow away, screaming again as the cat's claws pulled out of whatever they'd dug into.

The dealer continued screaming, his lips writhing, as he tried to shoot Shadow. But the cat seemed to fly around the cramped quarters of the pantry, crossing back and forth between shelves, trying to get at Shays again.

For a second, he hung on to Shays's back, his claws embedded into the side of the man's neck on the unbloodied side. Of course, it wasn't unbloodied after Shadow was done.

Shays twisted around, trying to aim his pistol over his left shoulder and between Shadow's eyes.

Sunny grabbed the nearest pot—good, old-fashioned, heavy stainless steel—and flung it at the dealer's head.

It hit with a satisfying *clong!* and knocked Shays off balance, his gun hand twitching. An instant later, the pistol went off. Shays staggered and spun, giving out his loudest scream yet. He stared at Sunny slack jawed for a moment. "Made me shoot myself!" he shrieked, barely audible over the ringing in Sunny's ears.

Then she heard something else. Approaching sirens.

Ron Shays must have heard them, too. His face became a bloody, torn devil mask of pure malevolence as he raised his gun.

Sunny flung herself toward the dining room in a hopeless leap.

And Shadow made an incredible bank shot, springing up from the floor, rebounding off one of the shelves, and fastening claws and teeth onto Shays's gun hand.

The weight of the cat pulled his hand down, and the pistol fired into the floor. The gun flew loose, going one way, the cat flying in the other. Shadow landed in a heap— Sunny did, too, half in, half out of the kitchen.

The pistol clattered on the linoleum floor.

Sunny saw her only chance. If she could get the pistol . . .

Ron Shays stood above her, his bleeding face contorted

in pain, moaning and cursing. He'd clapped his left hand over the shredded flesh of the hand that had held the gun. But that must have aggravated the self-inflicted wound in his shoulder. He rocked back and forth, his face pale.

She scrambled across the floor, trying to get the weapon. But her movement brought Shays out of his stupor. He swooped down, snatching the gun almost from under Sunny's nose. Shays straightened, reeling on his feet, needing both hands to aim the pistol.

It wobbled a little, but at this range it couldn't miss Sunny's head.

"Outta lives," he gasped. "Both you and that damn cat . . ." His hand steadied—

And the door behind him almost tore off its hinges as it shrieked open, slamming into Shays's back.

It crashed against him—right onto his wounded shoulder. That sudden pain was just too much for the dealer to deal with. His eyes rolled up, and he collapsed to the floor.

Will Price stood over him in the doorway, a snub-nosed revolver in his hand. His face was pale, with crusting blood smeared down one side. His eyes were wide and full of fear.

"Sunny!" he yelled. "Are you okay?"

She levered herself up. "Yeah!" she shouted back, her ears still ringing. "I thought he'd killed you!"

*

Shadow paid no attention as Will came in and hugged Sunny. All his attention was focused on the male on the floor. He wore a musky, spicy scent that should have been pleasant to smell. But under that, he was still marked with the poisonous stench, a hundred times worse than the Stinky One. This was the Other One, the one who had killed the old woman who had lived here, sheltering and feeding Shadow.

Until this one came and sent her down the stairs.

This was a Bad Place, a place of dread.

But now it could be a place of revenge.

With his battle song still rising from his gut, Shadow advanced on the form lying on the floor. His claws had done well, tearing one ear until the blood flowed—though even that stank with the Other One's taint.

But the killer had another ear. And Shadow knew he could make it bleed as freely.

*

A low moan snapped Sunny and Will apart. They looked down to find Shadow single-mindedly savaging Ron Shays's undamaged ear. The pain must have brought the drug lord around. Will moved quickly, kicking the pistol out of Shays's reach.

He had a much harder time shooing the cat away from Shays. The cat wanted another piece of him . . . a bigger piece.

Ben Semple burst in, gun drawn, followed by several other Kittery Harbor constables.

"We got a report of shots fired—jeez!" He broke off, staring around at the carnage spread out before him. "What were you trying to do, reenact the gunfight at the OK Corral?"

"The man on the floor is a drug dealer, Ron Shays,"

Sunny said, lurching to her feet and pointing. She needed the other hand to hold on to the countertop. "He's the one who shot those two guys that turned up dead yesterday."

Semple let his colleagues in blue have the job of stopping Shays's bleeding while also getting him into handcuffs. "And what happened to you?" he asked Will.

"Shays clocked me while coming in to try and kill Sunny," Will replied. "I came to, heard shots, dug out my backup gun, and tried to get in here ASAP."

"You missed a real Wile E. Coyote moment," Sunny told him. "Between Shadow and me, we managed to get Shays to shoot himself."

"But not before he shot the hell out of the place," Semple said. "He even killed the telephone." The constable shook his head.

Sunny looked over her shoulder. One of Shays's wild shots had indeed killed the old, 1960s-era phone hanging on Ada's wall. Only the backboard remained in place, with a big hole in it. The receiver lay on the floor, its coiled cord stretching up to the shattered body of the phone lying on the countertop.

And atop all the wreckage lay a piece of paper.

Sunny had to look twice before she believed her eyes.

It was a lottery ticket.

And, luckily, the bullet hole punched through it hadn't destroyed either the winning numbers or the date—which would expire tomorrow.

24

Ben Semple and the other constables quickly called two ambulances, one each for hauling Ron Shays and Will Price off to the hospital to be patched up. Getting Sunny down to the police station to explain what had happened turned into a much more ticklish job, however.

Shadow had positioned himself between her and everyone else in the room, back arched, his openmouthed hiss showing his willingness to attack anybody who even approached her.

It took a while for Sunny to calm the cat down. Finally she carried him down the stairs to the cellar, out to the backyard, and around the side of the Spruance house—to face what seemed like a wall of cameras and lights, all aimed at her.

Sunny just shook her head as the reporters surged forward, asking all sorts of inane questions. Luckily, Ben Semple got their attention by holding up the winning lottery ticket, now encased in a clear plastic evidence bag.

That's the nice thing about the television media, Sunny thought. *The cameras are so easily distracted.*

They arrived at the town police station at the same time as Sheriff Nesbit. He just sat quietly, running a finger over his silver mustache and shaking his head, as Sunny recounted her story.

Nesbit was probably fuming. On the other hand, though, despite nearly getting herself killed, Sunny had also managed to close out that embarrassing double murder case in the sheriff's supposedly crime-free county. And, of course, the perpetrator was a very nasty drug dealer—and an outsider.

Will looked properly heroic when he arrived with a bandage around his head, joining Sunny to answer questions at an impromptu press conference. Nesbit got in front of the cameras, too, finding lots of ways to spin the situation to his benefit.

Sunny was just eager for the questions to finally finish so she could put an end to this whole crazy adventure.

Except it still wasn't quite over.

The sheriff's office and the Maine lottery authority went to war over the ticket that had caused all the trouble in the first place. Nesbit said it was evidence, while the bean counters up in Augusta demanded that it be turned in to determine its authenticity.

Luckily, the amount of publicity surrounding the big prize ensured that some sort of reasonable accommodation would be reached.

That opened the way for an entirely different legal battle. Whose ticket was it? Obscure Spruance relatives whom Sunny had never heard of suddenly emerged to claim the prize—and argue with one another in front of the TV cameras. Mike Coolidge was delighted with the coverage, shouting abuse at the various contenders as they appeared on the screen. Sunny just shook her head, thinking, *Where is Jerry Springer when we really need him?*

Maybe it was watching all those seedy people fighting over so much money, but Mike began to show signs of Lotto fever. He suggested that Sunny should put in a claim for the winnings; after all, he argued, she was the one who'd found the damned ticket. Then Sunny caught him on her laptop, checking prices on pimped-out fishing boats, and laid down the law. That ticket might be worth millions, but it had brought worry and death to everyone connected with it.

Even though it might have made her life a lot easier, she told her dad that she didn't want a penny of the prize money. It would probably give *her* angina pains.

Maybe Mike felt he had to make up for that little episode, or maybe he couldn't resist the idea of scooping up a bargain. But after lengthy whispered negotiations with her dad hanging up the phone whenever Sunny came into the room, Sal came driving up Wild Goose Drive one evening in the maroon Wrangler and presented the keys to Sunny.

It still felt weird to drive around in an attempted murder weapon, but when Sunny asked her dad how much the SUV had cost, he'd just smiled mysteriously and said, "We can afford it."

Working in the office was a bit better, probably because all the free publicity for Kittery Harbor had led to a tsunami of interest from tourists. Apparently most of them were more interested in Lotto luck than mere murder. With Ron Shays's admission that he'd killed Ada Spruance and his complaint that the meth lab deal had died for lack of funding, it became clear that neither Ollie nor his money had been involved in the case. Sunny wasn't sure whether her suspicions about her boss represented paranoia or just a morbid wish-fulfillment fantasy.

Ollie the Barnacle even apologized for his bad behavior. "I was having a little cash-flow problem. Sometimes these hiccups happen, and, well, I suppose I kinda went off the deep end."

He didn't give her a raise, however.

So, just as everything was returning to normal again, Sunny was not happy to find a letter from a lawyer. This one was different from the usual legal garbage that had been clogging the Coolidge mailbox.

It was an invitation to attend the reading of Ada Spruance's will.

Fine, she thought. *So Ada leaves me her undying thanks, and then the whole shebang goes to Gordie, who probably died without a will. Which means her estate will either go to the state or into court for as long as those vulture relatives have money to fight over it.*

Sunny appeared at the lawyer's office, a place on Main Street in downtown Kittery Harbor. She was shocked to find Jane Rigsdale in the reception area, too. *Maybe the veterinarian gets Ada's thanks, too,* Sunny thought. *Wonderful.*

Jane reacted to the unexpected encounter pretty much the way Shadow had greeted the return of the Jeep Wrangler to the Coolidge driveway, by circling around suspiciously. At least Jane didn't try to sniff Sunny.

Finally Jane said, "After all I heard on the news, I guess I owe you an apology. Those guys really were after you."

"Let's just say you didn't pick the best time for a confrontation," Sunny replied. "I was wound a bit tight—frankly at that point, I was wondering if my boss was trying to kill me."

Whoops, maybe too much information, Sunny thought, taking in the look on Jane's face.

"Anyway," Sunny went on, "I hope we can be friends." *With just the occasional body slam and elbow in the eye when it comes to Will Price,* she finished silently.

Nobody else joined them in the outer office. Sunny and Jane kept glancing around, feeling weirder and weirder, until Peter Lewin, the attorney, came out, greeted them, and seated them in front of his desk with almost old-fashioned courtliness. "Mrs. Spruance came to me the day that the first story about her ticket appeared in the *Harbor Crier*," he said. "She was feeling very optimistic about finding it—an optimism that, despite everything, turned out to be well-founded," he added with a smile at Sunny.

"The terms of the will are actually very simple, so, if you agree, I'll just state them without the usual legal language," Lewin said. "There was a small trust fund set up for Gordie, provided he stayed clean and sober. As that apparently didn't happen, those funds go back into the main estate."

He turned to Sunny. "To thank you for your kindness

and promise to help, Ada offers you your pick of any of the cats living at her house."

Sunny couldn't help laughing. "Actually," she said, "one of the cats has already picked me."

"The remainder of her estate after taxes is to be invested into a foundation for the care of animals—especially cats. And Ada wanted you, Dr. Rigsdale, to run the show."

Jane looked as if she were about to fall out of her chair. "We'd talked many times about the specific problems that cats face—dogs get adopted much more often—and how Ada always hoped the town would have a no-kill shelter. But that was always pie in the sky!"

"Well, now you should have the wherewithal to accomplish some of those hopes," Lewin said. "I can hardly wait to hear the reaction from Ada's so-called relations."

"And that's it?" Jane asked. "It all goes to . . . me?"

"There will be papers to sign—lots of them," Lewin replied. "But that can be left to the future. I thought you should know the basic disposition of the estate."

Jane still looked a little shell-shocked as they stepped out onto Main Street. "It all seems just so . . . so *unfair*!" she burst out. "You not only found that ticket for Ada, you risked your life to find out who killed her and her son."

She broke off as a black pickup truck pulled up in the street and the window rolled down. Will Price stuck his head out. "Hey, Sunny!" Then he realized who was standing beside her and ducked his head. "Jane."

"You're just in time to congratulate us," Sunny told him, laughter bubbling up again. "We just heard the reading of Ada Spruance's will. I inherit a cat, and Jane here gets the millions."

Might as well let him know now, she thought. *Jane's hit the trifecta. Looks, personality, and buckets of money.*

"Actually," Jane broke in, embarrassed, "it's a foundation to benefit animals."

"Huh," Will said, looking a little shell-shocked now himself. He glanced over at Sunny. "Maybe we'll get that no-kill shelter you were talking about—even if it is a New York kind of idea."

Sunny felt a grin tug at her lips. So, he remembered that, did he? Maybe she had a chance after all, in spite of Jane's obvious advantages.

"Definitely," Jane said. She took Sunny by the hand. "I know it's not much, but I can promise you this. As long as I have any say, you won't ever have to worry about a vet bill for Shadow—ever."

Sunny was actually touched. "Thanks, Jane. I'll be sure to take you up on that. Knowing Shadow, he'll need more patching up than the average cat."

"It's little enough," Jane told her.

"Oh, no," Sunny replied. "I've gotten my payment."

She smiled, thinking of the look she would see on her dad's face when she told him *this* story.

"[A] wild, refreshing
over-the-top-of-Nob-Hill thriller."
—*The Best Reviews*

THE *NEW YORK TIMES* BESTSELLING SERIES FROM

• Rebecca M. Hale •

HOW TO MOON A CAT

A Cats and Curios Mystery

When Rupert the cat sniffs out a dusty green vase
with a toy bear inside, his owner has no doubt this is
another of her Uncle Oscar's infamous clues to one of
his valuable hidden treasures. Eager to put together
the pieces of the puzzle, she's soon heading to Ne-
vada City with her two cats, having no idea that this
road trip will put her life in danger.

facebook.com/TheCrimeSceneBooks
penguin.com
howtowashacat.com

M978T0911

There's a cat in the stacks with a killer to find . . .

FROM NATIONAL BESTSELLING AUTHOR
Miranda James

CLASSIFIED AS MURDER

- A Cat in the Stacks Mystery -

Charlie's librarian job goes from tranquil to terrify-
ing when his old, eccentric boss, the owner of a rare
book collection, turns up dead. With the help of his
cat, Diesel, Charlie must catch the killer—before
another victim checks out.

penguin.com
facebook.com/TheCrimeSceneBooks

BRIDGEPORT
PUBLIC LIBRARY

M960T0911

1230230318